Rebecca K. Busch was raised in north-eastern Michigan. Later she moved to Boulder, Colorado, where she earned her degree in English Literature at the University of Colorado. She continues to be an avid reader and currently lives in Denver, Colorado.

For my family

Rebecca K. Busch

DARK DRAGON

Book II

Suzanne,
Thank you for
reading

P.S. Fairies are still real!

AUSTIN MACAULEY PUBLISHERS™

LONDON ∗ CAMBRIDGE ∗ NEW YORK ∗ SHARJAH

Ordering Information
Quantity sales: Special discounts are available on quantity purchases by corporations, associations, and others. For details, contact the publisher at the address below.

Publisher's Cataloging-in-Publication data
Busch, Rebecca K.
Dark Dragon

ISBN 9781649791221 (Paperback)
ISBN 9781649791238 (Hardback)
ISBN 9781649791245 (Audiobook)
ISBN 9781649791252 (ePub e-book)

Library of Congress Control Number: 2021918986

www.austinmacauley.com/us

First Published 2021
Austin Macauley Publishers LLC
40 Wall Street, 33rd Floor, Suite 3302
New York, NY 10005
USA

mail-usa@austinmacauley.com
+1 (646) 5125767

I would like to say a special thank you to my parents whose continued support has been monumental in my progress getting here. Only a parent will take every opportunity, whether it be talking to a stranger on a plane, in an elevator, a waiting room, or even at a bar waiting for their table to be ready for dinner, to talk about their daughter – the author. I only want to make you proud.

Thank you to my wonderful friend and fellow author, Roni Lambrecht. Your attention to detail is extraordinary and you push me to be better.

Music is an instrumental part of my creative process. Without the epic sounds of Hidden Citizens, Methodic Doubt, Zack Hemsey, Chase Holfelder, Enigma, Sam Tinnez, Enya, Brandi Carlile, Smashing Pumpkins, Rag'n'Bone Man, and Moby to name a few, my imagination would not be nearly as colorful.

I appreciate every kind word, every critique, and every person that picks up a book in search of an adventure. You give me steam to go forward, and the drive to always improve.

And, of course, thank you to the fairies for their inspiration... In case you were wondering – yes, they are real!

Prologue

I am surrounded by darkness, and it is impenetrable. I cannot remember how I got here. One thing is quite certain. *I have never been in this place before.* Terror grips me with an iron claw. There is a tightness in my chest like a hand is reaching in and squeezing my heart. I can barely breathe. My body is heavy. It is a struggle just to stay on my feet and I cannot even extend my wings. A force is pushing down on me. *Have I been poisoned? Drugged?* No. No, this feels like something else. I drag my feet carefully with my hands reaching out trying to find my way out of the darkness. The ground is hard beneath my feet. It is like stone, but not smooth like the floor of someone's home. Loose rocks shift under my feet making each step unsure. With each labored breath, I smell some kind of perfume in the air. I can't place the scent but, for some reason, it seems familiar. The hairs on the back of my neck stand on end. There is something else. A presence.

I feel something lurking here. *I am not alone…*

Chapter 1

It is exactly how I remember. Flowers cover everything here: the trees, the bushes, the ground, and they are all vibrant. The flowers here are so different from what we have back at our village. Our wildflowers are usually dominated by the tall grasses, so they have become more resilient over the years. Smaller petals and thicker, thornier, stems. They are still beautiful, but nothing like this. Here, the rose bulbs seem never-ending with silky petals. There are fields of marigolds, lavender, and dozens of others all flourishing, and strong, but have a fragility at the same time.

The scent is sweet and fresh and unmistakable, and the air is so saturated, that it almost seems palatable. You almost expect honey to be falling from the sky. The buzzing gets louder as I come over the hill, and I see the hive suspended in all its splendor between giant tendrils of lilac.

"Oh wow!" Falon exclaims. It is the first time that he has been to the hive. I guess, in the past, before the relationship between the colony and our village became neglected, Vivek or my father were usually the ones that made these trips.

"I know," Jae says with his eyes fixed on it. "I forgot how pretty it was."

The hive is truly remarkable. The structure of it is formidable, but it is suspended by a narrow shoot to a branch of this enormous tree, so it looks like a massive castle floating in the air. The activity around the hive is just as impressive. The effortless, yet dizzying, dance of all the worker bees flying around the flowers and back and forth from the hive is overwhelming the first time you see it.

I remember coming here the first time. I was nervous just being in their territory alone, but, in addition to that, I had been there to ask the bees for their help in a war effort against the Skar tribe. This time, I am much more at ease and looking forward to seeing Asherah again. I can tell Jae and Khalon are much easier as well. They both stand casually, shoulders slouched just a bit.

Khalon has his hand resting on his belt in a relaxed way. I think Jae is secretly getting a little satisfaction watching his father's amazement and discomfort with this place. The noise and the activity are very uncomfortable the first time you're in it.

Suddenly, and without reason, all of the worker bees stop moving. They are still in the air, but they are flying in place rather than the usual zipping and zigzagging around each other from flower to flower. Instead, they are just focused on us.

"This is different," Khalon observes. He straightens up a little bit.

"Uh, Jae?" I look to Jae to see if he has any clue what is happening.

"Um, yeah…I mean, no. I have no idea what's going on." His brow is furrowed, but his eyes don't leave the thousands of bees all staring straight at us.

These bees could kill us with very little effort. We may be bigger, but their numbers alone could overwhelm us easily. This display is incredibly confusing since we are on good terms.

Out of the corner of my eye, I see Khalon's hand reach for his sword. My heart beats faster. I start to panic. The last thing I want is for Khalon to feel threatened by them, or for the bees to feel a threat from us.

Just then, one of her drones drops down in front of us. "Honored guests," he hums in monotone voice. "Welcome."

We all breathe again. This was not a show of force. This was a greeting; a very formal greeting as it turns out.

"Queen Asherah is so pleased you are here and has prepared a feast in your honor." The drone bows his head slightly.

I tilt my head to look him in the eyes. "We are honored to be here with you, dear friend."

His face, like all bees, is expressionless, but I'd like to think if it were not, he would be smiling.

He makes a small gesture with one of his legs and the worker bees take this cue and slowly line up, flanking on two sides, clearing a path to the hive. The drone nods and begins leading the way. We casually fly to the hive, acknowledging all of the surrounding bees along the way. Once we are inside, the frenzy outside continues as the workers go back to their jobs. The inside of the hive is just as I remember. A soft, yellow glow from the honeycomb walls; the sweet smell, and the honey is everywhere. The last time we were here, I had to watch Khalon very carefully. He had just been introduced to the precious treat and had been seduced by its sweetness. If I were to let him run wild, he may have eaten it straight from the walls.

"The Queen will want to see you right away," the drone explains.

We follow him through the tunnel, up to the Queen's quarters. It is also just the same as I remember. One grand room with her at its center. Her large lower abdomen resting on a pile of plush pillows and bedding. I forgot that she is truly immobile. Her body, which is this colonies most sacred and important necessity for survival, is so massive that moving her would be nearly impossible. Her eggs that have been laid incubate in the walls around her, she never lets them out of her sight. Her face is usually very unreadable, largely because her eyes are completely black, but today, when we enter, she smiles brightly, and I feel as though I'm seeing an old friend for the first time in a long while.

"Your Majesty." I bow to her. Jae, Khalon, and Falon bow behind me in a formal line. She reaches down and holds up my chin. "You never need to bow to me. You are my guests, my friends."

I smile. "It feels good to be here again. Jae and Khalon, you know, but this is Falon Redwood, one of our chief councilman and Jae's Father."

"Majesty." Falon nods to her again.

"I'm so pleased you could be here," she hums.

Just behind her, I see a small head pop up curiously, and then duck back down once I glance that way. The Queen sees me notice and the corner of her mouth lifts in a small smile.

"Majesty, it seems we are not alone," I tease, and there is a tiny giggle that comes from behind her.

"Come out, it's alright, these people want to meet you," the Queen encourages.

The onlooker slowly steps out from the cover of the Queen's protective presence. She is not as small as I thought. Her head and upper body are quite petite, but her lower abdomen is large, and she is quite tall. She looks very much like the Queen, just much smaller and younger. Her lower half, though it is bigger than the other bees, is not so big that she would have any trouble getting around.

"This is Abeille. She will be my successor someday," the Queen explains. "Abeille, this is Sigrun Livingstone, the Queen of the Northwoods, and her general, Khalon Blackburn, high councilor, Jae Redwood, and chief councilor, Falon Redwood."

The moment I hear her call me, "Queen," I start to feel flush and uncomfortable and, as I see the young princess start to bow to me, I take a step forward to stop the formal presentation.

"No bowing necessary. I'm not...I don't..." I take a breath. "In your home, we bow to you, Princess," I say finally, and then the four of us bow and fuss over her, which she loves.

Khalon takes my cue and does a very formal bow and ceremoniously kisses her hand, "Little Majesty."

She giggles again, and her eyes which are as black the darkest night, light up with a thousand stars. For such a ruffian, he can be very charming, and now it seems he has a seed-sized admirer. I like seeing his more playful side.

"Well, I'm sure you are very tired from your journey," the Queen motions for the drone. "Show them to their rooms please," she instructs. "Feel free to rest and freshen up before dinner and let us know if you need anything."

"Your Majesty," I give a small bow before leaving.

"Sigrun," she says almost curtly, "I told you my name is Asherah, and that is what you will call me." She smiles slightly.

"Yes, ma'am, I mean, Asherah. Thank you." I smile and leave the room.

Chapter 2

We were uncertain about what the sleeping arrangements would be when we were invited to stay for multiple days. The only rooms of the hive that I had seen before were the great chamber and the Queen's room, both of which were pretty basic and didn't have much in the way of furnishings, so I didn't know what to expect as they led us through the maze of tunnels within the hive. We come to a long, wide hallway and the drone motions to Jae, Khalon, and Falon to each take their rooms. He takes me a bit further to the last door at the end of the hall and opens it for me. It is very grand indeed. The ceiling is quite high and there are two large doors on the far end that open to the outside. They had built charming wicker furniture and the bedding looks very soft and is a deep plum color. As I walk in, two worker bees buzz in behind me with buckets of hot liquid. They pour it into a soaking tub on the other side.

"They will take your travel clothes to be washed for you," the drone informs me, "and there are clean clothes in the wardrobe for you. I will leave you now to wash and rest, and I will be back for you when dinner is served. Do you need anything?"

"No, no, this is more than enough. Thank you so much."

He leaves and the worker bees wait patiently for me to strip down and hand over my dirty clothes. I awkwardly disrobe and wrap myself in my wings until they leave. The tub is filled with a hot, milky liquid. It smells sweet, like oats and honey. The lilac from the tree wafts in from the large exterior doors. It is just lovely. I slide into my bath and sink into the warmth of it. There is a shelf next to the tub with jars of oils and soaps, each one more luxurious than the next.

After my bath, I make my way over to the wardrobe. I brought clothes with me in my pack but figure I might as well see what they set aside for me. Inside, I see they left me a beautiful silk nightgown, much finer than anything I have ever had before, some casual cotton tops and bottoms, and one dress that must be for tonight's dinner. It is dark blue and has a delicate sheer ruffle that covers the shoulders and the neckline. The back is low enough that my wings won't damage the delicate fabric. The front hem falls just above my knee and gets longer in the back so it is just below my calf muscle. It is much nicer than anything I have at home, even the dress Ainia made me last year. This one is much more formal. I usually hate dresses, but this one is really special.

I put on some casual clothes for now and go to the open doors. There is a small balcony and I step out and look over the lands. It is even more spectacular from up here; every variation of every color sprinkled throughout the countryside. The workers are still busily collecting pollen, going from flower to flower. It is quite something to watch from up here. The way they dance around each other so quickly and without incident is almost as though they read each other's minds.

Aside from the sound of the wind and the gentle hum from the workers, it is perfectly quiet. This is the first time in a long time that I don't have to be anywhere or do anything. I have no tasks that need to be completed, no problems to solve, no fights to fight, and it is almost uncomfortable. I have forgotten how to just sit and be. My mind begins to wander. I start thinking about the boys. I wonder what they are doing right now. Are they struggling with the inactivity as well? Likely not. Jae is probably loving the quiet. He also doesn't get much quiet time at home. Khalon, if he isn't eating, is most likely fast asleep. Probably taking the opportunity to enjoy a little 'bat-nap' before dinner. Just then there is a knock at my door.

"That didn't take long," I say to myself. I guess they are more restless than I thought.

I open the door to find Falon standing there with a tray in his hands. It surprises me to see him, and I take a half step back.

"Hi," I say unable to hide the wonderment in my voice.

"I hope I'm not intruding," he peers over my shoulder to see whether I am alone.

"No. No, not at all."

"I was wondering if you would join me for tea."

"Ah, of course! Please come in," I say a little surprised. I move to the side and let him enter.

The tray that he has with him carries a small white teapot, two very delicate cups, some sweet biscuits, and of course, a small pot of honey.

"Oh wow," he says looking around my room, "and I thought my room was nice." He sets the tray down on the small table by the open doors. I pull up two chairs and sit as he pours.

"Honey?" he asks.

"Yes please, just a little."

I sit in silence as he pours his own cup and settles into his chair. He's wearing a fresh, cream colored, casual day robe. The bees must have provided him with a wardrobe as well.

Watching him stir his cup, I'm still trying to figure out what brought him to my door in the first place. My relationship with Falon has certainly improved since last year. He was never warm to me when I was a child, but when he confessed to distrusting me to a point where he dispatched his own son as an unknowing spy to keep an eye on me, that hurt me more than I have ever admitted to anyone. I always held him in such high regards, so finding out that, for the majority of my life, he saw me as an enemy, or a nuisance at best, shook my confidence.

Usually being in Falon's presence makes me nervous. He is very intimidating, and he wears a seriousness that gives you the impression that he is not to be trifled with. Most days, he wears agility and focus like a comfortable cloak. Today, though, he seems more nervous that I am. He sits upright and rigid with his cup in hand. He looks out the open doors observing the colorful display outside while I observe him. His intense yellow eyes dart around fully taking in everything at great detail. He is very handsome. I see a lot of Jae in him. They have the same high cheekbones and broad chin, and when they are both relaxed, their mouths both twist upwards into a casual smile. Though, I tend to see that feature less in Falon these days. The skin at the corners of his eyes crinkle into deep lines and I amuse myself in the thought that, for a man with such deep laugh lines, he doesn't seem to laugh much at all. He takes a deep breath and keeps his gaze outside.

"We've been through a lot, me and you," he says at last. I'm not entirely sure what he means by this.

Does he mean he and I have been through a lot as individuals, or is he speaking to our turbulent relationship together?

"It's been quite a year," I throw out a generic statement.

He nods in agreement; looks at me and smiles a little.

"I remember the day my son met you. He ran into the house like a crazed animal, waving his arms wildly, 'Momma, Dadda, I met a dragon today,' he said. He was so excited, and I was so scared. Of course, I knew all about you and had been keeping a close watch since the day you were born. We didn't know what to expect. A dragon. A predator of the skies. There is no scarier thought for a fairy. If we are not even safe in the skies, where could we run to? It actually had been decided that we were going to eliminate the threat."

By this, I know he is talking about my own murder that I came very close to. His honesty is hard to listen to. I've known this truth for a long time, and it never gets easier, but I actually appreciate that he is opening up to me and so I sit in silence.

"I remember it was quite the dramatic scene," he continues. "About 12 other men, and myself, all came to your home with swords and torches. I was so mad at my brother for not coming. At the time, I was so certain that it was the right thing to do, and I couldn't figure out why he didn't feel the same. He held to the fact that there was a time when he and I would have been considered birds of prey and that made him more compassionate. When we arrived at your home that night, Baron came outside as though he was expecting us, like he was greeting his friends for a celebration. He knew why we were there, but he was always the gentlest man, and so he would never meet us in opposition. Instead, he just stood there with his hands in his robe pockets.

"He just looked over all of us standing there and simply said, 'Good evening my friends,' and I just felt awful. There I was, standing in front of my friend, who had just lost his wife, and I was there to murder his newborn child. All I could say back was, 'Good evening.' Then, he walked inside for a moment and came back with you in his arms. He said, 'I want you to meet my daughter.' He didn't address the reason that we were there. He didn't try to hide you from us, and he just trusted that we would see the goodness in you that he saw.

"You were such a happy baby. Your wings were alarming, that was true, but the rest of you was giggles and cooing, pink cheeks, big violet eyes, and a little bit of brown hair that went in whichever direction it pleased. I walked up to you with my dagger in hand and, just then, a piece of cotton fuzz from a tree wafted down and landed in your face and you sneezed. I laughed. I couldn't help it. I laughed out loud. You had this look of perplexity on your face like you were trying to figure out why you sneezed, or what a sneeze even was, and then you laughed because I was laughing. I melted a little right then. It made me think of Jae, who was at home with his mother, only a season or so older than you, and I suddenly felt very conflicted. I was still frightened at the possibility that you could become dangerous, but as you were then, at that moment, I, nor any other man there that day, could bear to bring a knife to you.

"I kept an eye on you, but from a distance, until that day when Jae rushed in after he met you, and now you were close again and that scared me. Well, it scared me for a moment, because right after he told me that he met a dragon, he said, 'And she is going to be my best friend.'"

I can't help but to smile at that. That sounds just like what Jae would say as a child. If he wanted you to be his friend, well, that's the way it was and there was nothing you or anyone could do about it.

He takes a sip of his tea and looks at me again. "He loved you so much," he says, and at first, I'm not sure who he means. Is he talking about Jae? "Your father, he loved you so much," he clarifies.

I feel a lump in my throat, and I swallow it down and smile. "I know."

"Do you think…" he pauses. "Do you think he knew?"

Again, I'm not sure what he means. I tilt my head at his question.

"About your brother, and his own death?"

I sit back in my chair and look outside to search for an answer that I already know. I have thought about this at length for many seasons now.

"My father saw a lot. I'm certain he knew. The last time I saw him, looking back on it, I felt like he was trying to say goodbye."

"I can't imagine how that was for him." Falon shakes his head at the thought.

"I wish he had told me, but he was as tough and stubborn as the oldest Oak. There was no bending his will, that's for sure. I used to get so frustrated that he would only tell me a little bit, he never gave me the full story about anything. My whole life has been a mystery, putting it together piece by piece like a puzzle. I never understood why he did that."

"He always had his methods."

"Yes, he did. I miss him though," I blurt out in a fit of honesty.

"Me too."

A knock at my door interrupts us. It's the drone. He has come back to let me know they will be serving dinner soon.

"Well, I should get going, let you get dressed," Falon says, making his way his way to the door.

"Thank you for the tea."

"Thank you for the conversation." He nods to me slightly and heads back down the hall.

Chapter 3

I look myself over in the mirror before I head to the dining room. The dress fits me well. Just after the drone came to let me know that dinner would soon be served, a small swarm of worker bees came in and began to fuss over me. In a swirl of black and yellow fuzz, I was scrubbed, buffed, dressed, and topped with a freshly made crown of flowers. My skin is glowing. My cheeks are pink. I don't quite look like myself, but I actually like it. Now that I'm away from home, I feel like I can pretend to be someone else for a while. I feel lighter here.

As soon as I step out of my room, I see Jae and Khalon waiting for me in the hallway. They have both cleaned up nicely. They both have formal clothes courtesy of the bees. Their dress robes are again much nicer than anything we have in our village. Jae is wearing a bronze-colored formal robe, a clean white linen shirt, and a nicely tailored pair of brown pants. Khalon's outfit is similar but shades of gray and silver. His pants are leather, and the fit of the shirt and robe are a bit tight across his chest and shoulders, which is to be expected. Gauging his size is not an easy task. It took Ainia several attempts to finally figure out how to dress him. I can tell he is not comfortable, but he is wearing it well and with respect. They both see me at the same time, and I can tell they are as surprised by my appearance, as I am by theirs.

"Wow," Jae stutters.

"You look…" Khalon fills in.

"Great," Jae finishes.

I shake my head and laugh at them. "Come on, you two, we don't want to be late."

Falon emerges from his room as well wearing a very striking dark red, like the color of a fine wine. He looks fit for a royal ball. He smiles when he sees me and extends his arm to escort me to dinner. I happily accept and look over my shoulder at the boys behind us. They follow closely with squinting eyes.

Since the Queen cannot really be moved, in the time that we were relaxing, her chambers were transformed into a magnificent dining hall. Flowers of all kinds have been brought in from the outside, glass votive candle holders hang down from the ceiling like glowing stars, and long rows of tables line up the path to the head table where the Queen sits. Abeille is already sitting next to her. They both smile when they see us come in and motion for us to sit with them at the head table. The Queen is adorned with jewels. Just as the hive is dripping with honey, she is dripping with gold. She has large gold cuff bracelets on both wrists. She is wearing the most elaborate necklace I have ever seen. It starts tightly around the middle of her neck and drapes across her shoulders and down into a dramatic 'V' shape down her chest. It is riddled with a lacing of jewels of assorted colors and one large ruby in the center. The weight of it must be extraordinary, and of course, a beautiful, golden crown in the shapes of flowers rests elegantly upon her regal head.

Abeille also wears golden trinkets, but they are not nearly as grand.

"This is wonderful," I say to the Queen, taking in the general splendor.

"Yes and thank you so much for the wonderful treatment and the beautiful clothes," Falon adds.

She smiles. "You are most welcome. We are so honored to have you here. Please sit."

She has me and Falon sit next to her on one side and Jae and Khalon on the other side, next to Abeille.

I turn to the Queen once seated and motion to her jewels, "Asherah, I must say that is the most splendid necklace I have ever seen."

She rests her hand on the jewels thoughtfully, "They were a gift from a mining colony many years ago. They needed a brief refuge and stayed here for a short while. I was very young at the time, but I do remember them. They had jewels from the mountains and gave this to my mother as a thank you, and these as well." She points to the wide gold cuff bracelets on each arm.

"They are magnificent, you look very imperial."

"Thank you. It is nice to have an occasion to wear them."

Workers are busily setting the tables with food, mostly sweets, and pouring the wine. Once my cup is full and the drones and workers have all been seated, I stand and raise my glass in a toast to the Queen and her colony.

"My friends, since last year, I learned more about our history together and of our two colonies' turbulent past. Our ancestors were careless with this relationship and, as a result, it was left at a shaky truce for many generations. Until one day, when I came to these lands in need of your help and in search of an alliance. I didn't know it then, but I also found a mentor and a friend. I am humbled by your efforts to welcome us here and I am so blessed to have your support and your friendship. I look forward to a long and prosperous relationship." I raise my glass high, and the entire room follows suit. "To the Queen!"

"To the Queen!" the drones and the head table cheer. The worker bees all pound their tables in unison as their way of joining the cheer. The vibration of it fills the room. The Queen nods in acknowledgement and I take my seat again.

My plate is filled with the most splendid fruits and sweets. And, just as my cup is filled for the second time, the Queen leans over to me.

"Thank you for that lovely speech," she says to me.

"Well, I meant it, I really do value you and everything that you have done for us."

"I must say though," she hums, "I do wonder which Queen they should be toasting."

Her black eyes are unreadable, but the slight lift of her head indicates that she is looking at the crown I wear, or lack thereof. The crown that was given to me as a gift when I took my council chair is at home on my dressing table, still resting in the same box that it was originally given. The crown of flowers that I was dressed in is more of a quick replacement.

"Oh, I, ah, decided to leave the crown at home. It is quite heavy to carry and if something were to happen to it, I would never forgive myself." I make a quick excuse. I begin to sweat along my hairline.

"Mmm. You should never be afraid to wear the crown, or of your gifts." She nods again and turns to a conversation on the other side of the table.

Something shifts in the room. I feel something like an invisible fog swell up around me. The candlelight flickers and the sound seems to evaporate from the room. I look around, but no one else seems to notice. A voice echoes around me.

One queen to rule them all.

"I'm sorry?" I ask.

The Queen turns to me, "What was that dear?"

"Did you hear that?"

"Hear what my dear?"

"That voice, did you hear that?" I turn to Falon who is looking at me quizzically. "Did you…" I begin to ask him, but it is clear no one else heard anything, other than their own conversations, "Never, never mind, I must just be tired."

"Yes, perhaps you should retire," the Queen says diplomatically. "You've had quite a long day and tomorrow we have many things in store for you as well."

"Oh yeah? What's on the agenda tomorrow?" Jae asks.

The Queen smiles a bit and looks to her drone.

"You'll be making honey with us." The drone explains.

"That sounds great!" Khalon explodes. His enthusiasm is not unusual given his delight with the sweet treat.

"Yes, you will be gathering pollen with the workers and then working with them through the process of making honey. We thought it might be a bit of fun for you," the Queen elaborates.

"That sounds wonderful, and I think you are right, I should settle in for the night."

I stand to leave and Falon, Jae, and Khalon all stand. Falon stands out of politeness, but Jae and Khalon both look eager at the opportunity to escort me back to my room. They both look at each other with a silent challenge.

"I can find my way back. You all stay. Enjoy yourselves." I'm not entirely sure that I can navigate my way through these halls without hesitation, but it seems to be a better alternative than having two Alpha Males trying to out show each other when I am already exhausted. I turn to the Queen, "Thank you again for everything. This was wonderful."

She smiles and nods to me. "Sleep well, and I will see you tomorrow."

The boys don't know what to do with themselves. Both of them were expecting this opportunity to spend time with me without the watchful eye of the other, and neither of them expected to be shut down so swiftly. Falon has a small half smile. I imagine he is musing at the notion of being young again.

The drone points me in the right direction, and I find my way back to my room.

*****

I am grateful for the quiet of my room. With all of the bees still feasting, the constant hum that has assaulted my surroundings since arrival is finally gone, leaving only the sound of the wind. I happily remove my evening dress and look over my wardrobe. The silk nightgown is simply divine and slips through my fingers fluidly. All of my nightdresses at home are simple cotton. This one seems too nice to sleep in. I slip it on and sit in the chair by the window. The moon is not quite full, but bright, nonetheless. The stars have also come out and wink at me one at a time.

Sinking into my chair, I find solitude for a moment. The only issue with the quiet is that it allows your mind to wander. *One queen to rule them all.* I know I heard it. At least, I'm pretty sure I did. Doubt creeps up on me. No one else seemed to. No one else seemed to notice the change in the room either. Exhaustion would be an easy thing to blame it on, but I don't feel all that tired. *Was it a warning? Asherah doesn't strike me as any kind of tyrant. I can't imagine that she would ever have ambitions to rule over anything but her own lands. Why was I the only one who could hear it?*

A knock at my door keeps me from finding an answer. Jae stands at my door with a steaming cup in his hand. "I thought you might want some tea," he says smiling.

"Thank you." I take the cup from him but continue to block my doorway. "Is the party still going on?"

"Yeah, these bees sure know how to celebrate—I don't see an end in sight. I had to duck out of there to save myself from a headache tomorrow. That wine is strong!" he laughs.

"Thank you for this," I lift up the cup. "I think this is what I needed to help me sleep."

He looks both pleased that he was part of a helpful contribution, and also a little disappointed that I am ending the interaction so quickly.

"Goodnight," he says and kisses me on the cheek before leaving.

"Goodnight."

I take my cup to the chair by the window and hold the rim to my nose. Floral and sweet. They certainly have a different bouquet up here. I barely get my first sip down and there is another knock at my door.

"What in the world…" I set my cup down and answer the door again.

This time, Khalon is standing in my doorway.

"I thought you might need this." He holds up a steaming cup.

"Tea! Thank you." I try hard not to laugh.

Khalon is a calculating man. He must have seen Jae come to my room first and then when he saw that Jae did not gain access, he thought he would try his own luck.

"Is everything okay?" he asks.

"Oh yeah, I think the excitement of the day just caught up with me."

"Just tired?"

"Yeah, just tired, and I have a little bit of a headache."

"Okay. I'll see you in the morning then. Sleep well."

"Goodnight."

He smiles and walks away.

I take a sip from this cup. Exotic and spiced. I set the cup down next to the one Jae brought me and smile. I blow out the candles on my table and jump into bed before anyone knocks at my door again.

*****

By morning, I am feeling refreshed. I thought that I would have a hard time sleeping in a strange place, but it was quite the opposite. I fell asleep the moment I shut my eyes and I don't think I moved again until morning.

I wash my face and pull on a casual white cotton top and a pair of dark green shorts from the wardrobe and head out. One of the drones is already standing outside my door.

"Oh!" I exclaim as I almost run into him.

"Good morning," he hums. "I am here to take you down to breakfast."

"Oh, great, thank you."

The breakfast hall is pretty much empty. Many circular tables throughout the room and, rather than chairs, they have pillows and cushions for seating. I noticed that the bees didn't sit the same way we did last night and that we were the only ones with actual chairs. Falon is already sitting at one of the tables reading a book and sipping his tea.

He smiles when he sees me coming and pours a cup for me.

"Good morning," he says. He has been in a far better mood these last few days than I think I have ever seen.

"Morning." I gratefully accept my morning tea. "Did you sleep well?"

"I did. Maybe even too well. I forgot where I was for a moment this morning. Don't tell Ulani I said that. She would be devastated at the thought that I could sleep without her."

"Your secret is safe with me." I smile.

Jae and Khalon make their way into the hall and, as soon as they are seated, the workers rush out with trays of warm rolls with honey and fresh biscuits.

"I could really get used to this kind of treatment," I say, sucking the remnants of a honey roll from my thumb.

"Me too," Khalon says patting his full stomach.

As the dishes are being cleared, a few drones fetch us from our table to put us to work for the day. Gathering pollen for honey doesn't seem like it will be a difficult task. Not until we are standing outside in front of a flurry of activity. I don't know how we are to navigate through this. The drone hands us each a pouch to tie around our waists. "This is for the pollen," he explains.

A worker hovers above us and waggles hurriedly in a certain direction.

"The worker is telling us which direction we should go to collect," the drone interprets. He speaks loudly to be heard over the buzzing, "She has already scouted the area and has found a good section of flowers to pick from."

"How do you know where to go?" Jae asks.

"See how she is dancing about, always in that one direction? That is how we know which way to go. The length of the dance lets us know how far. If the waggle is relatively short, then we know the pollen is closer. This way."

The drone takes flight in the direction that the worker indicated, and we follow closely.

Quickly, we come to a cluster of dark purple flowers. Many bees are already on them.

"You see how they are burrowing into the flower? They are collecting nectar," the drone points out.

"Are we gathering nectar too?" I ask, not entirely sure how we would get it, let alone transport it.

The drone shakes his head, "No, you will just be collecting pollen."

I watch the other bees. The fuzz that covers their bodies is now covered in pollen clusters that attach there as they burrow their bodies into the flower. Then they take their legs and brush and collect these clusters onto their back legs into pollen baskets. Looks easy enough.

I find a flower of my own and I reach into the center to grab at the yellow grains of pollen. They are stickier than I thought. The small balls adhere to my hand, between my fingers, and when I try to flick them off, they go nowhere. If I try to pick them off with the other hand, they just stick to those fingers instead. I have to use the bag to brush and pick them off. I look around to see where the men are.

Falon is observing more than collecting. Khalon and Jae are off at separate flowers going through the same struggle with the sticky substance as I am. I see curiosity get the better of Khalon and he puts a piece of pollen in his mouth to taste it. His nose scrunches and he spits it out. It isn't honey yet.

I have quickly exhausted the spoils from this flower, so I move on to the next. Flower after flower, sticky handful after sticky handful, we grab the pollen clusters and deposit them into our sacks. Once we have cleared out one section, the scout worker finds us and waggles in a different direction to pick from a new area. The work is hefty, and the reward is slight. We go through a lot of flowers and my sack is not more than halfway full. My back is starting to ache form the continual bending and my legs are cramping from kneeling all morning. I take a moment to rest. I wipe the sweat from my face and look over the fields. These bees are unaffected by this task. We are already starting to wane in our efforts while they forge on. To them, it is not a great task at all; it is just part of daily life. Our harvests in our village are hard work, but you see big results right away. Bales and bales of grain stalk. Basket upon basket of vegetables. It is easy to see the progress we make in our daily work. Here, you work so hard for the smallest reward, and it takes a lot of pollen and nectar to make a jar of honey. Bees really are the hardest workers.

I think the drone noticed us beginning to dwindle and he comes over to tell us that we have one more section to collect and then we can bring our sacks back to the hive to deposit.

The hive is busy. Continuous traffic to and from the hive never stops. The drone leads us to a room where more workers are building honeycomb. I follow the example of the other bees who are depositing their baskets into the honeycomb cells. They do this effortlessly. For us, it is a struggle to get the pollen out of the bag, because it just sticks to our hands. A worker sees me struggling and comes to my rescue. She takes her arms and brushes the pollen grain for me into the cell.

"Thank you." The workers faces are even more expressionless than the drones. Big, black, oval eyes staring at me. Their bodies covered by a fine layer of fuzz that I have wanted to touch since the very first time I came to the colony. I extend my hand without thinking and, very quickly, bring it back in.

"It's okay," the drone hums, "you can touch her. She likes you."

I slowly reach out again and the fuzz actually moves to meet my fingers. I feel a small tingling charge, similar to how the air feels right before a big lightning storm when the hairs on your arms stand on end anticipating the strike.

"That's incredible. How do they do that?" I ask.

"It happens when they fly. They move so fast that they build static. It helps the pollen stick to them." the drone educates us.

I turn to my companions, "You have to feel this."

Workers simultaneously cozy up to Falon, Jae, and Khalon to let them feel it for themselves.

"Oh, wow," they all remark in turn.

We are quickly interrupted by another wave of workers who have come to make their deliveries. One flies to the cell that Jae is working at and nudges him out of the way. He looks up in confusion.

"You have filled it with pollen and now he will fill it with nectar." The drone steps in seeing his reaction. "You need both for honey."

"So, how do they transport the nectar?" Khalon asks the drone.

"They have internal sacks for it."

"The stomach? They keep it in the stomach?" Khalon questions.

"That would be a primitive word to describe it, but yes," the drone replies.

"So, honey is essentially bee…vomit?" Khalon says a little disgusted.

"Again, a primitive word, but yes, I guess you could look at it that way."

The look on Khalon's face as he is trying to rationalize this process is both one of wonderment and uneasiness.

"Do you think that is enough to keep you from eating honey?" Jae teases, as he nudges Khalon in the side with his elbow.

Khalon takes a moment to consider and then finally blurts out, "Um, no, probably not. Yeah, definitely not. I probably would still eat honey even if you told me it was bee urine."

The drone clearly doesn't know how to respond and the rest of us laugh so hard, we have to wipe tears from our eyes. Even Falon, who is usually the picture of stoicism, is bent over with a laugh. We are quickly excused from any further work and given time to rest and recuperate before dinner. I think it was the drone's way of politely dismissing us from his care. I'm sure being our constant chaperone was becoming a draining experience and he needed a reason to retire as well.

Back in my room, I look out my window before getting in the bath. Bees still working hard for their community, and they let us be a part of it. I sink into the water and close my eyes.

Today was a good day.

*****

Not long after I freshen up, I get a visit from a drone. The Queen wants to see me before dinner. I enter her room and there is a pillow for me to sit placed next to her. She has a table set with tea and cake.

"Please sit," she motions for me to sit next to her.

A worker comes in and pours tea for us.

"I don't know how I will go back to my regular life after this. The service here is incredible," I joke.

The Queen smiles a little. "It isn't always this formal, but for guests, we like to show our best." She motions to her worker who then hands me my cup and a piece of cake, and then hands one to her. "One difference, though, is that I have to be served. That is my reward for being mother to all, I suppose."

"I'm not really sure that being served your daily bee-bread is a sufficient enough reward for what you have done for this colony. I can't imagine spending all of my days confined to one room."

"I saw the world when I was young. I didn't understand it either, how I would be able to disappear from it, but when my mother died, and I became queen, I gave birth to my first generation and there is no greater feeling than that. All of those lives possible because I was able to give it to them. I gladly trade every sunrise for the gift of building my colony."

She sips her tea and I watch her with amazement and jealousy. She exudes a confidence and self-knowing that I fear I'll never have.

"I do wish," she speaks again, "that I were able to visit you in your village. Tell me about it."

Her request is simple enough, but I'm not sure where to start. "Oh, well, our village is pretty simple really. The river borders our lands on the west and south sides. It is very heavily forested, most of our homes are built within hollowed trees, and our flowers are nice enough, but nothing like what you have here. We have grain fields, and a training field, which gratefully hasn't been used much lately."

"Ah, yes, the battle. Do you still think about it?"

"I try not to. I lost a lot last year." I touch my pendant.

"Yes. You also gained a lot too."

I stare at her with confusion for a moment. I can think of many big loses: my father, my brother, several good friends, but I'm coming up short in the gains category.

"You met new friends," she begins to explain, and she is right. I may have never met Khalon and even the friendships with those I have known my whole life may not have forged so strongly without the shared conflict that we had to wage together. "Our alliance became much stronger, and of course there is the development of your gifts," she pauses. "I wonder, do you think your fire would have emerged without being so cruelly forced? My drones told me the story about how it came about. How your brother died."

I swallow hard. I try not to think about that either. My brother died by my hand and it haunts me. "Yes, well, he didn't give me much of a choice," I say more defensively than I would have liked.

The Queen looks at me with a calm stoic gaze. "Do you ever wonder why he went down one life path, and you went down another?"

"All the time."

"I wonder if he was jealous of you and your power."

"But I wasn't powerful as a child. I was an outsider."

"You don't have to emerge in flames to be powerful. When I first met you, you had not yet discovered your gifts and I sensed a leader in you from the moment you set foot in front of me."

The memory makes me chuckle to myself. "I think you are confusing leadership with desperation."

She shakes her head. "It takes a leader to know a leader. I know what I see in you and, no matter how you may doubt yourself, I know what you are capable of. I think about your brother too. Had he won, my colony would be on its way to extinction by now. It would not have taken long before Mantus killed your brother himself, took control, and pushed his heathens this way to take our lands. He would have destroyed us. Conquerors like that don't ever stop. They continue stealing and killing until someone is brave enough to stop it. You didn't just save yourself, or your friends, or your village that day. You saved mine as well. I will always be in your debt for that."

My face feels flush. I search for anything to say in return, but nothing I can think of seems to be an appropriate response to such a grand expression.

"Well, we would not have saved your colony or ours without your help. Your bees put themselves in harm's way just as much as we did," I awkwardly reply. "As far as my fire, I think it had to be triggered somehow, by something big, and Merik's betrayal broke something in me." The Queen is silent, and her gaze remains calm and unreadable—as though she is giving me room to continue. "I wonder what my father knew. I know that he saw more than what he told me."

"Why do you say that?" she asks.

"Um, I have felt that way periodically throughout my life, but the night before he died, he seemed shaken. He had fought with Merik, what about, I'll never know, but afterwards, he seemed unsteady. I had paused outside of his doorway and considered going to speak with him, but I didn't. I will always regret not going through that doorway." As I'm telling this to her, I realize that I have never told that story to anyone, not even Jae, and saying it out loud now actually feels like a relief.

"Do you think it would have changed anything if you had?"

"No," I answer quickly. "I don't think so, but at least I would know that I tried."

"I knew your father a little, not very well, but enough to know he was a good man and that, if he ever kept you in the dark, it was for good reason."

I take a breath and nod, "I know. You're right. I just wish I could fully convince myself of that."

*****

Later, lying in bed, I find myself to be restless, though I'm not sure why. The rest of the day went by quickly and I was grateful that dinner tonight was much more casual. I am completely exhausted, yet I can't shake this anxious feeling I have.

The boys seemed to be tired as well. In fact, I didn't see Khalon again the rest of the day. He went to bed after the pollen collecting and slept through dinner. Jae and Falon kept the extent of their conversation to simple pleasantries during dinner and I could see the exhaustion beginning to take them over. It doesn't take long for the longing to be home to replace the excitement of being in a new place. Especially when you have a family to come home to. I no longer have any blood ties to my village, so the longing is not quite the same for me.

Nestling further into my bed, I know I will be happy to be home, but I am going to miss this place.

Chapter 4

The way home seems to be a slower journey. Not only because we are anxious and tired, but because we are weighed down with honey, wax, and other gifts that the bees sent us with. I left the majority of the clothes there for my next visit, but I did take the beautiful silk nightgown with me.

We have to stop more often to rest aching shoulders and tired wings. On one of these stops, we share a loaf of bread for lunch. We haven't said much to each other on this flight home, so when Jae clears his throat, he gets all of our attention.

"So, when you had tea with the Queen, was that just a formality or did she discuss any new treaties or bargains with you?"

The question surprises me. Especially coming from Jae. It would make sense for Falon, a community leader, to be concerned about colony affairs, but Jae has shown very little interest in anything political in the last year.

"No. It was nothing like that at all," I respond. "She really just wanted to ask about the battle and Merik. I'm sure she had a detailed report from the drones, but I think she wanted to hear it from me."

"Do you think she is nervous? About you?" Falon asks gently. "I mean, this entire trip felt as though they were trying to win us over somehow."

I shake my head. I understand what he means. The discovery of my fire could be very frightening, but she never seemed afraid.

"If anything, I feel like she was trying to encourage my acceptance of it. Almost like she wanted to push me towards it and help lift my shame."

"Shame?" Khalon pipes up. He looks at me intensely. He is so committed to defending me, he even takes an active role in protecting me from myself. "You have nothing to be ashamed of."

"Maybe that was a poor choice of words," I say flustered. I put my hands up to calm him down. "I just meant that she is, perhaps, even more comfortable sitting next to me knowing that I could ignite at any moment, than I am."

For whatever reason, whether it was satisfaction with my explanation or the unspoken agreement that there was nothing left to discuss, we finish our meal in silence and set off for the rest of a long day.

Chapter 5

I am surrounded by darkness, and it is impenetrable. I cannot remember how I got here. One thing is quite certain. *I have never been in this place before.* Terror grips me with an iron claw. There is a tightness in my chest like a hand is reaching in and squeezing my heart. I can barely breathe. My body is heavy. It is a struggle just to stay on my feet and I cannot even extend my wings. A force is pushing down on me. *Have I been poisoned? Drugged?* No. No, this feels like something else. I drag my feet carefully with my hands reaching out trying to find my way out of the darkness. The ground is hard beneath my feet. It is like stone, but not smooth like the floor of someone's home. Loose rocks shift under my feet making each step unsure. With each labored breath, I smell some kind of perfume in the air. I can't place the scent, but for some reason, it seems familiar. The hairs on the back of my neck stand on end. There is something else. A presence.

I feel something lurking here. *I am not alone.*

I jerk so suddenly I almost fall out of my bed. The tightness in my chest is still there, and I feel agitated, almost angry. I take in several long, deep breaths and calm myself. I've had nightmares before but nothing quite like this.

The morning light is still quite dim, but I would not be able to go back to sleep even if I tried. I quietly tiptoe into Khalon's room. He has completely taken over Merik's old room and made it his own. Though he still sleeps out on the branch outside of the large window most of the time, we did put in a bigger bed for him to accommodate his large stature when he does stay inside.

The bed in Khalon's room is empty, as I expected, and once I'm completely inside, I see him hanging upside down from his branch. He has his wings wrapped up like a shroud around his body and face. I had suggested in the past that we build something inside the room, so he may hang inside as well, but he says he likes being outside. My ever-watchful warrior, always on guard. I exit his room as quietly as I entered and go downstairs to make some tea.

The morning silence is a precious treat for me since later today will be anything but quiet. We got in late the night before and just in time. Today is, after all, Malyn and Vidar's wedding day. One of the more pressing reasons for our trip to see the bees was, not only to reunite with friends and allies, but to bring back enough honey candle wax for the celebration. Even though I should have stayed here to help prepare for the ceremony, I secretly desired a break from it all, and I knew my absence with the bees could have caused damage to our alliance.

As for Vidar and Malyn, they have been anxiously awaiting this day for three seasons now.

Once the ice broke and the snow started to melt, it has been practically all that Malyn talks about. Ainia has also been abuzz with excitement. She has helped plan just about every detail of the celebration, and she leapt at the invitation when she and I were asked to be bridesmaids. Though my friend's happiness is my primary concern, the excitement of a wedding is desperately needed in the village. The terror and heartbreak from last year's invasion damaged the spirit of so many. We all need good food, music, dancing, and the infectious glow of love.

I am only halfway through my first cup of tea when I hear heavy footsteps coming down the stairs. Khalon shuffles into the room. "You're up early," he says at the tail end of a loud yawn. "I thought you would sleep longer since we got in so late."

"Excited about the day, I suppose," I choose to omit the detail about my nightmare. "Why are you up? You must have just gone to sleep?" I ask him.

"I wanted to see you before you left this morning," he replies. His already deep voice is dragged down deeper still from the cling of sleep.

"Why? Is something wrong?" I can't help but think there is a lecture coming my way after my 'shame' comment yesterday.

He chuckles at me. "No, everything is fine. I just like having breakfast with you and I know you will be fully focused on the bride as soon as you leave here."

"Well, it *is* her big day, it seems only fair that she have my full attention," I say playfully.

He gives me a sideways smile.

I pour tea for him and grab some more bread and dried fruit for breakfast.

"Did you have a nightmare this morning?" he asks directly.

The cup in my hand teeters at his question giving me away. I do not usually tell Khalon the details of my dreams, simply because I know it bothers him that I am still haunted by the events of the past. I suspect he would not even know how to interpret this new dream, but he almost always can tell when I have had one, so lying is futile. I nod at his question.

"Do you want to talk about it?" he offers.

I shake my head. I can see his disappointment. "It's not that I don't want to tell you, I just don't know what it means—if it means anything at all." I know my explanation is not satisfactory for him, but he doesn't press me on it.

He sighs and shakes his head a little. "So, what do you girls have planned this morning, the usual pre-wedding pampering?" he asks after a moment.

"Pretty much," I smile at his willingness to change the subject, "I assume Ainia has various scrubs and rubs prepared to pamper the bride. What about you? What do the men have planned?" Jae and Ragnar are the only two standing up for Vidar as groomsmen, but I know a large group of our male friends are getting together before the wedding. I was very pleased when they invited Khalon. Ever since last year, they have really embraced him as a friend.

"Nothing crazy. We'll probably just get the groom stupid-drunk before the ceremony." My eyes must have widened with concern, because he started laughing at my reaction. "Kidding, kidding! We'll take good care of him, I promise." He raises his right hand as though he is taking an oath. "I think Vidar just wants to do a little fishing with all the guys, and just spend some time out on the riverside. Very mellow."

"Okay, well, I better get over to Malyn's house. Ainia is probably already over there." Before I could leave the kitchen, Mordecai comes through the front door with a couple of newly made fishing rods.

"Hey!" he said loudly to us both as he made his way into the room. He moved out into his own nest at the end of winter, so I don't see him every day like I used to. I miss having him here, but I am glad that he feels at home in our village, enough to build his own permanent home. He still has long black hair to match his black crow's wings, but his face has more color than it used to. You can tell he is happy. "Hi Sig," he says to me. "You ready?" he asks Khalon.

"I'm coming. Hang on. Let me just go get my things," Khalon grumbles.

"Just grab your knife, I brought you a rod." Mordecai offers.

"Ha! I don't need a rod. I'll use my spear."

"Once a savage, always a savage," I say jokingly to Mordecai, once Khalon is upstairs.

"No kidding!" He laughs.

"Do you know if Ainia is already over at Malyn's house?" I ask him.

"I'm not sure. She said she would be heading over there pretty early."

"Is she giving you a hard time with all this wedding stuff?" Khalon asks Mordecai as he enters the room again, spear in hand. "I bet she is just aching to get married."

"No, no, no, no. No marriage, not yet," Mordecai insists holding his hands up like barriers.

"Uh-huh," Khalon says suspiciously. "Are you telling me she hasn't brought it up since you built your own place?"

Mordecai just shakes his head a little and looks at the ground. I see a small smile on his face that tells me that Khalon is absolutely right.

"Can we just go fishing, please," Mordecai pleads through a smile.

"I'll see you later," Khalon says to me. He is smiling broadly on account of his small victory of needling his friend. He taps my chin with one large finger before they leave the house.

Chapter 6

Malyn's home is buzzing with activity. Malyn has a large family. She is the oldest of six children, and most of her extended family is already swarming. I can hear the commotion from outside. Ainia arrives at the same time I do. She is holding a very large billowy cloth bag that I can only assume is the wedding dress, and several other small bags that are slung over her shoulders.

"Hey, let me help you with that," I rush over to help unburden her.

"Oh, thank you." She peers over the top of the cloth bag. All I can see of her is the top of her head and her bright blue eyes.

The noise inside the house is truly overwhelming. Malyn's mother, Raya, spots us through the chaos and comes rushing over.

"Hello, hello. Come in, come in." Raya usher's us into the main part of the living room and gives us each a big hug. "The bride is upstairs," she says bursting with pride, "go on up. She is expecting you, and I have told everyone else that they have to leave you girls alone. I don't want anyone bothering my little sweet pea on her big day."

I am relieved that Raya has set boundaries for her family today. I am feeling dizzy just being here for two minutes. It is remarkably quieter upstairs and, by the time we make it up to Malyn's room, the frantic chatter from downstairs is reduced to a subtle hum.

Malyn is sitting at her dressing table and only her sisters, Evyan and Ava, are in the room with her. She looks beautiful and we haven't even done any of the preparations yet. Her skin is more luminous than the most beautiful pearl, and her cheeks are flush with a rosy glow. Evyan has just started pinning Malyn's fiery red hair up with white flowers.

Malyn is calm and quiet. I was expecting to see her zipping around the way she normally does, but instead she is completely at peace. She smiles brightly at us when we enter and stands, interrupting her sister's handy work, to welcome us.

"Well, I'd like to say, let's get you beautiful for your day, but you are already perfection," Ainia gushes fighting back joyous tears.

Malyn laughs. "Regardless, I will happily accept any tricks you have brought with you!"

*****

Hours of primping and a dull headache later, I slip out of the house, using the excuse that one of us should make sure everything is in order at the ceremony site. Between Ainia and Malyn's flock of siblings, the bride is sufficiently looked after, and I need a moment of quiet. Serenity wraps around me like a warm blanket the moment the door closes behind me and the noise drops out.

Malyn and Vidar chose to have an outdoor ceremony at our old training ground. At first, the families thought it was an inappropriate choice; holding a wedding at a location that had been formerly used as a place where we prepared for war, but this is also where they started to fall in love. This field is where we all came together as a community. Thinking about it now, a wedding is a perfect way to reinvent this place.

When I first set eyes on it, I cannot believe that I am standing in the same field. A year ago, the ground had been worn down by our stampeding and grappling. The trees on the perimeter had all been chipped and stripped from constant target practice, but now where arrows and knives once protruded, new bark scabs over closing the wound. Fresh, soft grass covers the ground. Pink blossoms on the trees, still lingering from spring, are just now starting to fall. With every subtle breeze, the air fills with soft, silken petals.

Four tall, wooden posts have been planted into the ground on the northern side of the field, outlining a large wedding alter. Flowered vines are strung across the top and wrapped around the posts to complete this romantic picture of elegance. Several other families work busily setting up the food tent, tables, and chairs, lighting candles, and putting the last finishing touches on the scene.

There is laughter coming from a tent in the distance. Laughter that I know very well.

As a joke, I cover my eyes as I walk into the groom's tent. "You boys decent in here?" I ask peeking through my fingertips. Jae, Ragnar, Ravi, Soren, and Khalon are all staggered around Vidar, who is slouching comfortably on a stool.

"Hey Sig!" they all shout collectively.

"We are decent," Jae says.

"But not for long!" Soren slurs. He is loosely clutching a half empty wine bottle.

They are all a bit of a mess: shirts unbuttoned, disheveled hair, faces aglow with too much wine. Their high spirits are infectious, even though I am looking at the groom, who is positively sloppy, it is impossible to be mad.

"You boys are a mess," I try to maintain a serious composition, but I can't help but to break out into a giggle. I point to Vidar, "Are you drunk?" His eyes go wide. My smile spreads.

"Oh, you are going to be in so much trouble!" I tease.

"Please don't tell Malyn." He looks absolutely frightened.

I laugh loudly and mess up his hair even more. "I'm not going to tell Malyn, but you're lucky I came out here early. Let's get you guys fixed up."

I grab the cork that's on the table and plug the bottle in Soren's hand. He is leaning a little to the left and has an unsteadiness to him, like the smallest tap could knock him over. "You need to sober up." I lecture him a little more seriously. "Why, don't you go get some water?"

He snorts at the suggestion. "Yes, Your Majesty," he taunts with a mock bow. Heat rises in my chest.

The jovial mood has shifted. Jae stands up from his chair so he's behind me. Khalon moves quickly and calmly over to Soren and puts his arm around Soren's shoulders. "Come on. Let's get something to eat." Khalon ushers him out of the tent smoothly. Once they are gone, my temperature cools down.

"That was intense," Ragnar says under his breath as he relaxes his posture once again.

"I'm sorry," I say to Vidar. "I just…you know how I feel about that."

I did accept a role of leadership in the village. I sit on the council, and I treasure the golden crown that was gifted to me, but I refuse to be queen. It is not a role that I am prepared to fill, and I hate being called 'majesty.' I kept those feelings to myself when I saw the Bee Queen out of respect, but I have no intention to wear the crown.

"Don't apologize. He was out of line," Vidar assures me.

I give him a faint smile and let out a breath. "Okay, let's get you fixed up."

*****

One at a time, I dust off their shirts, comb and straighten their hair, pin fresh boutonnieres on their dress robes, and send them out of the tent one at a time to stand in place. Vidar and I are the last two in the tent. A look crosses over his face that can only be described as sadness. I know instantly what he is thinking. It is something that only people who have had tremendous losses understand.

"You are thinking of your father, aren't you?" I ask.

He gives me a half-smile, and nods.

"Osiris and I had our problems for sure, but I know he was a good father, and he would be so proud of the man you have become." I look at him, and his light gray eyes are beginning to show the promise of tears. "Because you used to be a real jerk."

He laughs. "I know."

I smooth out his lapels and give him a kiss on the cheek. "Well, I think it's just about time. I better go check on the bride." I look over my shoulder at him just before walking out. He looks happy.

*****

The bridal tent is the same frenzy that Malyn's home was, except now, instead of being spread out in a home, it is crammed in a tent. Finally, Malyn's father comes in and shoos out everyone except for me, her mother, Evyan, and Ainia. Now that the tent has cleared out, I can see Malyn fully for the first time. The dress that Ainia made is truly a masterpiece. White silk drapes lightly at Malyn's shoulders and cinches tight at her waist and then billows out slightly like an upside-down lily all the way to the ground and beyond. The silhouette is simple enough, but the color gradually goes from a soft white to a beautiful blue, like un-veined turquoise, at the bottom. Her red hair, delicately pinned in easy waves, is adorned with fragrant white flowers. I don't think a bride has ever looked more beautiful. It was clear that Vidar thought the very same thing when he saw her for the first time at the ceremony. His eyes fixed on her with such love and wonderment. He did not break his stare until he was given permission by Vivek, who was officiating the ceremony, to kiss her for the first time as his wife.

The entire village cheered as they took their first steps together as husband and wife. The music starts almost instantly, and food and drink are plentiful. Every household brought something, whether it was food, wine, flowers, or other various gifts. A wedding is not just about two families coming together. It is about *all* families celebrating love. This party is something everyone needed.

Just after the food and drinks are brought, the band begins to play a particular song. I recognize the tune right away. It is a formal dance for couples, full of arm linking, twirling, and lifts. I immediately want to disappear, I'm miserable at dancing. Jae, Khalon, and I stand together awkwardly, until Wren pops up out of the crowd.

"Hey! Wanna dance?" She elbows Khalon in the side.

He looks positively terrified. "I don't. I've never." He looks over at me, hoping for a rescue.

"Don't look at me, I'm a terrible dancer. You'll be in much better hands with Wren," I say, with a small smile, taking a small amount of satisfaction in his squirming about.

"Come on," she grabs him by the wrist and pulls him out to the dance floor.

She walks him through the steps quickly and then they are in the middle of the dance with the rest. I see Wren's face twist a few times when one of Khalon's misplaced feet lands on one of her own. It's like watching a bear dance with a bird, but I must admit he is picking it up rather quickly. The couples stand in two lines, then step forward and link arms with their partner and spin around together. When they release, they link arms with a different partner and spin with them before finding their way back to their original partner for the lift. The male lifts his lady counterpart and, once she's in the air, spreads out her wings and catches just enough air to float for a moment, before landing back into her partner's arms. It is lovely to watch. Malyn and Vidar are, of course, dancing together. Ainia is actually dancing this one with her father. It's very sweet to see them together. Ainia is a really beautiful dancer, and you can see how proud he is of her. Khalon is so strong, I worry that Wren might end up in the trees on the lifts. She goes higher than any of the others, and a couple times I see her eyes go wide, I think she might be nervous he might toss her into the sky as well.

I giggle to myself as I watch.

"Shall we?" Jae says as he nudges me.

"What? No." I shake my head and take a step backwards away from the dance floor.

"Yes. It'll be fun."

"Nope. No, it won't. I'm horrible, and I haven't done this dance since I was a little girl. I barely remember it."

"Oh, stop being a baby," he rolls his eyes and grabs my hand, leading me to my doom. My temperature starts to rise the moment we get on the floor. I find my spot in the line and clumsily go through the moves. Stepping on his feet, bumping into his shoulder. It isn't until the second time through that I finally start to find some confidence. The good thing is anyone can look great when they are dancing with Jae. He moves easily and leads very well. He knows just how to touch me to get me to move where I need to. By the end, I even find myself smiling. He picks me up in his arms and kisses me on the cheek. He looks into my eyes. He looks happy. I feel my face flush and his eyes dance down to my neckline.

"I haven't seen that happen for a while," he says with a sideways smile.

I look down and see that the rose is blushing. I close my eyes and shake my head. It has been a while since my emotions have been on display. I forgot how embarrassing it is when it shows. He smiles and kisses my face again.

Well into the reception, I find myself sitting, rubbing the balls of my feet, I'm not used to this much dancing. Watching the scene on the dance floor is almost as entertaining as being part of it. Ainia and Mordecai are pretty much inseparable. With the exception of the dance, she had with her father, they have not left each other's arms. Malyn and Vidar have barely had a chance to hit the dance floor themselves, busy zipping around from table to table, person to person, expressing their gratitude to everyone who came. The real spectacle though, is watching Jae maneuver his way around the droves of young girls all pining for his attention. He had his hands full enough trying to entertain Malyn's sisters, but then all the girls trickled onto the dance floor and, before he knew it, he was overrun. Occasionally, he will shoot me a glance beckoning for a rescue.

I hear a deep chuckle behind me. I look up to see Khalon watching the same show I am.

"Looks like Jae's gotten himself into a real situation," he says, as he sits in the chair next to me. "Aren't you going to go save him?"

"Nah, he's fine."

He looks at me a little surprised.

"He's enjoying himself more than he's letting on," I justify. "He's loving the attention."

"You're probably right." He picks up the foot I was rubbing and starts to massage it for me. I can't help but to let out a small groan of relief.

"I don't think I have had a chance to tell you that you look really beautiful tonight," he says, looking up from my toes that he is expertly rubbing. Ainia also made complementing dresses for herself, Malyn's sisters, and me. They are all the same turquoise color, but each one is a little different than the next. Mine is about mid-thigh in length and has a high neck and a low back.

"Ainia did a really great job with all the dresses," I admit.

"The dress is nice for sure, but that wasn't really what I meant." He stops rubbing my foot and pulls my chair closer to him. I smile at him. He leans toward me. I feel my heartbeat in my throat as he gets closer to me, our eyes locked on each other. I hear my heart thumping in my ears. My insides are rippling, but he looks a calm and easy as the most placid pond on a day with no wind. Before he can touch me, something runs into my chair, jolting my attention away. Soren is standing next to us. He is swaying and has to hold on to the back of my chair to keep steady.

He clearly finished off that bottle from before and likely started on another.

"Sig, dance with me," he slurs at me. His eyelids are drooping so low, I'm amazed he found his way over to me.

"No, I don't really feel like dancing right now, Soren," I try to be diplomatic.

"Come on," he pushes on the chair and trips over himself.

I stand and grab him to keep him from falling. He puts his arms around my shoulders. They are heavy and careless. The smell of wine and sweat has turned sour. My stomach wretches.

"You're not still mad at me are you, Sig?" He asks, not letting go.

"No, I'm not mad." I try to shrug out of his grasp, but he is not budging. I see Khalon over Soren's shoulder. He wants to step in, but I hold up my hand to stop him.

"Then let's dance." Soren moves me closer to the dance floor.

"Soren, I don't want to."

He's not listening to me. Instead, he stumbles his way over to the middle of the dancefloor with me in tow. Everyone has stopped dancing to look at us.

It's embarrassing. My temper is rising. I have been trying to hold it in since the moment jeered me in the groom's tent. My body feels hot, but there is something else building as well; something darker. Whatever it is, it is being held in by something fragile, like a thin pane of glass, and whatever it is, it's tapping at the barrier looking for the weak spot, threatening to break loose at any moment.

The pendant that my father gave me is usually cool to the touch but, for some reason, now it is burning my chest. Soren starts to spin us around in circles. He finally starts to let go a little and I squirm free.

"Come on," he pleads. He grabs my arm hard and pulls me back to him.

My body starts shaking. I desperately try to regain control. *Hold it together.* I tell myself, but it's too late. The glass barrier inside me breaks and I am suddenly immersed in a feeling. A rush tingles through all of me. Static vibrations touch every nerve, raise every hair, and finally reach the top of my head before exploding in a divine release that can only be explained as enraptured. I feel stronger. I am stronger; more powerful. Similar to how I feel when I am on fire but amplified. I look at Soren again.

He is nothing, a simple boor.

I grab him by the shirt and toss him, easily, across the dancefloor into a table of food. The table collapses under him. Honey rolls and spice cakes litter the ground beneath him. His eyes are wide and fearful, as they should be. He looks sober for the first time tonight. His helplessness feeds my exhilaration. I am angry.

Hurt him. Hurting him will feel good.

Crossing the space between us with only the intention of crushing him with my bare hands, I anticipate the sound of his bones cracking, the breath leaving his body, and it fills me with pleasure. Picking him up off the ground is easy, like lifting a doll. He is too stunned to move. My hands wrap around his throat, and I squeeze.

"Impudent creature," I growl, astounded by his presumption that he was allowed to touch me. "You are slime, worthless and disgusting. How dare you address me—a queen." The vein in his neck pops out, straining against the

46

constriction of my grasp. I feel the slowing of his pulse against my thumb. This exertion of power is the most intoxicating feeling I have ever had. The exhilaration that I feel is only stifled by the uncomfortable burning of my pendant.

I look into his eyes and then, suddenly, there is a flicker of something. I blink and see Merik's eyes the day I killed him. I blink again and see Soren scared and struggling to breathe. It is only then that I fully realize I am about to end his life. I rock back onto my heels. My new strength fails me, and Soren drops to the ground. He gasps and coughs. My own breath is labored as well.

Looking around, I see scared and confused faces. Even Khalon is in shock. The broken table, wasted food, and broken gifts are evidence of my tirade. I did this. The music has stopped and, with the exception of crying children huddled together under one of the tables, there is only silence.

Malyn pushes her way through the crowd until she is standing in front of me. She is careful to keep a good distance from me. She just looks at me with pain in her eyes. Whether it is for her, or me, I'm not sure.

I feel like I might get sick.

"I. I'm so sorry," I manage to say to Malyn. I look around at everyone else and I feel tears slip from my eyes. "So, so very sorry."

Khalon takes a step toward me, and I take a step back, afraid of myself. I take off into the night sky and retreat home.

Chapter 7

"What is wrong with me?" I ask myself, while staring at my reflection in my dressing mirror, studying my every feature, looking for an answer.

He was drunk and stupid. He had it coming. The darkness tremors through me giving me justification. *I should have crushed him.*

No! I grab fistfuls of my hair, trying to pull the anger out. This rage is unlike anything I have ever felt before. It gives me power and pleasure, but I know it is wrong.

Once I calm down and force the rage out, heartbreak rushes in to fill its place. I ruined Malyn's wedding celebration. I remember her face; confused, scared, eyes brimming with tears.

Shame grips hard at my chest, and the overwhelming tightness finally irrupts into sobs. Hot tears break free, streaming down my face uncontrollably. I try to stop, but that only makes it worse.

There is a gentle knock at my door.

"Sigrun? Can I come in?" Khalon asks nicely.

I struggle to collect myself long enough to answer. "I think I should be alone right now." I finally manage.

"Let me in, Sig." His tone is more insistent.

"No, I really—"

"Do I have to remind you that I can break this door down?" he interrupts. "Easily," he adds for emphasis.

I take a deep breath. "Okay, just give me a minute."

I strip off my dress and put on my nightgown. As I'm folding the dress, I see a burn mark the shape of a circle near the neckline. It is from my pendant. I touch the marble, and it is cool again. My skin is a bit tender beneath it, but it is already healing.

Strange.

I check my face in the mirror. It's a mess; my nose is runny and the skin beneath my eyes is red and blotchy from the tears.

"Sigrun?" he calls again.

"I'm coming." I wipe my face quickly with a rag and go to the door.

Khalon is leaning into the frame of the door as I open it. His eyes are intense and concerned, his brow furrowed in confusion. I look away from him and down to the floor, feeling ashamed. He reaches out to touch me, but I take a step away from it. Tears are brimming in my eyes again and I know any comfort from him will unleash them. He retracts his hand, and he looks sad, but this sadness is more for me, than for him.

I retreat further into my room and sit on my bed. He follows and sits on my vanity stool so he can face me. He leans in close to me and puts his hands on the outsides of my knees. As I predicted, just this little bit of contact has brought back my sobs. He lets me cry. He says nothing He only wipes my eyes with a soft rag. This kindness is better than I deserve.

After a while, I finally calm down enough to find my voice again. "How's Malyn?" I ask, afraid to hear the answer.

"She's okay. She wanted to come and see you, but we convinced her to stay. She's worried about you. Everyone is."

He looks at me intensely. His eyes burrow into mine looking for an explanation that I don't have myself. I shake my head and lower my gaze to my hands.

"I don't know what happened," I answer the unasked question.

He shrugs, "Soren was pushing you all day. You just snapped."

I appreciate Khalon trying to dilute the situation to make me feel better, but I know that there is something else. I just don't know what. Instead of explaining that to him, I nod my head at his generous excuse for my awful behavior.

"Yeah, sure. He was definitely getting under my skin."

Khalon's eyes squint a little. He sees everything in me, and he always knows when I'm not telling him something. I suspect tonight is no exception. Since I'm not feeling like digging into this new development, I try my best to put on a convincing smile and shift the topic.

"So, did you bring me any cake," I ask.

"Do you think you deserve cake?" His eyes are still squinting, but he has the hint of a smile.

"No," I speak candidly, but with humor.

"Good. You don't, but I brought it you some anyway. Come on, it's downstairs." He picks up my hand out of my lap and leads me to the kitchen.

Two large pieces of spice cake with raspberry sauce are sitting on the table. My stomach rumbles at the sight of them. I haven't eaten much today. The commotion of the wedding has kept me busy all day and I was so preoccupied talking to everyone and dancing at the celebration that I forgot to eat.

"You want me to make tea?" he asks.

"I think I might need something stronger."

Khalon raises his eyebrows. I rarely drink wine.

"I can do that." He walks over to the cupboard and pulls out a dark green bottle.

Chapter 8

Murmurs coming from my kitchen lure me out of my wine-induced coma. The brightness of the sun and how it is assaulting my eyes tells me it is either very late in the morning or early afternoon. My mouth feels dry, like I spent the night chewing on sand, and my head is throbbing. I stumble to my vanity table, looking for water. Both the pitcher and cup are empty. I feel even thirstier now, than before. I look at my reflection even though I know it will be a disaster. Disaster doesn't even cover it. My eyes are swollen and bloodshot, my hair is disheveled irreparably, and the healthy tan I usually have in the warm seasons has abandoned me and left a pasty, sickly, green color behind. The last thing I want to do right now is face the world, but the need for water forces me out the door. Once I'm on the stairs, I hear Khalon and Jae in the kitchen.

"You know that was something different," Jae says to Khalon.

"Yes. Jae, I know." Khalon sounds tired.

"And the voice." Jae starts, "you know that was different, it didn't sound anything like her."

My voice was different? It sounded like my voice to me. I don't know where the words and thoughts came from, but the voice was definitely mine.

"What did she tell you?" Jae presses.

"Nothing. She was concerned about Malyn, and she was upset. I gave her an excuse that Soren was being too aggressive, and she lost her temper. She agreed and then we had some cake," Khalon says casually.

"You had some cake?" Jae repeats stupefied. There is a long pause. Khalon knows Jae wants more of an explanation, but he has none to offer.

"Do you think she knows what happened?" Jae finally asks.

"I do," Khalon admits, "but I didn't want to push her last night. She felt awful. Whatever triggered, whatever that was," he doesn't finish his sentence.

I don't think he knows how to. I feel sick. Khalon is right. I do know what happened, but then, at the same time, I don't. I remember losing control and letting that darkness take over. I remember how good it felt to surrender to it, but what it is or why it happened, I have no answer.

I take a deep breath and enter the room. Their faces are muddled with embarrassment when they realize I probably overheard their conversation and something else that resembles pity.

I don't like it. In fact, it makes me a little edgy.

"Morning," Khalon says first.

"Morning," I respond coolly.

"How are you feeling?" Jae asks, clearing his throat.

"Fine."

I walk over to the kettle and pour myself some tea.

"Okay. Well, I just wanted to make sure you were alright. You left so suddenly, you know, so I wanted to check," Jae fights his way through his explanation.

I press my mouth in a line. I don't know what to say.

"It looks like you are okay," he pauses and looks me over. "Except, your hair. Your hair's a mess."

Even Khalon laughs at Jae's all so true observation. Jae tugs on one of my wayward locks and squeezes my shoulder before he heads out the door. Once he's gone, I look at Khalon who is returning my look with analytical, squinting eyes.

"You know what I think?" he asks.

"I'm afraid to ask."

"I think you need a good fight."

"What?"

"Yeah, I think you need a workout. You've been sedentary for too long. You're edgy, pent-up. You just need an outlet for all that energy. If you think about it, you've tapped into an energy that no one has ever seen, and it has just been welling up with nowhere to go. I bet you will feel a lot better if we start doing some regular training."

I guess his idea makes sense. I don't really feel "pent-up," but it doesn't seem like it would hurt anything to blow off a little steam. It might feel good to throw a sword around a little bit. It's worth trying anyway.

"Okay," I agree.

"Okay," he smiles, "just do something about that hair first."

I grab a piece of bread that is on the table and throw it at him. He swats it away and laughs.

*****

The field still has remnants from the night before; leftover shreds from the paper lanterns, some candy lost to the grass by playing children, the occasional wine bottle strewn. Then, I see the spot by the edge of the dancefloor where I tossed Soren. Cake is still smashed into the ground from when the table collapsed. All of these things are evidence of a happy day, until I ruined it. My stomach drops.

Khalon nudges me with his shoulder, bumping me out of my misery. I look at him. He has a smile that says, 'I know what you're thinking—let it go.'

"Alright," he says handing me my sword, "let's see what you remember."

He takes his place opposite me. An arrogant half-smile spreads across his face. I hold my sword ready. It takes a moment to remember what it is like to fight with a sword. A year ago, I was training every day. After a while, the weapons became an extension of my own arm, but we haven't had any need for swords, or bows, except for regular hunting and fishing. It didn't take long for me to forget how the grip of the hilt feels, or the weight of the blade. Khalon taps the end of my sword with his to start the match. Instantly, I feel the acceleration of my heart, my blood pumping a little faster, a little harder. I dig my heels into the ground, bend my knees, and stand ready. He swings broad and wide from overhead. I block with my sword and move to the side. He swings again. I block. He comes at me with his sword on the right side, the left, from the top, and from underneath. He swings hard and wide, and fast and small. I keep blocking. Over, and over. Again, and again.

The morning sun is getting hotter. My hands are getting sweaty making my grip unsure. My arms are getting tired. He, on the other hand, doesn't seem to show any fatigue. Aside from the perspiration on his forehead, he looks as rested as he was when we first arrived. He won't let this fight end until I have won it in some way. I wipe the sweat from my brow, and spin my sword around in my hand, getting a new grip. He smiles, knowing I'm getting tired. I think back to the first time I fought Khalon. We were training like we are now. He got the best of me over and over, until I finally figured him out. I have to attack. I swing suddenly, and his eyes go wide, but he looks pleased.

53

"There she is," he says, blocking my swing, "there's my fighter." I swing again. He blocks my swing with his sword in his right hand and grabs my wrist with his left. "I thought maybe I lost you for a minute," he smiles and grits his teeth as he pushes me away, hard.

Heat builds in my chest. I go after him again, but this time I don't stop. I keep swinging and push him back further into the field. The repeated clang of the steel drowns out all the sounds of the forest. I can see it now. He is starting to tire.

Our swords lock up, both of us pressing our blades toward the other. He grunts and pushes, one hard shove that not only breaks the hold, but the hilt of his sword pops up and hits me hard in the mouth. I see stars for a second and stumble backwards.

"Oh! Are you alright?" Khalon lowers his sword and rushes over as I spit blood on the ground. "I'm sorry. You okay? Here, let me take a look." He reaches out to touch my chin, and I snap. It doesn't go dark exactly, but the rage fills me and runs through me, and my vision, along with all my other senses, shifts. Everything is sharper, more defined, and all I want to do is hit him back.

I swat his hand away and throw my sword again, he isn't ready this time, and though he recovers quickly I can see he is surprised and confused by me now. It feeds my anger, and I continue to go after him.

"Sigrun! Hey, calm down," he tries to reason with me.

But I won't be reasoned with. "You always think your better," I growl.

"What? Sigrun."

I swing at him again. He blocks.

"But you're not! I'm the leader of this colony, *me*!" I swing hard again. He moves to the side, escaping the blade. "I'm smarter," I swing, "I'm faster," I swing again, "and, I'm stronger!"

I lean back and bring my leg up, thrusting hard, my foot connects squarely with his chest. The force of it knocks him back so far that he rolls backwards and has to dig his hands into the ground to stop.

Finish him. The voice purrs in my head.

I run towards him, sword drawn and ready to cut him down. His eyes are wide with shock and disbelief. I run faster. Rather than bring up his sword to defend himself, he slams it point down into the ground and throws his hands up in surrender.

"SIGRUN, STOP!" he shouts.

His voice rattles through me, shaking me down to my bones. I do stop. My senses go back to normal, and I look at him. He is on his knees with his hands in the air. He is breathing fast, and his eyes are wide. I drop my sword and fall to the ground. My head is throbbing, my body is shaking, and my chest feels constricted. I struggle to breathe.

"It's okay, you're okay," he rushes over to me and holds me tightly to his chest. His heart is beating faster than normal, but after a few moments, it slows down to its regular rhythmic beat. Like a lullaby, it soothes me enough so my breathing calms down and my tremors start to subside. I try to match my breathing to his; slow and steady. His body is warm, and I almost feel as though I could melt into him. He is, and always has been, such a comfort to me. Why did I get so angry? We've sparred many times, and I've never reacted this way to him before. I would never hurt him, or any my friends.

"So, maybe a workout was a bad idea," he jokes.

I chuckle.

He holds me tighter, cradling my head in his large hand, stroking my hair. He kisses my head, and though I know he wants to an explanation, he doesn't ask for one, and I am grateful for it.

*****

Jae and Ainia are standing in front of my house when we return. Ainia seems a little surprised to see us walking up with weapons in tow, though she might be more alarmed by my disgraceful, muddy, and stained appearance.

"Hey," she says to us. "How are you?" she asks me.

I sigh deeply. I don't really know how to answer. "I'm okay. Thirsty."

Khalon's mouth slightly twitches towards a smile, "We just thought we would do a little training," he says, explaining our appearance. "Trying to stay loose."

Jae looks skeptical but doesn't say anything. I usher everyone inside and head for the water pitcher. Everyone awkwardly stands in silence while I drink a full cup.

Ainia clears her throat.

"So, Malyn and Vidar are having a family and friend dinner tomorrow night and they would like you to come," Ainia speaks almost diplomatically.

The invitation surprises me. I ruined their wedding. I threatened one of our friends. I frightened the entire village. Again.

"Are we sure that's a good idea?" Jae questions.

Now I realize why they are both here. Ainia has been tasked with inviting me and Jae is trying to protect either me, or the entire village; I'm not sure which, and their goals are conflicting.

"I mean, is that safe? For everyone, for Sigrun?" he continues. All of us look at him with varied expressions. Khalon looks baffled—I don't think he ever expected Jae would speak out against me. Ainia looks a little grateful that he said it, but also a little annoyed since he is arguing the other side, and I must have a wounded look, because that's how I feel. What's funny is that I agree with him, but hearing him say it out loud, hurts.

"Do you expect her to lock herself up forever?" Khalon fires back.

I'm surprised that Khalon is taking such a strong stance on my behalf after what just happened at the field.

"This just happened yesterday." Jae is getting defensive.

"I know, and the sooner we address it the better."

Watching them battle it out in front of me is uncomfortable.

"Look guys," Ainia cuts in, "Malyn and Vidar asked for her to be there."

"Jae might be right," I say at last. Jae looks relieved. Thinking about how I just almost beheaded Khalon at the field, I'm obviously still a little raw.

"No, he's not," Khalon says through his teeth. He is trying to appear calm, but his clenched jaw deceives him.

"I'm not really comfortable seeing everyone right now. I think I should stay behind this time."

"Well, it's not about you and what you think. It's about them and what they want," Ainia throws back at me. It stings.

Who does she think she is? I could rip her wings off with one hand if I wanted to.

Seething anger flares up in me. It rattles through me all the way to the surface of my skin.

I take a breath and try to clear my head.

"Go and get cleaned up and rest," she says with a smile, "we'll see you there tomorrow night."

I take another deep breath. I don't like being handled like a child.

Jae shakes his head but says nothing more. They leave together.

"Are you okay?" Khalon looks me in the eyes. He is serious, and I can tell he is trying to figure out what I'm really thinking.

I purse my lips into a hard line and nod. He doesn't speak but keeps staring. Finally, I turn and go upstairs. This seems like madness. I don't want to go. I don't want to see anyone. I don't want to deal with the stares and fake niceties, but Malyn is one of my closest friends. I owe it to her.

*****

Khalon and I stand in front of Malyn and Vidar's new home. I nervously fidget with the strap of my purple dress—the nice one that Ainia made for me. I thought I should make an effort to look nice for the occasion. I wish I felt better about being here. My legs feel heavy, like I am rooted here as part of the landscape. Khalon looks at me and squeezes my hand with encouragement. I give him a small smile and walk towards the back garden.

The house is pretty big for just the two of them, but knowing Malyn, she'll want a big family someday. The outside garden is truly the best feature of the home. Malyn worked tirelessly planting the most beautiful flowers and a large vegetable garden before they settled in. I hear many voices chirping in the back. It sounds like everyone is already here.

There is one very large, long table that seats about 18, and a couple of smaller tables for the kids. Just about everyone has already been seated. The food is out, and it is a feast as abundant as the wedding night. The flowers, both in the garden and on the tables, waft a delicate perfume, and the candles glow softly in the failing sunlight. It's beautiful, and I don't belong here.

The conversations all stop as soon as we are noticed, and we are standing in awkward silence. Something grips at me like an invisible hand reaching into my chest.

Peasants. They should be bowing rather than staring.

I squeeze my eyes shut. When I open them, at the far end of the table, I see a bright red head of hair pop up. It is Malyn. Immediately my anger subsides. She smiles as she zips over to me, and she hugs me so hard I almost fall over. The tightness in my chest is gone and tears stream down my face.

"Thank you for inviting me," I say through sobs. "I'm just so sor—"

She puts her hand up to keep me from finishing my apology. She smiles, "I'm just so glad you came."

We find our places at the table. The reactions from the rest of the group are mixed. The majority seem cautious, but most of my friends are happy to see me. Naturally, Soren is much more reserved, and I notice he declined wine this evening. I feel some of the children are afraid of me, which makes me incredibly sad. I'll have to find a way to make it up to them. I say nothing during the meal. Instead, I listen and laugh and try to remain as far in the background as I can. I listen to the retelling of old stories and what everyone has planned for the summer months. Even Malyn, to Vidar's horror, tells a few funny moments from their wedding night. Overall, the mood of the evening is jovial, and I start to forget why I was nervous in the first place.

At the end of the meal, the laughter settles down just enough for me to notice Soren staring off in the distance. I pick up one of the small cakes in front of me and two forks. I get up from my seat and walk over to him.

"Friends?" I ask standing in front of him with the cake extended as a sugary peace offering.

He chuckles a bit and motions for me to sit next to him.

"I'm really sorry," I say to him. "I don't know what happened," I want to say more, but I can't seem to make sense of it.

Soren shakes his head, "No, I was really out of line. I should have never grabbed you like that, so I'm sorry too."

I smile and nod as I hand him a fork, and we both take a big bite of cake. I look over the rest of the table. Most everyone is caught up in their own side conversations. I catch a wink from Khalon, and a smile from Jae. I smile back and look over my shoulder to see a little girl running right toward me. Except, she doesn't see me. She is looking behind her at the little boy that is playfully chasing her in some kind of childish game. So preoccupied by her miniature pursuer, and so deafened by her own squealing giggle, no one is able to stop her before she slams into me leaving the contents of her juice cup that she had in one hand and the piece of cake that she had in the other, both in my lap.

There is a moment when we look at each other, her big blue eyes are wide with surprise. I sit frozen looking at the sticky mess that drips down the front of me. My dress, a gift from one of my dearest friends, ruined. The little girl looks from my face to my lap, and she covers her mouth as she lets out a small chuckle. The rest of the table falls silent. My hands begin to tremble, and I see red.

Little brat.

Furious, I snatch her up easily by the front of her dress. She shrieks as I hold her inches from my face.

"Not laughing anymore, I see," I growl at her.

Panic and fear are laced in her eyes. I hear a small cry down on my left side, it is the little boy, the co-conspirator in my humiliation. I grab him by the arm as well.

"You." I turn my attention to the boy. His face still smeared with cake, too afraid to cry, "You disgusting little creature! Do you think it's fun to chase little girls?" I release him with a hard shove. I pull the little girl close enough so our noses almost touch, "And you need to watch where you are going."

I put her back on the ground. She runs to her mother sobbing and hides behind the protective folds of her mother's dress.

"S-Sig," Ainia barely mutters. She lightly touches my elbow.

I pull away from her quickly. "Don't. Touch. Me." I warn, speaking clearly and slowly, through clenched teeth, "I told you I didn't want to come here, but you didn't listen, did you?" I shake my head for her. "You need to start listening."

I look over the faces of the rest of the party. Their dumbfounded looks strike a chord even deeper in my rage.

This has gone on too long. They are lazy, disobedient, urchins who have taken you for granted.

"You all need to start listening," I say pointing at the lot.

Chapter 9

It wasn't until I was back in my room that I realized what had just happened. *What have I done?*

Their faces. The silence. It was just like the other day, but worse. How can they possibly forgive me now? My breathing runs away from me—getting faster and faster. The loss of control makes my head spin. Where is this anger and hatred coming from, and why do I keep surrendering to it? I lie in the darkness of my room. I desperately try to quiet my mind and ease the sickness in my belly, but it seems that it's all in vain. It gnaws at me like a rabid rodent. I close my eyes and try to think of nothing, because nothing is the only thing that does not hurt. My dreams come for me quickly. Just after the moment my eyelids resign, I am transported back into that dark place from before.

Everything is the same: the rocky ground, the heaviness in my body, the familiar smell, the darkness. At least, this time, I know it is a dream. Despite the force which tries to keep me down, I manage to walk forward. As my eyes adjust to the dark, I notice that the rocky earth covers every surface. I'm in a cave. It is not a cave anywhere near our village, I know that for sure, and the earth is different than the Southlands. *Where am I?*

They don't deserve you. A voice speaks to me, but it sounds like my own. *That little girl should have been begging for forgiveness. They will learn their place before the end.*

I look around for the source of this proclamation, but it is only me. I am alone.

There is a loud thrumming coming from the other end of the tunnel. It is not from any instrument that I have ever heard, and it hurts my ears. Every step is harder to take. It feels like an invisible shield keeps pushing on me. The tightness in my chest returns and the pendant starts to burn. It sears my flesh. The pain brings me to my knees. The thrumming is getting louder, and louder. Now the pounding is inside my head. Then there is screaming from the tunnel.

I spin around wildly trying to find the source. It seems to come from everywhere. They are so terrified; so full of pain, like someone is fighting for their life. It hurts me. I can't take it. *I can't take it!* I find myself sitting upright in my bed at the tail end of my own scream. Khalon comes rushing in a moment later, sword in hand. His eyes are wide and he's breathing hard. As soon as he sees that I am alone in my room, he begins to slow his breathing and he sets the sword down against the wall. I start to calm myself down as well.

"Are you alright?" he finally asks. He looks exhausted.

"Yes," I catch my breath, "I'm sorry I startled you."

"Startled?" he laughs, and then let's out a big sigh. "You scared me into a murderous rage, that's all," he chuckles again and takes another breath, centering himself. "I've never heard you scream like that before. All I could think about was carving up whatever intruder was in here." He plops down on the bed next to me. The weight of him jostles me around on my side.

I had not really thought about it before, but he must still harbor guilt from when I was abducted. As far as we know, Mantus is still alive, and vengeful, and most likely planning his retaliation. Until recently, I had finally begun to feel safe again, but knowing Khalon, he is probably on guard all the time.

"Do you want to tell me about it?" He asks. I gather from his tone he also means my outburst at dinner.

I shake my head.

He clenches his jaw in frustration. "Sigrun, you have to start talking about it. I know the dreams have been getting worse. I can hear that you are restless. It is affecting you. Badly." He does not usually push me to talk about things. Now that he is, my agitation starts rising again.

"I guess I'm just battling old demons." I use a vague explanation in hopes that it will do for now.

"Okay, tell me about it."

Clearly, he is not giving up. The heat in my chest is building. "I really don't want to talk about it."

"I don't care," he says firmly, "you need to try, or else it won't get better. You aren't even talking to Vivek anymore. You used to tell him everything," he pauses, then shakes his head at my silence. He looks at me seriously, "Even though you almost killed me today, I am not afraid of you. They all might be, but I am not, and I'm not leaving until you start talking."

Now I'm angry. *He just keeps pushing. You need to get him to get him to stop.* The voice hisses. Without warning something snaps within me and I move on impulse. I turn to him and kiss him forcefully. My emotions are tied to my flames so tightly. Even enjoyable emotions, like passion, can be dangerous for those around me, so I have been very careful to keep them subdued. This time, his safety is the least of my concerns. I don't care if I ignite. In fact, I want to feel the fire. I crave the power and pleasure of it, and I just want him silenced.

He is absolutely taken by surprise. He was not expecting to be kissed. It takes him a second to realize what is happening, but as soon as he sees this door is open, he accepts it willingly. He kisses me back and pulls me closer. His kiss is softer, more loving than mine. It irritates me. I bite his lip hard.

"Ow." He pulls away and looks at me with confusion. His eyes search mine for an answer, which I don't like. I kiss him again to get his gaze off me. This time, he kisses me back hard. The passion feels good, and the anger is feeding it. The divine rush that I felt at Malyn's wedding tremors through me once again. I surrender to it. My nails dig into his back and drag across his flesh.

"Ah!" He tosses me off him. He looks wounded, not physically—it is just a scratch—but emotionally, I have hurt him. The anger is gone, and I crumble.

"This isn't you," he says to me bewildered.

"I know." *It wasn't me. It wasn't me!* I'm screaming inside my head. I can feel tears building up again.

"I want to help you. How can I help you?" he pleads. He is almost desperate. He picks up one of my hands and holds it between his. His hands are always so warm. I don't deserve his kindness. The tears break free.

"You have to go."

He hangs his head—defeated.

"Please," I beg. I'm trying hard not to cry, but failing, "you have to leave me. I don't know how to explain it, but if you stay, I might hurt you."

"You won't."

"I could," I say darkly, with intention behind it.

He stands slowly, picks up his sword, and walks to the door. "I'll be right there," he points to his room, "if you need anything, or want to talk." He waits for my acknowledgment before he walks through the door. The most I can manage is a small nod.

Exhausted, I lie back down and stare at my ceiling. I forbid sleep to come, afraid of what awaits me there, so I lie there for the rest of the night, simply trying not to cry.

*****

It takes an eternity, but morning does finally come, and with the arrival of the dawn, it also brings Jae. Khalon is already outside splitting firewood. The strike of the ax has stopped. I go to my window.

"Morning, Jae. Two days in a row, what a pleasure," Khalon says calmly, his words are kind, but the meaning is not. He holds the ax casually in in his hand.

"Honestly, I wish wasn't here today either."

Khalon's brow furrows with confusion.

"I don't know what to do," Jae sits on the wood stump, "I'm just trying to understand."

"She's not talking to me about it either." Khalon confesses as he rests the ax against the wood pile.

"How can I help her if I don't understand it?"

"Maybe it's not something you can help me with, Jae," I say standing in the doorway. The morning air is still cold. I shiver in my nightdress.

"I don't think I can accept that," he challenges.

"Jae—" I start.

"Listen," he cuts me off, "I'm nervous because this is behavior that I have seen before."

"What?" I exclaim, reaching back into my memory for any other moment where I ever acted this way. I come up blank. "I've never had anything happen like this before."

He shakes his head, "You're right. You haven't, but we have seen this from Merik." This revelation is like taking an arrow to the heart. Even Khalon takes a small step backwards.

"Sig," Jae stands and holds his hands out to me almost like he is pleading with me, "I'm not trying to upset you, but I have to be honest. The moods, the temper, and the violence are very similar to him."

I'm starting to shake, but it is not from the cold.

"I hate saying this to you, Sig, but maybe this is some kind of sickness; something that affects your family, or some kind of guilt?"

I feel worse now than I did before. His question: *What if this is some kind of sickness? A family trait? A tragic flaw just for being a Livingstone?* If that is the truth, then my brother wasn't evil after all. If he was sick, that makes me a murderer.

"Jae, I don't think that's what happening." Khalon tries to smooth it over.

I put my hand up to keep them both from speaking. "You both need to listen to me. Go home, Jae. I don't know why all of the sudden I am having these feelings but being around you and everyone else is not helping." I look at Khalon directly as well. He needs to know that I need distance from him as well. "It's making it worse. I need to figure this out myself. I need to be alone."

The wounded looks coming from them both would normally cause me pain, but not this time. I know I must send them away. I go back inside and close the door.

Chapter 10

Days have been slipping past me. I'm not even sure how many have passed. The days bleed into the night and I have locked myself in my own solitary. I refuse to see my friends. I know that hurts them, but I will not risk losing control around them again. Khalon and Jae take turns trying badger me out of my room. I must be nasty to them so they will go away. I'm not sleeping. I'm so tired. All I want to do is sleep, but every time sink deep enough into it, I end up in that cave, and the darkness comes for me.

It is sometime in the middle of the night. I'm not sure how late or how early, and I cannot lie here and stare at the walls any longer. It is still a little chilly, so I wrap a blanket around my shoulders and retreat to my father's den. Since I have cut myself off from the rest of the world, all I have been doing is reading my father's books. I've already read most of them, but I keep searching, hoping to find an answer. I lift a heavy book of remedies off the shelf with a groan and take it to the desk.

Foggy. Drowsy. Unfocused. I'm not even reading the words. My eyes can barely stay open. I want to sleep so badly. I am desperate for it, so much so, I feel like I might cry out of sheer desperation. I run my hands through hair in frustration and get up out of the chair. I'm so exhausted, my feet don't even come off the ground when I walk. I shuffle my way down the hallway. I look into Khalon's room. He's not there; not that I was expecting him to be. He is usually up at this time anyway, but I miss him. I have not really been in his presence since the night I kissed him. He leaves food out for me, and tries to get me to come out, but I have avoided being in a situation where I might make eye contact with him. I don't know what triggers my recent anger and I'm just trying to avoid anyone and everything to prevent an episode. If I'm being honest, I'm also avoiding him because I'm embarrassed. He has been so patient and beyond understanding and it only highlights how bad my behavior has been. I know everyone has questions. So do I. Until I have answers though, I have nothing to say.

Answers. I would do anything to find them. My whole life has been surrounded by questions, but I had never concerned myself with it, because there was always someone who had the solutions. The void is unbearable. I miss my father so much. He would know everything. I'm certain of it. With a word of wisdom and a cup of tea, he would have everything sorted. Before I know it, I am down the stairs and through my front door. The grass is cold under my feet. The night air breezes through me, and I pull the blanket around me a little tighter. The village is completely quiet and absolutely oblivious to my late-night walk-about. I'm not sure where I'm heading. I just keep walking, and it isn't until I am standing in front of my father's grave that I realize, this is where I needed to be all along.

I haven't been back here since the day we buried him. That day, it was raining hard. After the service, I remember exploding in my grief and flying up into the storming skies. It should have been frightening flying into the storm, watching stems of lightning strike around me, but I actually felt strong and clear in the middle of the turmoil.

I kneel down and put my hands on the grass that covers the grave. I spread my fingers wide hoping to feel something. A flicker. A touch. Some kind of warmth. Anything to pull me away from this agony. I desperately wish for him to emerge from the trees and say, "Hello, Petal," that sweet and delicate nickname that used to drive me crazy would be the best gift in the world to me tonight. Instead, I put my hands back in my lap and take a deep breath.

"Hello, Dadda. I'm sorry I haven't come sooner." I shake my head. I know better. He would never make me feel guilty for not visiting enough. I don't know why I said it, other than knowing I had to start somewhere. "A lot has happened. Malyn just got married to Vidar, if you can believe that. I have met the Bee Queen and her colony and some other new people, some new friends," thinking about Khalon and Mordecai. I wonder what he would have said about them. More specifically, how he would have reacted to me bringing them to the village. I think he would have been accepting and proud of me and my decisions, but I'll never really know.

"I'm sure you know about Merik. I don't know what to say about that, except I hope he has finally found peace, and I would like to think the two of you are together; wherever you are."

Any veil of self-control that I had is gone now. At the foot of my father's resting place, I fall to pieces. The sobbing comes without limits. I am utterly raw inside and out. "I need help," I whisper to him between sobs. "I wish you were here. I'm really struggling, Dadda. I can't sleep. I keep having these overpowering outbursts that keep getting worse. What is the point of having these visions or these feelings, if I can't control them or interpret them? I am losing my mind and I can't talk to anyone about it because no one would, or could, understand."

It takes a good long time for me to finally stop the convulsion of anguish. I stand up and wrap myself up again.

"I love you, Dadda, and I miss you all the time."

*****

I sneak back into my house. I'm not sure why I feel the need to be quiet. I know that no one is home, but I feel like I still need to take extra care. My emotional outing has wiped me of any remaining alertness that I may have had. I shuffle up the stairs and towards my room, but at the top of the stairs, I veer into my father's old room instead. Mordecai used to sleep here, but when he left, he took all of him, and only left the memory of my father behind. It's dark inside. Only a sliver of moonlight is shining through the open window. *I don't remember opening that.* I go to it and I look out. Everything is quiet. The stars are out. The crickets and frogs are the only sounds I hear. A breeze rustles through the leaves and then washes over me. I feel heavy, woozy. I don't even realize I have closed my eyes until I teeter and hit my head on the window frame.

"Ah," I rub my temple. I close the window and turn to walk away, but before I can drag my feet two steps, I stub my toe, hard, on a lifted floorboard.

"Ow!" I grab hold of my injured digit and fall onto the bed coddling myself. It's not bad, just a little scrape on the corner of my nail, but the pain shoots all the way up my leg. I lie there for minute chuckling at myself. In the last year, I've been punched in the face, stabbed through the hand, slashed by a Gila, but a stubbed toe has me whimpering like a baby. Once the pain subsides, I get down on the floor to face my opponent. The board is mostly under the bed, but the end that is sticking up has a corner missing. The wood is smooth like the corner was sanded down intentionally. Pulling on the board, it comes up easily. I reach into the floor and my fingers clumsily stumble onto something. Perhaps a box, in a cloth sack? When Merik came back to the house he tore everything apart searching for something, which I always assumed was the Red Book. I am surprised that he never found this. I struggle with it at first since I am reaching through the narrow space under the bed. I am able to turn it sideways and then it squeezes through the thin space of the floorboard. Eagerly, I unwrap it. It's not a box. It is a large, black, leather-bound book. I have never seen it before. I flip through the pages and instantly recognize my father's handwriting.

A new resolve washes over me. I am not tired any more. In addition to my excitement, I also wonder why this was hidden. The secrecy of this book makes me nervous. I quickly replace the floorboard and take the book back to my room. Eagerly, I light candles on my bedside table. I sit on my bed with the book in my lap and open it to a random page. I was expecting more of his medicinal recipes or perhaps a book of some lost history, but a few sentences in I realize it is his personal journal. This entry is dated *720.3.40*. He was a young man when this was written, only about five years older than I am now. There are about 100 days in a season, 40 days into the third season, so this was written mid-autumn.

720.3.40

I have returned. Our journey was not easy or expected. There were several times that I thought we might not make it back. Those woods are not like ours, easy to get lost in. However, we did manage to find the plants and the serum is being made. We have already lost so many. The extra days it took to get back, cost lives. For that, I will forever atone. Once the illness lifts, I will go back. I have to find her again.

A new record of my father's life brings a lump to my throat. I thought I had lost all of him, and all I had left was what I already knew. I look out my window and thank him. He must have heard me and led me to this. It may not have my answers but having another part of him is a bigger gift than I could have asked for.

I turn the page.

720.3.43

This disease is unlike anything I have ever seen. The nausea is causing intense dehydration. The advanced cases can barely drink enough water to stay alive. They are in so much pain. Sores and pustules cover their bodies making it extremely contagious. The caretakers have to be incredibly careful. The fevers are so high, it is causing hallucinations. Some of the more extreme reports are when the caretakers come into the rooms, the infected mistake them for monsters or worse. Unknowingly, they fight their loved ones injuring themselves and spreading the disease.

More and more are getting sick every day. The serum is helping, but I have to make batches all day, every day, to keep up with the increasing sickness. The serum is only part of it. I have to find the time to gather the spices for the teas, and the plants for the compresses. I have to prepare everything, and distribute everything, and when I do find time for sleep, I lie there thinking of everything I still have to do, or worrying that is not enough, and we will lose the village to this plague anyway.

I hate to call it a burden, but sometimes being a Healer feels that way. Every loss hits me hard and personally. "What could I have done differently, or better, or maybe if I had figured it out sooner?" I constantly wonder if it is enough.

I've never known my father to show despair. He always seemed so sure of his gifts. He always knew what to do, he never floundered in his decisions, and people always knew he had the answers. It was, and is, always a lot to live up to. Knowing that in his younger years, he struggled makes me feel more connected to him. It makes me feel better about my own struggles, that maybe I'm not as lost as I feel.

720.3.56

It took several days, but the serum has made a tremendous difference. It seems the worst is over. I take a small comfort in that. The wake of the disease has left many families with tragic losses, and I feel all of them.

We buried Falon and Vivek's parents today, and I fear their family may have another loss still. I can treat the wounds that I see, but the hearts of my closest friends are badly broken, and there is no healing for that.

Now that I'm getting some relief from the constant demand, I'm able to sleep again, but the dreams are getting stronger. I feel more and more anxious to go back. The first snow could come anytime now. I cannot wait until spring.

The knock on my door startles me.

"Sigrun?" Khalon asks.

I slam the book shut and slide it under my bed. I'm not sure if I feel like I need to hide it because it was already hidden, there doesn't seem to be anything that needs to be kept secret, but if my father took such care to tuck it out of sight, I feel I must do the same.

"Come in."

He opens the door slowly, and he has a look of concern. "I saw the light through your window when I was coming back." He only takes a one step into my room. I haven't let him in for days. He doesn't know what to do anymore. "Are you okay?"

"Yeah," I say. For the first time in weeks, I feel like that isn't a complete lie.

He shakes his head like he doesn't believe me. "You really need to get some sleep." Just hearing the word 'sleep' makes me drowsy again. "I know, I just feel like I can't."

"Will you please talk to me about it?" he pleads.

I find myself sighing and nodding without even realizing. He is surprised and maybe even excited that I am not shutting him out again. He sits on the bed next to me.

"I just. I'm having these dreams, nightmares, and they affect me. I don't really know how to explain it."

"What kind of nightmares?"

"I'm always in this place that I've never been before, I don't know where it is, but it's dark and cold, and there's this…" I pause trying to find the right way to make sense of it, "…feeling that I get, like I know it's bad, but it feels good."

He listens intently.

"And, so far, every time I have this dream, I wake up filled with this rage and then I have those crazy outbursts. It's almost like the dreams are the fuel. I don't know how else to explain it."

"So, these aren't old demons like you said the other night?"

I shake my head, "No, this is new."

"Well, I don't understand it, but I'm glad you're talking to me about it." He gives me a small sideways smile. "You really do need to get some sleep though."

I know he's right, but without knowing what may come for me, it seems daunting.

"What if I stay with you," he suggests. Obviously, he is picking up on my hesitation. "If you start getting restless, I can wake you up, before it gets bad."

His idea makes sense, though it still makes me nervous. I also want to get back to reading my father's journal. My eyelids deceive me and start to get heavy again.

"Sigrun?" He turns his head slightly to the side. He knows he is winning this one.

"Okay," I concede.

He lies down and moves over to make room for me. I nestle into the nook of his arm and rest my head on his chest. His body is warm, and I actually feel safe. He tucks the blanket around me and blows the candle out. I quiet my mind and only hear the slow steady beat of his heart, which quickly lulls me into the first restful sleep I have had in weeks.

Chapter 11

Once Khalon leaves the house, I dig the book out from under my bed. I start reading again. The majority is about an illness that plagued the village long ago. He talks about the remedy he made from the plants he gathered, and few references about a mystery woman. I have to assume he means my mother. I know she was from a different village. Perhaps they met in search of these special plants. He writes entries every few days, just about everyday things. It doesn't seem strange at all, until I notice the dates go from *720.3.88* and the next entry after that is *729.2.35*, almost ten years later. I spread the pages of the book further. I see several pages have been ripped out, not ten years' worth, but enough to know a big part of the story is missing.

729.2.35

Something is wrong. He is not like the other children. He is emotionless except for a temperamental moodiness that comes without warning. Other than that, he shows no real joy, or pleasure in anything. I cannot think of one time that he laughed or giggled. Only, sometimes, I see a smirk on his face, but it does not resemble happiness. He is only content when he is with Maia, and content is all.

He is talking about Merik. By the date, he would have been only two years old, if that. I always thought it was just me he hated so much and that was why he became so enraged. Reading this and discovering that he may have been born that way makes me feel bad for him, but better for me.

731.1.76

Last night I had a vision. I don't fully understand it. Maia is going to give birth. Not to a child, but to a dragon. Naturally the thought of having more children seems like a bad idea since my relationship with Merik is estranged at best, but this would come at a cost that I don't think I could bear. She made me promise to tell her my visions, whether I understood them or not, whether they were sad, joyous, triumphant, or catastrophic. She made me promise. How can I possibly tell Maia how she will die?

Knowing the story and reading the emotional words coming from my father in real time are two completely different truths. Since the time I was able to understand, I have known the consequences of my birth, but they were washed out versions made more palatable. I'm starting to realize why this was hidden. I don't think he ever meant for me to see this.

My stomach rumbles for the first time in days. I don't want to stop reading, but the thought of a nice piece of bread and some raspberry jam seems like perfection. I grab my breakfast from the kitchen and start to make my way back upstairs when there is a knock at my door.

"Sig?" Jae tentatively pokes his head through the door. He smiles when he sees me. He seems relieved to find me here rather than locked up in my bedroom. "Hey! You're..." he doesn't know how to finish his sentence, "you're up." He's nervous and it makes me smile.

"Yeah, I'm up," I look outside, the sun is quite high. "It is late in the morning after all."

"Right. I...uh...well, I'm just glad to see you up and around. It's really nice today. I thought it would be nice to go do a little gathering, maybe go to the waterfall."

It is a nice idea, I have to admit, but the book sitting in my room is almost pulling me back upstairs.

"Just for a little bit," he promises. Clearly, he saw me drifting in thought.

"Okay," I nod and look down, I am still in my nightgown, "let me just get cleaned up a bit."

I run back upstairs and dig a pair shorts and shirt out of my closet. I look in the mirror. I don't look that bad, really. That little bit of sleep mostly erased the dark circles under my eyes. My hair is unruly, but it always is. I run my fingers through it, wipe my face with a wet rag, and head back downstairs.

It is a beautiful day. It is just warm enough that the sun feels good, rather than roasting, and the breeze is light and cool. The blackberries are just ripe enough for picking. Khalon has adapted very well to our way of life. He is an excellent fisherman, and he is great with harvesting, but he has not quite mastered the art of gathering, so that usually falls on me. I like it though: the sun on my shoulders, digging for the best fruit, occasionally rewarding myself with a sweet berry warmed by the sun.

Jae looks happy too. We haven't seen each other as much recently. Even before I barricaded myself in my room, he had been helping out with the farming and planting since the ground thawed. It has been interesting to watch him evolve. I never could quite figure out what would make him the happiest, but I now see that he loves to make things grow and get his hands dirty. The satisfaction of nurturing something into a sustainable item for the entire community fills him with a sense of purpose. As for me, I have been mostly occupied by council matters, until just before Malyn's wedding. Dealing with the day-to-day squabbles between villagers takes up more time than I would have thought. Between all of that, our paths rarely cross anymore. I miss him. Things between us used to be easier. Though, things often are when you are children. Every so often I catch him looking and smiling at me. I'm sure he is glad that I am out of my house, but I know his looks mean more than that. He has not shown any special attention to any other girls in the village, even though I know there are several who would pounce on the opportunity. I suspect he is still waiting for me to 'catch up' as he once told me.

"I'm glad you came," he says finally.

"Me too."

"Are you feeling better?" he asks a little hesitantly.

It is not an easy question to answer. In this moment I do feel better, but I don't feel as though this is a lasting solution. Finding my father's journal has given me some new hope that I did not have before, or at least a new distraction.

"Um, I am. Today has been really nice. Thank you for convincing me." I smile at him. He smiles back looking very pleased with himself.

He goes back to his task, and I take a moment to steal a look at him. He is still unnervingly handsome. His feathers always shine like bronze in sunlight, and his mouth twists up into a confident half-smile—like he knows a secret.

I shake my thoughts back to berries and continue picking. Once we are through with blackberries, we fly over to the Butternut Trees to gather some white walnuts. Fingers sore from the picking, I rub the pad of my thumb. Jae takes my hand and kisses it. "Let's go to the cavern, I haven't been there all summer," he says.

I look up at the sky, we still have a lot of day light left, so I nod, and we head that way.

As beautiful as ever, the crystals shimmer and the water laps gently on the sides of the pool. The last time I was here was just before we left for battle. I had needed to see this place one more time just in case I didn't make it back. Despite the warmth and joy that this place brings me, a cold, somber, wave rolls over me.

"What was today actually about, Jae? Are you keeping an eye on me?" I ask, not in an interrogative way, but more as a joke.

"A little bit," he confesses with a smile, "I also just like being with you."

His eyes are warm. He straightens the neckline of my shirt, bunched up from the swim in, carefully and tenderly. I immediately feel my face flush. I focus very hard to keep the rose from blushing and giving me away. This was also the place that he kissed me for the first time. I remember being surprised by it, feeling guilty about it, and wanting it, all at the same time. I struggle with myself even still.

"I can't give you an explanation," I say breaking the tension, and addressing what I think he really wants to know, "I don't know what's happening."

He listens patiently.

"What I do know, is that it makes me physically stronger, and unreasonably angry. I think it is connected to my dreams somehow. I wake up edgy when it happens. It rushes over me and takes over, but it's still me. It's so hard to make sense of it," I shake my head. "When it happens, I feel powerful. It feels good. I like it," I confess. Just saying it out loud makes me feel guilt and shame.

I look down at my hand, which at some point made its way to his intertwined in a way where I can't tell his fingers from mine. He rests his lips on my forehead and breathes out heavily. Wrapping me in a feathered cocoon, he hugs me tightly and keeps his head resting on mine.

"We're going to figure this out," he promises. He moves my hair away from my temple.

I nod against his chest, silently saying, *I hope so.*

*****

It is several hours later when I notice the setting sun and take flight back home. It did feel good to get out, but I was more eager than ever to get back to the journal.

Khalon is in the kitchen putting his rations away when I arrive. He smiles when he sees me. He is pleased to see that I have been out of the house.

"Well, what have you been up to?" His eyes divert to the overstuffed bags I'm carrying.

"A little gathering." I spread my spoils on the table. His eyes light up as soon as he sees what I have brought home. He goes straight for the berries—he loves the sweets.

I make tea for us both and we have a casual supper together. The conversation is light, which I'm grateful for. There is a minute where I forget about books, and bad dreams, and an unexplainable darkness that is lurking in me. It feels good to just be. I am enjoying this time with him, but eventually, I find my thoughts drifting. I really want to get back into my room and continue reading. I blame it on sleepiness, which he is all too willing to except. We clean up the kitchen and I retire to my room.

Chapter 12

731.1.78

My wife amazes me. I tell her everything. How I see her and her swollen belly, beautiful and glowing, until the last day; the day she gives birth. Her flush, rosy cheeks drain of their color. The soft fullness of her face withers away to gauntness in moments. Then comes the pain and the screaming. All childbirth is terrifying. Women go through pain that men will never understand, and men go through helplessness that women will never understand. I am utterly lost. I want to fix it. I want to make it better, but I can't. All I can do is tell her to keep breathing and she will make it through this. Only, this time, she won't. The baby tears through her flesh like a sword on fire. From the charred womb of my beloved, a creature unlike anything I have ever seen, emerges. Green scales, sharp talons, expansive wings, two rows of horns going from head to tail, and the biggest violet-colored eyes I have ever seen.

Maia listened quietly, and when I was done, she nodded in acceptance. How can anyone so calmly accept a fate as brutal as this? I certainly do not.

731.1.84

She says I am only postponing the inevitable. My refusal to touch her intimately only makes her shake her head and laugh—this baby will come—she says to me. I love my wife, I want to hold my wife, but loving her will bring her death.

731.1.99

She showed me the book today, the red one. We had agreed to destroy it, it could cause more harm than good, but in the end, she felt it may be needed some day. Like always, she was right. She read me a section that she thought may ease my mind. 'An Object of Fire,' that's what our child will be. Of course,

I focus on the more concerning parts such as, 'the misuse of its power could destroy all the good in this world.'

So do I. Especially since I fear it might be true.

But then she smiles and takes the book from me and reads, 'Powerful and elemental, a leader for all.' If the misuse of its power could be so devastating, then I must believe that the latter could mean that I may sire the greatest leader of all time.

She sleeps now as I write this. Beautiful in the moonlight. She just barely moves as I touch her stomach—my unborn child.

I sit back. It's funny that my father and I struggled with the same passages from the Red Book, which sounds like actually belonged to my mother. Strangely it makes me feel more connected to her. I do wonder what he meant by the Red Book could cause more harm than good. Vivek had not been able to translate more. He said the language was mostly unknown to him. The parts that he could somewhat piece together seemed to be recipes of some sort. It didn't appear to be a danger to anyone.

I keep reading and find that the next several entries focus mostly on a record of my mother's pregnancy sickness. Apparently, I was not an easy child to carry; though, anyone could have guessed as much. A yawn finally forces me to acknowledge that I'm so tired, I'm starting to see double. I put the book down for the night and nestle into my bed.

I jolt suddenly before I fall asleep. Only as I look around, I realize I'm not in my bed. I'm on my knees in the cave. The thrumming starts again, attacking my ears all the way into the center of my head. This time I take a deep breath. *This is only a dream—the pain is not real.* Instantly the pain lifts and I am able to stand. I desperately want to get out of this place, but this might be the only way to get any answers. Something keeps bringing me here. Something is twisting my insides with rage. I need to know what, and why.

The air is cold and damp. There is a sound of water coming from one of the tunnels. I follow it. My body still feels heavy in this place. It takes a lot of energy just to walk. The tunnel was quite narrow at first, but the further I go, the bigger it gets. It is dark. I step carefully and keep one hand on the rocky cave wall. The sound of water gets louder, and the darkness starts to lift. Once

I get to the other side of the tunnel, the mouth of it opens up to an oasis with a waterfall in the center. Vegetation along the edges, and the walls of the cave lead to a narrow opening at the top. I must be inside a mountain. The walls glitter with some kind of metallic mineral. It's beautiful. I notice that, for the first time, I am not in any pain, and I do not hear any screaming or pulsing, just the hypnotic sound of the waterfall.

Walking farther into this place, I see something on the other side of the pool. A figure of someone. It is a fairy. A young woman in a white dress with long dark hair. She is kneeling by the waterside filling a jug. She sees me also and stands. Her jug slips from her hand pouring its contents back into the earth. She has white feathered wings and bright green eyes. My knees go weak, and I fall to the ground.

Mother?

Her eyes go wide and suddenly pain grips her. She screams and clutches her head as the pulsating rushes in. The pressure pushes me farther to the ground. We look at each other, and then she looks behind her. She is terrified. She screams.

I sit upright. I'm back in my bed, nightgown soaked in sweat, and struggling to breathe. My heart is beating so wildly, I feel as though it may burst through my chest. *My mother, I just saw my mother.* Throwing the covers off, I race over to my vanity table where the journal rests. I madly flip through the pages. There has to be something in here. My eyes search for anything, any kind of explanation. I think about the dream I had the night before my father died. I had that same heavy feeling making it hard to walk. I saw his blood. I saw his death. *Is she alive? Is she in danger?* Page after page—nothing. I find no answer. My rushing blood boils over into desperation. Worthless! I throw the book hard against the wall. It collapses into a mangled pile on the floor. I grab my hair by the roots in frustration. Anger bubbles up in me.

Stay calm. Just breathe.

Finally, it subsides, and I am left with only a few stray tears that have shaken free. I take a deep breath and go over to the journal. My outburst managed to tear the binding a bit. This is one of the few treasures that I have left of my parents. I should have never been so careless. I sit back at my table to see if I can mend it.

The corner of the back cover has come loose at the binding. I grab a candle to see if maybe I can repair it with some melted wax. My fingers run along the tear to see where it starts. Something bulges out between the leather and the backing. It looks like a folded corner of a piece of paper. I try to pull it free, but it is stuck. I dig out my father's dagger from my drawer and carefully separate the cover enough to pull the paper free. My hands shake as I unfold it. This must be my answer.

To my disappointment, I find no words, only pictures and symbols. At second glance, I recognize it as something else—it's a map. It is not a land that I know, but it is clearly a map to somewhere. There is a heavily wooded area on the west and south sides, which lead up to a pretty significant mountain range with one very prominent peak. Nestled within the mountain range, there looks to be a small village completely secluded from the rest of the world. This cannot be an accident that I found this. There is likely only one person alive who knows where this place is.

Chapter 13

The sun is just beginning to rise when I knock on Vivek's door. He answers sleepily, still in his sleep shirt and robe, with eyes squinting against the newly shining light. He shakes his head when he sees me.

"Well, what have you found?" he asks. His directness catches me off guard.

He shakes his head again, and motions for me to come inside. He has a small smile as he shuffles into the main room. "Every time you call on me at strange hours, you've found something, or figured out something, or had some implausibly revelation," he sits in one of the large armchairs in front of the hearth, "So, what have you found?"

"This." I hold up the folded square.

He leans forward and reaches out for it. I don't know what he was expecting, maybe neither did he, but from the puzzled look on his face, he didn't anticipate this. It takes him a moment once he has it unfolded to figure out what it is, much the same way I did, but slowly his furrowed brow breaks and light shines in his eyes. He recognizes it.

"Where did you find this?"

"In this." I pull the journal out of my sack. "It was hidden in the binding."

He takes the book from me and flips through the pages. As soon as he sees the writing his hands begin to tremor. Carefully he smooths over the pages. He runs his hand over the words and smiles like he is saying hello to an old friend.

"He had the journal hidden in the floorboards under his bed," I explain as he flips through the pages.

Vivek nods as he skims a few passages, "I suspect he meant to keep it out of Merik's hands. This is a painfully honest account of his feelings towards the boy. He certainly didn't dress anything up, but it *is* accurate." He breathes in slowly. "My heart always broke for your parents. They were the most deserving and loving people, but they had one child who was incapable of love, and another who was very loving, but robbed of opportunity to fully know it."

A lump rises in my throat. I swallow it back and remember why I came here in the first place. "The map, do you know where it leads to?"

"Yes," he smiles. "It is your mother's village."

I sit on the edge of my chair leaning into his every word.

"You must have already read about the sickness that plagued the village. It was unlike anything we had ever seen. Almost every family had at least one person that was infected. Fairies were dying so quickly," he pauses, "we lost our son."

A sharp pain needles my heart. "I didn't know you had a child."

He nods, "Egan, named for my father. The eldest son of the eldest son, but he was a fragile child. It was a miracle that he was even born." He drifts off into his memory. A small smile appears while he thinks of his boy; the joy he must have brought them, and then his smile fades into heartbreak. He shakes his head and clears his throat as he continues with his story. "Your father knew of a plant that could potentially cure it. One of those family secrets passed down from generation to generation, but it didn't grow here, and he only had a vague idea about where it was. So, he and I traveled together to find it. Like I said he only had a vague idea where it was, so to no surprise, we got lost on our way. The plants were small, forcing us to stick to the ground to look for them. Days spent going in circles, or so we thought and, before we knew it, we were lost in the middle of a vast mountain range. We were exhausted and hungry, and when we finally caught sight of candlelight off in the distance, we flew straight to it hoping for food and shelter. The people were kind, but very nervous. They were wary of us since we were strangers, but once they settled that we were no threat, they took us in for the night, fed us soup and bread, and let us sleep in front of their fire.

"The next day, as we were helping ourselves to their main water well, that's when he saw her. It was like lightning struck his heart. He went right to her, like a bee to honey, and it is a good thing he did—she was the one who told us where to find the plants. Before we left that day, she drew this map to help us find our way out, but actually, I believe it was so he could find his way back to her.

"By the time we made it home, many more were lost, and my son was beyond saving. When he died, that was when Yoana stopped talking. Her heart was broken, and we were never able to have more children. The only consolation was that we were able to save so many others."

82

"Why didn't he ever tell us this story? Why keep it a secret?" I ask almost frustrated.

"I'm not exactly sure, but I think it was because of Maia's family, and to keep her, and you kids, safe."

"Keep us safe? From her family?"

"Like I said, they were jittery people. I think something bad happened there, but I don't know anything else. Your parents made me promise to not talk about her village, and we agreed to destroy all copies of the map." His mouth twists into a forgiving smile, "But, it seems your father did not keep his end of the bargain." He doesn't seem all that surprised that my father didn't keep his word.

"Do you think they are still there?"

"I don't see why they wouldn't be. Why do you ask?"

"I've had a vision of my mother."

Vivek looks surprised, but he doesn't interrupt.

"I've been having the same dream since before Malyn's wedding. I'm in a cave and there is this heavy dark force there, like an evil presence, and when I wake up, I feel changed, and angry, and powerful. Last night, I had the same dream, but I forced myself deeper. I was drawn into this really beautiful part of the cave and that's when I saw her. She was alone and afraid, and I felt like I needed to save her."

He is focused on my every word, unmoving and intense.

"Is it possible she is still alive?" I finally ask.

He breathes, breaking the stillness, and sadly shakes his head. "Sigrun, she's dead." It hurts him to say it.

"But I saw her."

"It was a dream, Sigrun."

"But—"

"You've never seen her. How do you know it was even her?" he cuts me off.

"I could feel her. I just know. I-I can't explain it rationally," I'm struggling to make him understand and I'm beginning to feel desperate.

"What did she look like?" he quizzes.

"Fair skin, long dark hair, bright green eyes, wings like a white dove."

"That does sound like Maia," he sits back in his chair considering for a moment the possibility. "The birthmark, did you see the birthmark?" he asks excitedly.

I search my memory hard for anything.

He interrupts, "She had a small brown birthmark on the inside of her right wing. It almost looked like a sideways heart."

I shake my head.

"Her wings were folded. I never saw the inside of her wings." He rubs his chin pensively then finally waves his hand shooing away any prospect of my crazy idea. "Sigrun, she died," he speaks slowly and carefully, "I was there. I lowered her body into the ground. She's gone. Whatever you saw, wasn't her. It was just a dream." He's looking at me as though he would rather tell me lies to give me hope, than break my heart all over again, but we both know he can't. "I'm sorry, Sigrun."

My bottom lip starts to quiver, and I try to smile to hide it. "It's okay. It was a silly, bizarre, idea. I think I was just hoping," I can't finish my sentence. If I keep talking, the tears might break through.

He smiles kindly, and hands the journal back to me, "This is a gift. I know it does not replace him, but to have a direct line into your father's mind is very special."

"I know."

"Stay for breakfast?"

"No, I should get going, but I was wondering if I could get the Red Book back from you."

"Of course!" he springs out of his chair to grab it off the side table. "I wish I could have translated more of it for you."

"You did great. I think you figured out the most important bits anyway." I tuck both books and the map in my sack and head back home.

*****

He's wrong. It was her.

Flying home, I think about the dream again. The pain. The screaming. Her fear. I know now, more than ever, that my father led me to his journal for a reason. He wants me to find her. It isn't until I reach home that I realize I'm clutching the map.

Chapter 14

I don't need much in the way of supplies. I should only be gone a few days, but I go through the plants in my father's den for the basics anyway. Lemongrass for cleaning wounds, calendula flower for swelling, and white willow bark for pain.

When I go down to the living room, I realize that I should bring some kind of weapon. I will be heading into a forest that I've never entered before. Who knows what I will encounter? I should take my father's sword—it is the better weapon to take. I lift it from its resting place above the mantle. The weight of the sword feels good, sturdy, the hilt fits my hand perfectly. I remember the last time I held it. It had just been pulled from Khalon's chest. I had turned my back on the enemy and when I came back around, I had almost lost a friend forever because of it. After the battle, I put the sword above the mantle, and I hoped that I would never have to take it down. It rested here, serving as a reminder to never hesitate again. If something evil ever came for us in the future, I would cut its heart out before making that mistake again.

A warm flutter tickles my veins at the thought of blood. A rush to my head makes me almost euphorically woozy. I rest my hand on the mantle shelf until my head stops spinning. Once I settle myself and put the sword back on the wall. It is too heavy, I tell myself, it would just slow me down.

I put my dagger in my belt and run back upstairs. I fling open the top of the wooden trunk that Ainia and Khalon gave me as a gift before the battle. It's the trunk with my armor. My back harness is resting on top with my kama carefully strapped in place, freshly cleaned and sharpened. I buckle myself in and make sure my wings are not constricted. My kama are secured between my wings. It's strange that I feel a kind of comfort putting them on. It would make more sense that a weapon harness would feel restrictive and heavy, but it feels as soothing as a warm hug from a good friend.

I grab some bread and nuts from the kitchen and figure I can gather more supplies on the way. Normally, I would never leave for this kind of trip on such thin supply, but I'm rushing. Khalon has not come home yet from whatever scavenging he is up to. I cannot lie to him. It is not a matter of principle. I would tell him a direct lie to his face without flinching, if I could, but the man seems to have direct insight into my mind and would see the holes in my story, and then I would never leave. When I go to put the food in my sack, I see the Red Book is still in there. My fingers trace the risen hide of the book. I should leave it. Keep it safe. Though, as far as we can tell, it is only a book of stories and recipes; hardly anything of great importance. I will take it with me. If this book did come from my mother's village, then maybe someone there can read it, and I will finally know what it really says. Once justified, I grab the map and head out.

The last time I left home like this I was looking for Merik. I was so blinded by the grief over my father's murder that I wasn't concerned with much else. I was aimless and I didn't know what I was doing. This time I know exactly where I'm going.

Our river runs north to south and then bends to the west, dividing the land from the Deadlands in the south where the Skars were camped. I suspect that this map begins on the eastside of the river. The heavy woods suggest a prominent water source and I've never seen any mountains to the west near bee territory. This village must be east of our river.

I feel guilty for a moment when I fly away from home. Khalon and Jae will likely be worried, but this is too important, and I don't think they would understand. I have to do this. I have to find her.

*****

I stop at the river to fill my canteens with water. I'm not sure how close I will be to fresh water on the other side. Once I am on the other side my guilt lets up a little. Now I am only looking forward.

When Vivek and my father made this journey, they had to stick to the ground to look for plants. Since I do not, I will be able to fly and hopefully get there much faster. The weather is mild today. If I push through the night, I should be there by morning.

At first, the terrain looks very much like home; large trees, flowering bushes, very green, very fragrant, but slowly it begins to change. The trees become more severe looking, fewer leaves, and more spikes on the bark. The delicacy of the flowers begins to disappear. The plants are tougher, more robust, and thorns cover most of them. Bird calls become fewer and fewer. Even though it is still quite early in the day, darkness begins to shroud the land. It's as though the territory itself had to develop a thicker skin.

It is colder here also. We are in the hot season, but I feel a chill in the air. I fly higher. As I do, the air gets warmer toward the top of the tree line, but it also gets heavier. I push to the top. My breathing is labored, and my wings are struggling. It's like flying through water. I am surrounded by resistance. I just need to get to the top. Once I get my bearings, and I can see exactly where I am, I'll be able to continue. I see the top. I just need to push a little harder. My wings are aching, and I'm starting to get dizzy, but I'm almost there. I finally make it, but I'm in a fog. A thick heavy mist is blanketing the forest. I can't see anything. I am in a wall of gray. The air is so thick and warm, and it's so hard to breathe. Feeling lightheaded. Can't. Move. Anymore.

Everything goes dark.

I start to move again. My eyes open slowly. It takes a minute to regain focus. My body aches. I look up at the trees and see the broken branches that outline my fall back to the ground. That fog was unlike anything I have ever seen, or felt, before. I have never heard of a fog above the trees before. I struggle to sit up, and as I assess the damage of my aching limbs. I realize that I have lost my sense of direction. That fog disoriented and paralyzed me. I can't fly to the top. I would lose consciousness again. This must be why my father and Vivek got lost. This forest is one big trap.

My strength is coming back, and it seems that I don't have any major injuries. I have to figure out where I am. It is already dark here, but the light is fading fast. I get the map out of my pack. I retrace where I started from tracing my route with my finger. I should be right about here. My finger rests on what looks like a tea stain right where I think I am. I look closer. Unless it is not just a stain—maybe that's the fog.

"Thanks, Dadda," I shake my head, "A note section might have been helpful. Something like, 'Hey, stay away from this bit. This is a crazy, scary forest that has fog that paralyzes you.' Just giving you a little heads-up."

I sigh heavily and look back at the page. At least it looks like a relatively small portion of the map I can probably make my way through it, if I can just figure out the direction. The light dims again. I won't have enough light to find my way out of here today. Frustrated, I go through my sack for something to eat. Just as I get my hands on some bread something takes a bite out of me.

"Ouch!" I slap the culprit that has just assaulted my right thigh. It is a really large mosquito, much bigger than the ones we have in our village, and much hungrier, I expect. I flick it from my palm leaving only a bloody smear. Within seconds the spot where I was bitten, an ugly, purple, welt rises up. Before I can tend to it, I hear the buzzing. The swarm is around me in seconds.

They are biting every bit of exposed flesh. The only part of me that they can't seem to penetrate are my wings. I wrap myself in them trying to shield my body, but they are small enough to find their way through the barrier to the soft parts of my flesh. The stings are certainly uncomfortable and a little painful, but I am starting to feel some minor effects of their venom. My joints are beginning to stiffen, and I can feel my heart rhythm is off. A few of them are no threat, but the swarm will be deadly. Once enough venom has me immobile, they will suck all the blood from my body. My limbs are cramping and the mobility in my fingers is now completely gone. I can't open my hands, and now my arms and legs are seizing. There are too many. I have to get them off me. Swatting didn't seem to work and soon, I won't be able to move at all.

Fire. Let's see how they like fire. I stop moving long enough for the swarm to overcome me. The pain is starting to get bad, and it sets me off into the right mood. Angry. I ignite. Blue flames dance along my flesh torching the pests leaving only bits of ash behind. The bugs are dead, but a searing pain brings me to my knees. It is my pendant. The marble that holds the rose is burning me. I quell the fire and the marble begins to cool. It did this the day of Malyn's wedding when I ignited too. *Why are my gifts suddenly being kept from me?* It is almost completely dark, and I suspect those mosquitoes are not the only critters looking for blood in this place. I set my fingers ablaze just long enough to light a fire. The pendant burns my flesh all the while.

While I sit by the fire, I watch the threatening flames and I contemplate my own. This just began around the time that I started having the dreams. I wonder, if like my increased anger, this is another unwelcome side effect. The welts on my body from the mosquitoes are bad, but not as bad as they should be. I have used up some of the plants I brought, and they are healing quickly, and the joint pain was almost gone once I set fire. The heat of the flames must have burned up the venom in my blood. Clearly my body isn't rejecting the fire. It is something else. I'm so tired. I just want to sleep, but I don't trust this place. The sounds are eerie and unfamiliar; movements in the shadows, eyes in the dark, I don't know what is real and what is just fear getting the better of me. I doze off for a moment in rising light. Finally, I force myself up. The sooner I find my way out of here the better.

It takes some time, but I finally find the path on which I came in. One of the downfalls of flying, is that is much harder to trace back your steps. Now that I found where I came from, I can reassess where I am headed. This little setback will cost me a substantial amount of time. I was hoping I would be through the woods yesterday, and now with all the backtracking, and loss of flight, I will be lucky to get out of here by the end of today. I put the map back in my sack and continue.

It takes the better part of the day, since I am restricted to the ground, but hours later, I finally I feel a difference in the air. It starts to get lighter again, breathing gets easier, and I am able to fly. As I continue east, the trees and plants become fewer and fewer. I stop for a midday bite and look over my supplies. If I decrease my portions, my food rations should hold, but I am getting low on water and, by the looks of this place, water might be hard to find. I pull the map out again.

On the map, the tree line is heavy all the way to the foot of the mountain range. That's odd, the forest shouldn't be thinning out this much. I launch back up above the trees with desperate hope that I am closer than I thought, only to be disappointed to see nothing that resembles a mountain anywhere. I can barely make out the fog behind me, and every other direction is either forested or flat. Discouraged, I go back to the ground to finish eating so I can continue on, because it seems I still have a long way to go.

*****

The forest continues getting leaner. The green is almost wiped out entirely. The only trees that still remain died long ago, leaving behind only twisted, hollow corpses of what they used to be. The rich dark earth has turned hard and gray; completely void of any nutrients needed to grow anything sustainable. Even the bugs have retreated from this place.

How could anything live out here? Something about this place feels incredibly familiar. I start thinking about last year when I stumbled onto the Deadlands. The Skars had depleted the land until it had become unlivable. That is how they live, and this land looks like it has been sucked dry too. My stomach feels like it is in my throat. What if they have already been here? What if the Skars have already wiped out my mother's people? Maybe that's what she is trying to tell me. As far as we know, Mantus is still alive. Maybe he came back here. I'm suddenly feeling very foolish for coming out here alone. Even with my fire, I don't know if I could defeat him. I shake my head. Too late now. I'm too close. I have to keep going.

The day is almost over. The sun is almost gone, and the temperature is dropping quickly. If I stay out here, I will have to build a fire so I don't freeze but, with the terrain as open as it is, a fire would be a beacon to my exact location. It doesn't seem like anything, or anyone, is out here, but I can't risk it. Something about this place feels wrong.

I keep moving forward, but soon the cold makes it hard to fly. My shorts and light summer shirt are feeble against the chill. At least on the ground, I can wrap my wings around me for some protection from the elements. It has been so warm lately, it never occurred to me to bring heavier clothes. Occasionally, I use my fire to shake the chill from my bones, but the pendant burns me every time, and I can't hold it for long.

It is well into the night, maybe even into early morning, when I finally see the ground begin to change beneath my feet. I'm not sure how long I have been walking. I have been so preoccupied with keeping warm that I probably would not have noticed if I hadn't stubbed a toe on a large rock. The ground is still gray and ashy, but there are large rocks staggered about. I pick one up. It is a solid piece of granite, heavy crystallized, like remnants of a volcanic eruption, not some kind of hard clay or petrified wood. This is something that came from a mountain. I put it in my pack.

Excited, I move faster. I must be close.

It is still too dark to fully see them, but I can make out the outline of the mountain range in the distance. By the time the sun starts to rise, I see the village. I fly toward it with vigor. I hadn't thought about it much until now, but I hope I don't frighten them. I forget about my dragon wings, since my village is used to them and it doesn't really affect them anymore, but there was a time when people were afraid of me because of my wings. The thought of frightening a group of unsuspecting villagers is interrupted by another. What if there are others like me here? I rush forward, but stop short of the village, not by my hopeful epiphany, but by the deafening sound of silence. I don't hear one voice. There isn't one child laughing or crying, nothing but the howl of the wind charging through empty dwellings.

The homes look somewhat similar to ours. Some are within large trees. Others built on the ground with stones and wood, but they all look like something from a nightmare. All have been abandoned and neglected for a long time. They have been grown over, but the new growth has died, leaving snarled roots and dried up vines wrapped around and warping the structures. The smell in the air is sour, but the rot died out long ago.

Cautiously, I enter each home calling out, "Hello," though I know I will not hear anything back. Many of the clothes have been left behind. They sit in drawers and on shelves, folded and undisturbed. Most of them are in pretty good condition, only some are worn by idle time, or eaten through by larva. I do find a pair of brown pants that fit, and some arm covers that are in good shape. I tuck them in my pack.

Any food that was here has all been either picked over by other invaders or has rotted many years ago. Many of the other items in the homes remain: books, cooking pots, tools, all left behind. I pick up many of the items, hoping that one of them will give me some idea about what happened here. Obviously, the fairies that lived here either left in a hurry, or they were taken. The Skars weren't here, this much is certain. They would have used everything and, what they didn't use, would have been burned right down to the dwellings themselves. With the exception of the occasional critter, I might be the first person who has come through here.

The search for food and water bares no success. My own rations are running thin, and my water supply is down to drops. All the wells have come up as dust and the rain buckets are all dry. It takes most of the day to search all the homes. Tired, I shuffle through the hallway of one home and come to a bedroom at the end of the hall. The floorboards are warped and uneven. They squeak under my feet. The room is small, but comfortable with a small bed in the far corner. The covers have been pulled back and there is a small toy resting face down. I sit on the bed. It's soft. I pick up the forgotten toy. It is a stuffed doll in the shape of a rabbit made out of an old, brown, cloth sack. Stitched with twine, it has large floppy ears, and the cotton tail was likely hugged right off by whatever child loved this bunny the most. It's surprising that this was left behind.

My eyelids get heavy. Exhaustion washes over me, and I hardly even realize that I have laid down with the rabbit still in my hand.

*****

Sleep came easy, but the dreams seem blocked. Normally, I would welcome this and just allow myself to slip into the dark abyss of slumber, but I am searching for answers. Something is in my way, and I cannot seem to find my way back to the cave. I do get one strong image—a mountain. It is dark and formed by sharp, jagged peaks. It looks like the home for evil itself. I try to see more, but everything goes black.

When I finally wake, I am surrounded by the same silence as when I first arrived. It takes me a minute to get up and start moving again. Still so tired, I feel as though I could sleep for days. The sun is setting. I should keep moving to see if I can find water.

Since the village has been wiped out, I head toward the mountains, hoping for snow melt or something. I only make it a short distance before I see something out of the corner of my eye. At first, it's a blinking light in the distance. It isn't until I see the faint smokestack, that I realize it is a shack that has a fire going. The basic need for survival vanquishes any hesitations about marching up to the home of a complete stranger in a foreign land. I walk steadily toward the light like it is my pharos. The closer I get, the more I wonder about who could possibly live out here in this uninhabitable land alone? What kind of Fae would isolate themselves here? I don't give myself time to consider it. I just keep walking and pull my dagger from my belt.

Khalon

Chapter 15

He can live on their food. The plants and berries, but his blood still craves flesh from time to time. His eyes roll back into his head when he takes the first bite. Still hot from the fire, it burns his mouth, but the salty, smoky taste, marbled with buttery ribbons of fat are worth it. Greedily, he eats the meat right off the bone.

He doesn't tell anyone that every so often he goes out in the middle of the night to check his snares, hoping for some late-night feast. He was only just cleansed from his barbaric reputation, so no point in upsetting his new shining image quite yet. This time, he was delighted to find a small wild pig. Most of the time, he only finds rodents or the occasional rabbit. There isn't much game in this part of the land, so this was a *real* catch. Even though there is plenty of meat for another few days, he picks the animal clean, licks his greasy fingers, and sits with his belly full, staring happily at the fire.

This is happiness. The village has been the best home he could have ever hoped for, especially with his violent past, but he relishes these nights alone. Quiet. Uncomplicated. Able to disappear from the world.

His carnal bliss is soon buggered by a guilt he knows too well. It's not a lie. He isn't necessarily hiding anything, but he just isn't telling her everything either. Shaking his head, he surrenders the bones and scraps to the other critters to pick over and for the earth to swallow up. He covers the burning embers with dirt and goes to reset his snares for the next victim. Before returning home, he tries to find edible plants, so it looks like he spent the night scavenging for food, rather than spending it in his own gluttonous paradise. Usually, he ends up at the river fishing since he still doesn't fully understand which plants are food, medicine, or poison, though all would serve some purpose, in his eyes. It is late morning by the time he has a good string of fish and enough flora to look like he's been out on a successful venture.

Sigrun is not home when he arrives. This isn't all that strange. She goes off on her own all the time, but she has been such a recluse lately, he's not used to her not being there. Selfishly, he has enjoyed it. He hates seeing her unhappy but, as long as she's home, she is not running around with the golden boy as much. His jaw clenches as his jealousy flares up. He tries very hard to be aloof, give her space, but sometimes the idea of her sharing herself with anyone else drives him mad. He's never had feelings like this before. Females in his previous clan were, at best, fellow soldiers and, at worst, merely objects to be exploited and discarded. Affection was completely foreign to him when he met her.

He often thinks about the day he first saw her. He had been tracking the Gila for a long time. He knew it was close and a fresh chunk of meat would be all that was needed to distract it long enough to get the drop on it. His plan was solid and his timing perfect, but then she came along. The intention was to trap it alive and secrete its poison as they yield more when they are alive. At first, he was annoyed by the stranger's interference and thought for a fleeting moment he should just let nature take its course, but the moment he heard her scream, something unexplainable happened to him. It was like something reached into his chest and touched his heart for the first time. Saving her was all he could to do.

He truly did not know if she would still be alive when he was rolling the beast off her. It took every bit of his strength, but finally he managed. She was dirty and bloodied, clothes torn, and unconscious, but she was the most beautiful thing he had ever seen. Strong body, high cheekbones, beautiful skin, and dragon wings. He had never seen anything like her before. Her wings were mostly green, but in the sunlight, there was a subtle purple iridescence. Carefully, he moved a loose strand of hair away from her eyes. Immediately he felt differently about her than he had felt about anyone else. It made him very uncomfortable. He was grateful that she remained unconscious as he carried her out of the Deadlands and while he bandaged her wounds. It gave him time to think about how to handle this unexpected event. Looking back on it now, he didn't handle everything as well as he would have liked, but she just asked so many damn questions! He wasn't prepared for that. His outburst at her surprised him as much as it surprised her. He had never been that emotional before, but what he was the most unprepared for, was the fear that she would leave and that he would never see her again. When she didn't leave, it gave him hope, which made him made him even more uncomfortable. Caring about anything almost made his skin hurt, but she found a way in.

Any thought of her in danger sends him into a panicked state. The worry has not been as strong lately, since she can clearly handle herself, not to mention she can set herself on fire, if things get really dire, but today, he has a sick feeling when realizes she is not home.

He shakes off the edgy feeling that something might be wrong and heads back outside to gut and smoke the fish. By the time the fish is cooked, and the rest of the plants have been cleaned and stored, the afternoon light is fading. She's still not home. Anxiety might be the most frustrating feeling of all. It comes out of nowhere and is not easily dealt with.

I'm just tired, he convinces himself.

He goes out to his branch and wraps up for the day. He never understood why other fairies say hanging upside down makes them lightheaded. To him, it's just the same as being upright, only his muscles stretch out and relax all at the same time. Nothing feels better after a long day, or night. His wing shrouds his face blacking out the sun.

She'll be back by the time I wake up, he thinks, as he drifts off to sleep.

*****

He wakes with the sun. Unusual for him to sleep through the night. He was more tired than he thought. After a tree shaking yawn, he stretches out and climbs back in through his window. The house is still quiet.

Maybe she is still sleeping.

Walking quietly so to not disturb, he peeks down the hallway and sees her door is open. She never sleeps with her door open. His nerves start to rise. He quickens his paces and ascends into full blown panic when he reaches her bedroom door and notices that her bed is still made from the day before, and nothing in her room has been touched. She never came home.

He runs downstairs to see if maybe she fell asleep in one of the living room chairs, only to be disappointed again. He goes back upstairs just long enough to put on clean clothes and then he jumps out his bedroom window and springs to flight.

Not sure at first where he is going since she has left no clues, he flies in no specific direction. He just can't stand still, while he thinks about where she might be. His first thought was that maybe she stayed over at Ainia's house but given the tension between her and all of her friends, that doesn't seem likely. Ainia might even be too frightened of her right now to be alone with her for any period of time. He saw the look on Ainia's face that night at Malyn's house. She was terrified. All of her friends have been too apprehensive to even come to the house. Well, almost all of them.

Jae. She must be with Jae. The thought makes him irritable, but just knowing she is safe would make it tolerable. He alters direction and heads toward the Redwood family home.

Jae's house seems quiet. He feels a little uncomfortable knocking on the door in the first place, but it's especially awkward since it is so early. Falon opens the door in his robe, but he is holding a cup of tea, so he feels better knowing he was already awake.

"Khalon?" Falon asks, surprised to see him standing at his doorstep.

"Have you seen Sigrun?" he gets straight to the point.

"No, I haven't."

Khalon's brow furrows.

"Is everything alright?" Falon asks.

"Is Jae at home?" Khalon ignores Falon's question entirely.

"No. He left at first light to get down to the fields," Falon explains. He sees the immediate confusion in Khalon's face and knows right away what he is thinking. "I know, who knew my son would take to farming, but he really likes it," he shrugs.

"Okay, thank you," Khalon says stepping away from the front door.

"Is everything alright?" Falon asks again, as Khalon lifts into the sky.

"Everything's fine. Thank you," Khalon replies, before disappearing from sight. Everything was not fine, but he didn't want to raise the alarm until he had exhausted all rational explanations.

Flying toward the grain fields, he can't help but think about the last time he had to go to Jae and tell him that Sigrun was missing. Asking for help is something he almost never does, and asking for help from someone who, to him, is the equivalent to a mouth sore, makes him grit his teeth. Despite this general animosity, Jae is certainly someone he can trust to have Sigrun's safety as a primary concern.

He swore he would never be in this vulnerable place ever again. The feeling of helplessness does not rest well with him. Was she taken, or did she leave? It didn't feel like Mantus' work. He would never come back just for her. If he did come back, it would be for the entire village. Regardless, any number of terrible things could have happened to her, and her recent behavior has been so out of character, that the certainty of knowing her so well was beginning to wane.

Up ahead at the fields, he sees Jae immediately. Jae has the same surprised look his father did when he sees Khalon fly up to the fields.

"Hey," Jae says, a little confused by Khalon's presence.

"Were you with Sigrun at all yesterday or this morning?" Again, Khalon gets straight to the point.

"No, I haven't seen her for a few days." At first, Jae is just answering a question, but then the implications begin to arise, and the question of why Khalon might asking gets his full attention. His stance stiffens.

"What's going on? What's wrong?" Jae asks.

"She's gone."

"What do you mean she's gone?" Jae puts down is fielding tools and grabs his shirt from the ground.

"She wasn't home when I got back yesterday morning, but it was late enough that I figured she was out with you," he swallows hard as he says that, "but when she was still gone this morning, I knew something was wrong."

Jae looks ill. He is clearly as worried as Khalon.

"Do you know of any place that she might be?" Khalon asks.

Jae's eyes light up a little like he has thought of something. "Maybe. Why don't you go back to the house in case she did go home, and I'll look in a couple other places and then meet you there."

"Sounds good. I will swing by the old training field on my way and see if maybe she is there."

They both take off in a hurry. Khalon makes it to the training field to find nothing but new grass growing and remnants of Malyn's wedding. Picking up the pace, he rushes home to see if maybe she's there now. The house is as silent as it was when he left this morning. Just as he goes back outside, Jae flies up. Alone. He is a little bit out of breath and his hair is wet, which seems odd, but Khalon does not care enough to ask why.

"Is she here?" Jae asks.

Khalon just shakes his head. The disappointment is heavy on both.

"Any other ideas?" Khalon asks.

Jae pauses for a minute, "My uncle, she spends a lot of time over there."

Khalon does not waste time replying, he just flies off toward Vivek's house with Jae just behind him.

*****

For the second time in two days, Vivek finds visitors at his doorstep early in the morning.

He smiles when he sees his nephew. He has not seen him much in recent months, but when he notices Khalon is the other person, his smile fades a bit and his eyes dart between the two for a moment in confusion. Seeing Jae and Khalon together is strange. The two are hardly friends. They both vie for the attention of the same girl, and neither of them would miss an opportunity to discredit the other, so seeing them together—united—causes concern.

"H…hello boys," Vivek says awkwardly.

"Morning, Uncle. Sorry to drop in on you, but we are looking for Sigrun. Has she been here?" Jae doesn't waste time with any pleasantries.

Vivek's face goes gray. He knew when she left his house that it was not over for her. He hoped it was, but deep down, he knew better.

"Come inside," he invites them in calmly, and lazily walks back inside his home.

Neither Jae nor Khalon know how to react to Vivek's easy demeanor. They look at each other a little perplexed before following him inside. It should be a comfort that he is not frantic, but in a strange way, it seems more distressful that he knows exactly what's going on.

"Would either of you like some tea?" Vivek offers as they enter the room.

"Ummm, no, no thank you," Khalon declines.

Jae shakes his head at his uncle's offer. Vivek simply shrugs his shoulders and refills his own cup from the steaming pot.

"I saw her yesterday," he finally answers their question. He motions for them to sit in the chairs by the hearth. "She had some questions about her mother."

"Her mother?" Jae asks.

"Yes."

"Why?" Jae asks again.

"She's been having dreams of her."

100

"What kind of dreams?" Khalon leans forward as he asks.

"The kind that made her question whether or not she is still alive."

Now Jae leans forward, "She's not though. Is she?"

Vivek shakes his head, "No. She is not, which is exactly what I told her, but you know how she is."

Jae and Khalon both nod with a mutual understanding. They both know how impulsive and headstrong she can be. Once she has something in her mind, there is nothing anyone can say to talk her out of it.

"I think," Vivek continues, "she is out trying to prove me wrong."

"What? How?" Jae's face is twisted with the absurdity of it.

"She found a journal that her father had hidden away. It had some pretty powerful things in it. A very honest account of Merik, and some very hard things regarding her mother." He takes a sip of his tea, sits back in his chair, and directs his attention a bit more toward Khalon. "Jae knows a little bit about this, but our village had a devastating plague tear through it many years ago and that is how Baron met Maia. Baron and I went scavenging for a certain type of plant that was rumored to be a remedy, but it didn't grow here, and we stumbled onto Maia's village in search of it. He saw her and that was that. As I told Sigrun, the two of them where just drawn to each other—like magic." He smiles at the memory.

"I don't remember hearing this," Jae interjects. "I mean, I've heard about the plague, but I didn't know that was how Baron and Maia met."

"They never spoke about her village. It was all kept very secret, and no one ever knew why. They even kept the location of her village a secret. Baron and I each had a copy of the map leading back to her home and we each agreed to destroy them." He stands up out of his chair and walks over to the desk on the other side of the room where the tea pot sits. He fills his cup again. "While she was going through this journal, Sigrun found the map, so it would seem my trusted friend did not keep his word," Vivek looks over his shoulder and gives a half smile, "but what my friend didn't know," he opens the desk drawer and pulls out a weathered piece of canvas, "is that I didn't keep my word either."

He lightly shakes the fabric like a man triumphant and gloating that he has the upper hand. Jae and Khalon both eject from their seats to look at this new treasure. Spreading it out carefully on the desk's surface, they look at it, trying get a sense of the landscape. The map is old, and certainly looks it, but the ink is still very readable.

"Our village is over on this side," Vivek points to the left side edge of the map navigating them through it. "You will cross over the river and head through a lot of forest, and her village is tucked away at the foot of this mountain range. It is hidden away, and you almost need to know what you are looking for to find it. It was really lucky that we found it in the first place."

Khalon bends over the desk to get a closer look. His massive hands touch the canvas lightly tracing the route, hopeful to hone in on Sigrun's current location. He stops when he reaches a certain spot on the map. He rubs it gently. "Is this a stain?"

Vivek reaches for a magnifying glass and looks it over. "Oh! Right, I almost forgot, watch out for this bit. You will want to go around." He moves his finger, mapping out an alternate route.

"It might seem like the long way around, but trust me, you do not want to go through the fog. There is something unnatural about it. This is why we got lost in the first place when we were looking for the plants. The fog disorients you and makes it very hard to move and breathe, and if you try to fly up out of it, it paralyzes you, and knocks you unconscious. The forest, itself, does not want you to find your way out."

Khalon had started to relax once he found out that Sigrun was just trying to discover her roots, but now hearing that she is traipsing through an evil forest, his comfort is dwindling.

Looking at Jae and Vivek's long faces, he can tell that he is not the only one concerned.

"May we take this?" Jae asks.

"Of course," Vivek surrenders it willingly. "Go, bring her home," he puts one hand on Jae's arm and the other on Khalon. He knows fully, it will take both of them to do it.

As Jae and Khalon are stepping out of the house, Vivek stops them.

"Boys, one more thing," he breathes deeply searching for the right words, "we were told to never ask, and we never did, but when Baron came back with Maia, she was half-dead. He had to carry her most of the way and he was weakened himself. When he left our village, he had hair as dark brown as Sigrun's and when he came back it was as white as a moth's wing. Whatever he saw turned his hair white. Look out for each other and come home as fast as you can."

Chapter 16

"We leave today," Jae says as they walk away from Vivek's front door.

"We leave now," Khalon counters.

Jae nods in agreement and they both fly off to quickly gather supplies. Khalon wastes very little time. Vivek's words as they were leaving were a warning, adding urgency to this quest. He focuses more on weapons, than food or medicine. His sword, he is taking for sure. A bow, he can make easily in the woods, if he needs to, and he tucks a dagger in his belt for good measure. He throws a loaf of bread and a satchel of nuts in his travel sack and sets out to meet Jae.

They find one another at the edge of the village on the east side just before the river. Jae is similarly attired. One sack strewn across his body, which likely carries food and other supplies, and he has his sword hanging from his belt as well. Jae casually rests his hand on the hilt. Khalon smiles a bit when he sees it. It used to be his. Many battles were won, and much blood was spilled, by that sword. He still remembers the feel of it as though it were an extension of his own arm. Jae notices Khalon looking at it and awkwardly moves his hand away.

"We should go," Jae says, clearing his throat a little, "she has a full day's start on us. We should push through the night and see if we can't catch up with her."

"Let's go," Khalon says in agreement, but he still finds being with Jae irksome. The two have hardly had a good relationship. If it had been up to Jae, Khalon would have been cast out when he first arrived, and it's no secret that Khalon would have gone to bloody measures to deal with Jae. They have managed to co-exist merely due to the fact that they both care for Sigrun, and her continued affections hinge on them getting along.

Jae pulls the map from his bag. "We just head east until we get to the fog."

"Simple enough."

They both fill up water canteens and take off over the river.

*****

The day passes in silence. Khalon has nothing to say to Jae. His presence is tolerable. He knows Jae has always meant well and he respects him for that, but he has never had a desire to be friends, and he expects Jae feels the same way about him.

The forest flies past them in a blur. Khalon's mind veers away from where they are going onto *why* they are going. *Why can't she just stay put?* Irritation knots up in his stomach. At the very least, she should let someone know where she is going. It is almost cruel to take off with no explanation, especially after what everyone has been through in the last year. Her thoughtlessness annoys him.

Emotions are complicated. He is not used to having so many, and even less used to dealing with them. Soldiering had been his entire life: you follow orders, do what you're told, and fall in line. In the past, if someone annoyed him, that would earn them a justified drubbing or worse, depending on the severity of the annoyance, but this is different. This agitation is not born from some drunken ravings of a halfwit, or the misguided foolishness of an adolescent's issue with authority. Something like that is as easily handled as swatting a fly, eliminating a pest. Sigrun, on the other hand, is the furthest thing from a pest to him. Not dealt with as easily at all, and he does understand on some level that she wants answers about her family, but damn it! Why does it always involve her getting into danger!

Somewhere during his reeling, the forest had changed, but it wasn't until he heard Jae struggling for breath that he noticed his own breathing was labored and how dark and cold it was. Jae seems to notice that Khalon is struggling as much as he is, and he motions to land.

"We must be getting close to the fog," Jae gets out between breaths.

"It's so cold here," Khalon says, wishing, for once, he had worn a shirt. He folds his wings around his shoulders like a cape.

Jae pulls out the map from his pack and lays it out on the ground. "Okay, I'm thinking we are right here," he points to the edge of the blurry bit of the map. "I don't think it matters which way we go, so let's take the southern route around it and hopefully we will make our way through it by early morning."

They both take a quick drink of water and prepare themselves for the long walk ahead of them. The air is better on the outskirts of the fog. It's easier to breathe, but the cold still persists. The aching in their bodies clings to them the same way the chill does. They walk steadily for several hours, yet this forest feels never ending.

Nighttime comes quickly in this place, and with it, the cold and the dark get more intense. The darkness is thick. Even with his superior nighttime vision, Khalon still cannot see properly here. The moon should be full, but as far as Khalon can tell, the moon does not exist in these lands. Even with torches, they are stumbling clumsily through the terrain. About twenty toe stubs and three or four twisted ankles later, Jae stops walking.

"I hate to say it, but I don't think we are getting anywhere tonight," Jae says defeated. Khalon's own body is aching, he is tired and hungry, but he would never admit it. More than anything, he is grateful that Jae finally folded, and he can keep his own struggles to himself.

"Yeah, we will be able get through it easier in the morning," Khalon replies coolly. "I'll get a fire going."

Khalon eats his bread sitting on the opposite side of the fire from Jae. Khalon takes a few moments and watches Jae on the other side. Jae is gazing off into the distance focused on something that isn't there. Eating his food out of habit, rather than desire. Khalon has not spoken more than a few words to Jae since this journey began. Then again, neither has Jae. They don't have much in common. They come from completely different backgrounds and don't speak to one another unless forced, but Khalon knows that they will go from bored to mad if they do not find a way to pass the time.

"What was she like when she was younger?" Khalon asks, grasping at the only mutual topic that they share.

Jae looks stunned for a moment. He was not expecting to Khalon to speak, let alone ask a direct question. He chuckles to himself and rolls his eyes. He knows instantly Khalon is asking about Sigrun. "Smaller."

Khalon chuckles.

"She was hardheaded. You couldn't tell her 'no', or that she couldn't do something. She would have to prove you wrong."

"So, not much has changed."

Jae laughs a little, "No, she is definitely the same person now that she was then. Only now, she's pretty good with a weapon." His eyes wonder off for a moment as he seems to reflect on childhood memories. A small smile crosses his lips. "You couldn't ask for a better friend though." Khalon leans forward resting his elbows on his knees.

"When we were kids, Vidar was a bit of a bully. He has a little too much Blue Jay blood in him," Jae continues. "For some reason, one day he was really going after Ainia. Looking back on it now, he probably had a crush, but didn't know how to get a girl's attention without being a toad about it. Anyway, all it took was Ainia running to Sigrun with tears in her eyes. I told her to just blow it off, but oh no—there goes Sigrun. Not only did she go charging after Vidar, but she took on Soren and Ragnar as well. She came back with a split lip and a black eye, but she had her head held up high and Vidar never picked on Ainia again."

The story makes Khalon smile. Even though he never saw her as a little girl, he sees her perfectly. He imagines her walking with a determined little strut into an almost certain beating with meaty little hands clinched into tight fists, eyes squinting at her opponent, and her refusal to accept anything less than exactly what she wants.

"I never understood her willingness to excuse Merik," Jae shakes his head. "If anyone of us had a sibling like him, she would've marched right up to them and made it very clear that their continued health was contingent on them being a better brother or sister, but whenever one of us would start to fight for her, or try to protect her, she would turn around and defend her brother instead."

"What would he do to her?"

"There were so many things. Of course, there was punching and hitting, but it was more than that. He just held an unnatural hatred for her," Jae sits up straighter and folds his arms across his chest like he is protecting himself. "One thing I remember was one of the older kids telling us a story about just after Sigrun was born. The entire village was in an uproar over her to begin with, her mother's death being so brutal and all, and that kind of scandal generates a lot of curiosity. Many kids would try to sneak into the Livingstone home to get a glimpse at 'the monster'," Jae rolls his eyes. "This boy, who was probably not much older than ten, crept into the house one afternoon and found Merik, who was only about five years old at the time, bent over the cradle with his hands over her nose and mouth. He was trying to suffocate her. The boy shouted at Merik to stop, but Merik didn't even acknowledge that the boy was there and just continued to suffocate her." Jae's jaw clenches as the fury wells up in him. He takes a breath before speaking again, "The boy had to pull Merik off of her kicking and screaming, and he said that he would never forget the terrified gasp and the horrific wailing that came from her when she was finally able to breathe. It wasn't until Baron came running into the room that Merik stopped trying to run back to the cradle and finish it. Then he just ran away. The boy told Baron what happened, and I guess Baron just nodded and then began to comfort his newborn daughter.

"The funny thing is, I bet if you were to ask Sigrun, even to this day, after all she's been through, she would probably say the same thing, that 'He had just lost his mother and didn't understand, blah, blah, blah.' she would never admit that he was just pure evil from the start. She just couldn't see it," he pauses and gazes off into the darkness. "I think she still struggles with his death."

"I'm sure you're right about that," Khalon nods in agreement. "What did the boy think about her?"

"Huh?" the question catches Jae off guard.

"The boy, when he saw her, did he say what he thought when he saw 'the monster?'"

Jae smiles, "Yeah, he said that when she finally settled down, Baron let him hold her. He said she was smiley and strong, she had pink cheeks, a little bit of dark-brown, fuzzy hair, and really wicked wings."

The corner of Khalon's mouth twitches into a smile.

"Well, we might as well get some rest. It's going to be a long day tomorrow," Jae says, settling down on the ground to sleep.

"Go ahead. I'm going to stay up and keep the fire going. I'm not very tired."

Jay shrugs his shoulders and mumbles something inaudible before turning away from the light of the fire.

Sigrun

Chapter 17

The figure is merely a shadow at first. A movement in the window, then a quick dash to the door.

"W...who's out there?" the voice is a little shaky and sounds like one belonging to an old man. With the light behind him, I can only make out his silhouette. He is very thin, and though his wiry appearance may look feeble, I gather he is quite formidable being out here all by himself. This does not seem to be an easy place to live, but the knife in his trembling hand suggests he does not get many visitors.

I raise my hands up and stop walking, "I mean you no harm. I'm just looking for water and a warm place for the night."

He looks around nervously.

"I'm alone. I promise you," I say, trying to ease him, which may not be possible seeing as how I am strapped in armor and loaded with weapons.

After another moment or so, he finally lowers his hand with the knife and nods slightly.

He goes back inside leaving the door open. I continue standing there, unsure about what to do.

"Well, are you coming in, or not?" he shouts annoyed from the house.

"Oh," I hustle up to the door and close it behind me.

The house isn't more than one room constructed from straw and clay with old, worn, wood floors. The door is a heavy wood, and the windows have very rustic looking shutter doors. His bed is in the far, right corner. It's small and he doesn't have much in the way of bedding, but it is neatly made and clean, as is the rest of the home. Everything is tucked away and in its place. He only has a few items, but the cups and dishes are stacked on the shelves next to the few food stores he seems to have. His books, all worn out and cracked, sit next his clothes, which are all folded and resting on a bench next to his bed. Even though he was certainly not expecting company, it looks like he tidied up for the occasion. This is a man with very little, but he has a lot of pride.

There is a small table and two wooden chairs near the hearth, which has a good fire going and a small pot cooking on the spit. He barely seems to notice that I am even there. He has his back to me, and he's pouring water into a cup. Hopefully it's for me.

He is rather old indeed, though I expect that he is aged more by life, than time. His hair is wispy like gray cotton and seems to stick out whichever way it pleases. His clothing looks older than he does, tattered and stained, but again, I can tell it has been freshly washed. He has feathered wings mostly a gray-brown color, nothing remarkable, and they are thinned out by malnourishment and daily hardship, the same way he is. He turns back to me, and I see his face clearly for the first time. Deep creases shape his forehead into a sad brow. He has a prominent nose and a small mouth, but more than anything he looks kind. He takes a step toward me with the cup in his knobby-knuckled hand.

"You must be thirsty. There isn't wa…" he stops suddenly when he looks at me for the first time in the light. His eyes are wide, and his lower jaw hangs open just a bit.

I tuck my wings back neatly behind my back, "I know they look fearsome, but I'm no danger to you."

The cup in his hand tips forward slightly, as he has forgotten that he is holding it, spilling a few precious drops of the liquid onto the floor.

"Oh gosh," he shakes his head, recovering himself, and stabilizes his hand, "I'm sorry about that." Embarrassed that he spilled water on his own floor, he pushes the cup into my hands and grabs a rag from the table to wipe the floor. He stands back up, looking even more nervous than when I first arrived. He motions to the chair in front of the fire for me to sit.

I smile slightly. This is not the first time that someone has been alarmed at the sight of my wings. I still remember the first time I went to school. Several children had stolen a glance of me before, but it was the first time I was to sit amongst them fully vulnerable to their merciless stares. A dozen or so pairs of wide eyes invasively roaming over me. At first, I remember feeling naked. Without the body of my father to stand behind, I was utterly exposed. That was also the first time I felt that glint in my chest. I squinted my eyes and thrust my wings out to full expansion. The children all let out a collective gasp. One little boy jumped so much he fell backwards out of his seat.

I stood there, wings fully out, hands on my little hips daring anyone to give me any trouble. They all sat there with wide-eyed stares, except for one boy with brown wavy locks and golden-brown wings. He walked up to me, reached out with one curious finger, and touched the green scales of my wings.

"Wow," he said, before taking my hand and walking me over to sit next to him. That was the day Jae became my best friend.

The old man stands up after cleaning the spill and wrings the tattered rag nervously in his hands. Not looking at me directly, he motions again for me to sit in one of the chairs. Happily, I oblige. I unstrap my weapon harness and carefully place my kama and dagger on the ground. I settle into my chair. The fire feels good on my aching body. Eager and thirsty, I start drinking the water, but am stopped by the foul taste and smell. It resembles metal and rot and stings my tongue a little.

"I know," the old man says, "It tastes bad." I must have made a face when I drank. "The land here is cursed. Even what little rain we get is acidic. I boil the water, so it won't kill you, but it still tastes bad." While he is talking, he is dishing out two bowls of soup from the pot over the fire. He places one bowl in front of me and shrugs his shoulders in an apologetic way, as though he is saying, 'It's all I've got.'

"Thank you," I say gratefully. "You have saved me tonight," I add, lifting the bowl as acknowledgment of his generosity. He says nothing else, but nods and waves his hand at me, uncomfortable with my gratitude.

It isn't much. Mostly a broth with a few boiled, weedlike roots. The smell is still pungent like the water, but it is hot and salty and just enough to subdue my hunger.

"Did you get lost?" the old man asks.

"I'm sorry?" I ask in return.

"I was just wondering what brought you out to this wasteland. I'm assuming you must be lost."

"Actually no, I'm right where I want to be. I think." I pull the map from my pack and lay it out on the table. His trembling hand traces the map carefully.

"Where did you get this?" he asks mystified.

"My father. Well, I found it in one of his books. He passed away." I don't know why I felt I needed to disclose that my father had died, but he nodded with an empathetic understanding. "I just came from here," I pointed to the village, "But it looks different than the map. The tree line is much scanter than I thought it would be."

He raises his eyebrows and nods, not taking his eyes off the map.

"What happened here, why are all the people gone?"

Slowly, he moves one thin finger and rests it accusingly on the map—squarely on the tallest mountain peak. "There is evil there."

"On the mountain?"

His head nods heavily. "It is like a poison," his brow furrows. "It seeped into the ground and slowly reached out to everything. The wells dried up, the crops died, the animals fled, it kills everything it touches," his voice is tired and shaky. His eyes stare through the map like he is looking into another place. "Everyone left. There was no other choice."

I cock my head to the side confused, "But, you stayed?"

He presses his already thin lips into a thinner line.

"Why?"

He turns his head to the window, "My wife," he takes a breath, "she died on that mountain. I couldn't bear to leave her." Sadness shows itself in his dull blue eyes. He turns back to me, and the corner of his mouth twists up into an apologetic smile. "In fact, I moved here and built this shack because this was as close as I could be to her without feeling the sickness."

"So, we are close to the mountain then?"

"Oh yes, you can't see it because it is dark, but once the daylight comes in, you will be able to see it right through that window." He points to the window on the east facing wall.

I walk over to the window and throw open the shutters. He's right, all I can see is the dark—thick and impenetrable. "I can't see the moon."

"No moon. No stars. The sun never really comes out either. Every day is just another dismal shade of dreary."

I want to urge him to leave. I'm sure his wife would not want to him to stay here. This land is dying and killing every living thing on it, but he already knows this, and I suspect there is nothing I could say to make him leave.

He wipes down the dishes and stacks them back on the shelf. "Well, you must be tired," he points to the small bed offering up his own bed to me.

I put my hands up in protest, "Oh no, if it is alright with you, I would rather sleep by the fire. Still feeling a bit chilled," I lie, but I have put this man out enough for one night. I certainly cannot take his bed as well.

He squints his eyes at my polite decline and pulls the blanket off the top. "You take this at least," he orders. He lays it carefully on the floor in front of the hearth.

I nod my head in compliance, "Thank you."

He waves me off again and grumbles lightly as he settles in his bed.

I lie down in front of the hearth. The fire does feel good. The hypnotic dance of the flame quickly lulls me to sleep.

*****

The morning comes faster than I expected. The old man is already up and putting some water in the kettle for tea. I look outside. The old man wasn't lying—it *is* just another shade of dreary. The skies are a dark gray. It looks like a storm could break lose any moment and the air carries a stinging cold on it. I shudder.

"Looks like it might rain," I say.

He shakes his head and tosses another log on the dying fire. "It looks like it is going to rain, but the rain never comes."

I turn back to the window. There is a mist off in the distance, but I can see the faint outline of the mountains.

"The morning mist will lift in a bit," he says, almost like he can read my mind, "then you'll be able to see it." He points to the tallest peak, "That's Dragon Claw Mountain," he looks at my wings and touches his bottom lip for a second. "Ah, no offense."

"Oh, none taken," I reassure him.

He walks over to me with a steaming cup. It isn't so much tea as it is hot water with a kind of bark and a few dried leaves of some sort. "It's not rose hips, or dandelion, but it will help keep you alert." He pushes the cup into my hands.

"Thank you." It is bitter, but I do feel a sharpness to my senses after a few sips. "Well, I better get going." I hand the cup back to him and grab my pack and weapons.

He walks me to the door. "So, it is just that way," he points east. He looks as though he wants to say more to me, some warning or wisdom, but only manages, "Okay, then."

"Again, thank you for everything," I smile and start to walk away, then something occurs to me, and I turn around quickly. "Your name, I never got your name."

He lets out a light chuckle. It seems he had forgotten about social graces as well. "Aryl," he says finally.

"Thank you, Aryl. I'm Sigrun."

"Nice to meet you."

I nod and start to fly off toward the mountains.

*****

I don't get far before my wings start to ache. They feel heavy and stiff like they are turning to stone. My joints are locking up. I am once again forced to the ground. This must be what Aryl meant when he said, 'the sickness.' It feels like I have aged 70 years. Everything hurts and it's a struggle to move. No wonder everyone left this place.

Ahead, I see the mountain. It is forbidding indeed. It's no surprise how it acquired its name, Dragon Claw Mountain; sharp and jagged like a claw reaching out from the earth attempting slice into the sky. It seems crazy that all this force is coming from that one place. Crazier still that this is the one place I am trying to get to, and it's still quite far away. When Aryl said the mountain was visible from his window, I thought this would just be a quick flight. Now that I am grounded for the foreseeable future, this is going to take much longer than I thought.

Walking the distance would not be as daunting if the elements were more forgiving. The wind is whipping through the mountain range making forward progress almost non-existent. It makes my already laggard pace feel outright glacial. I have to keep my wings tucked very tightly behind my back. Any extra resistance catches the wind like a sail and flings me backwards. Merely keeping my head up is a challenge. The wind assaults my eyes every time I look up, forcing out tears, which blurs my vision even more. I block the wind enough with my hand to track my progress. Almost every time I look up, I find that I have gotten off course and the correction takes extra time.

Every part about this journey makes me want to turn around and go back to where I came from. Going forward is painful and there is nowhere and no way to rest. Every step forward, I feel heavier and heavier. My shoulders ache.

It feels like I have an iron chain wrapped around my neck pulling me down. The air is thin, and I start to feel dizzy. I fall to my knees for a moment to catch my breath.

I close my eyes. *Maybe I should go back.*

The idea of turning back feels good and terrible all at the same time. This trip would be harder the second time; so much so, that I don't know if I would try it again. The wind picks up again, winding between the range, and with it, a voice carries my name with the wind.

Sssigruuuunnn.

The hairs on the back of my neck stand up. I look around me. I am very much alone. I shake my head. It must be exhaustion, I convince myself. I must keep going.

I look forward again. One more pass and then I should be there. I should be at the foot of the mountain. I struggle to my feet and start walking again. One slow, heavy step at a time.

Chapter 18

The entire day has gone. Night is flooding in, and I have finally made it to the base of Dragon Claw Mountain. The peak is a very long way up. The wind is as violent as ever, whipping sand and dirt into my eyes and now the failing light makes it even harder to see. Straining to see all the way to the top, my eyes finally land on a small opening near the tallest point.

"Of course, it would be all the way up there," I say to myself.

There doesn't seem to be a pathway anywhere. Flying is still not possible. The wind has been getting stronger the closer I get. I take a few moments to see if there is any passageway, something hidden, something I missed. Walking around the foot of the mountain, I try to see if there is a more desirable route. I reach out to feel the granite with my hands. Something jolts in me with the touch. A flicker of rage ignites in me just long enough for me to feel a drunkenness, but not one of spirits. This is a high brought on only by power. I let go and the feeling subsides. Cautiously, I reach my hand out to touch the mountain again. The rock itself is hard, unforgiving, and freezing to the touch, which is not encouraging, since it seems I will be climbing my way to the top, but more than that, the heaviness on my shoulders increases by double. My knees buckle and I almost fall to the ground. I let go of the mountain and the extra weight goes away. I look at my hands. Aside from the dirt, they look fine. I touch the rock again. Once more the force of something pushes on me, but I am ready for it this time and able to remain standing. It is uncomfortable, but tolerable. There is something here. That is definite. No place would have so many barriers to keep someone out, if there was no one inside. This mountain is a natural prison. I am more certain than ever that, either my mother is here, or she is driving me toward this place for a reason.

I wish I still had sunlight. Climbing this in the daylight would still be incredibly tough but climbing at night seems like suicide. My body is so tired. It just wants rest, but there is no resting here. There is nowhere comfortable to lie down, and the wind would make it impossible to find any solace. Dirt and grit are being thrown against all my exposed flesh. The force of every grain of sand cuts like a tiny knife. Thousands of them slicing me.

My only options are to go back, which I refuse to do, or seek the nearest shelter and the nearest shelter is atop the mountain.

"Keep it simple. Keep it small," I give myself a pep talk. "It's just one step in front of the other." I look up to my destination. "Only vertical."

The footing is rough. The rock is sharp and many of the boulders are loose and shaky beneath my feet. Every step must be carefully taken. The wind, though constant, has irruptions from time to time, forcing me to burrow into the mountain side as much as I can until it passes. My wings are useless here. I cannot fly against this wind. If I were to fall, it would not be without injury, so I have to keep myself as flat to the mountain as possible, so I'm not blown backwards.

*****

The night has fully arrived. Enveloped in darkness, every unsure step is even more weighted with caution. My pace is slow. It feels like I have been climbing for hours, but I'm not even near the halfway point. It's getting harder now. The joints in my hands are stiff and my fingertips are raw from holding the rough, rocky surface. Even though I haven't looked, I know my feet are bleeding and my knees are banged up and bruised. I can't tell if the weight around my neck and shoulders has gotten worse or if I'm just getting more and more exhausted, but every move takes outrageous effort. The wind has not become any more forgiving. The soft skin on my body, particularly my lips and cheeks, are so chapped that they are cracking, and I am not at all surprised when I taste blood on my lip.

"I must be getting close."

Looking up, it seems so far away still. I know I shouldn't look down, but my curiosity gets the best of me. Twisting slightly at the waist, I turn just enough to see that I am probably about halfway up the mountain side. A small accomplishment goes a long way right now.

Halfway is a marker I can celebrate.

I relax my body for a moment, and the top of my right wing pops up just enough to be caught by a whipping gust that came without warning. Frantic, I

119

try grasping for anything to keep me from falling but it is too late. I am ripped from my footing as easily as a dried leaf from tree in autumn. I can't get my wings open in time, but even if I could it wouldn't do much good anyway.

Falling is much different than flying. Helplessness and panic overwhelm me. Desperate, I grasp at the void hoping for something to snatch me out of the air, but there is nothing. I crash down on my back and jagged rocks dig into my flesh. The slope is so steep that I continue to roll over onto my side. My attempts to stop the fall are in vain. The rocks I try to grab either slip through my hands, or come loose, and fall along with me. I roll a few times before slamming down on my left side on one of the sturdier rock ledges. My left arm takes the brunt of the fall.

I'm not dead. That's for sure. It hurts too much to be dead. My hands were in bad shape before, but they're really torn up now. My palms are scratched and raw and it looks like I might be at risk of losing a fingernail or two. My pant leg is ripped on the right side, and I have a pretty nasty gash on my leg, but it isn't anything that I can't patch up. The left arm that I landed on is in bad shape. I move it carefully at all the joints. It does not appear to be broken, but every part of my body cries out in pain. It could have been much worse. Fortunately, my wings protected me from a lot of the sharp edges. Khalon was the first one to point out their shieldlike quality. Feeling grateful for that at least.

I take some cloth from my bag and wrap up my leg as best I can to stop the bleeding. Bandaging my hands is a little more difficult. I manage to wrap up the two fingers that are in the worst shape. My fingertips throb with pain as I tighten the knot.

I didn't fall that much, but the halfway mark where I was seems quite far now. The struggle just to get that far was so acute that this small setback seems tremendous. I shake off the impulse to cry from sheer frustration and look up as I take my first shaky step towards the middle.

*****

I thought that once I reached the middle, the second half would be easier. It is quite the opposite. The heaviness continues to intensify. It takes every bit of strength for every step. I have to rest between each step, so it is taking much longer than I planned. The intense gusts of wind are more frequent, and the howling of the wind is almost deafening. What's worse, is my pendant is starting to burn.

It was an irritation at first, but with every bit farther, the sensation gets stronger. It is fully burning me now. The skin that it rests on is completely red and threatening to blister. I get to a flat spot and rest on my hands and knees for a moment.

I should take it off, I start thinking. The pendant is having a very strange reaction to this place. I don't want to take it off, but I can't bear the pain much longer.

Maybe I could just carry it in my pack? I reach behind my neck to untie the cord. My hands are shaking. I haven't eaten much in a couple days, and I am utterly exhausted. The cord slips through my clumsy fingers and the crystal marble slams down as hard as an iron hammer on the rock's surface. The impact is so hard that the granite beneath the marble cracks and I feel the tremor all the way through my body. Amazingly, just in the same moment the heaviness on my body lifts. From the moment I set foot on this mountain I felt as though I was carrying an extraordinary length of invisible metal chain, and suddenly it was just snipped away. All that weight—that extra burden—came from my pendant.

I go to pick it up, and sure enough, it's a real struggle to get it off the ground. Even if I were to try to carry it in my pack, I might as well strap one of these boulders to my back, because the effort would be the same.

I have to leave it here. The thought of leaving it behind crushes my heart. This was the last gift my father gave me. I can't possibly leave it behind. I go to touch it again, but the marble burns my skin.

I'll get it on the way back. I promise myself.

Chapter 19

Once I surrendered the pendant to the mountainside, I've been able to move much easier. Daylight is just beginning to break as I reach the opening at the top. The ledge at the opening is a good distance from where I am at. There is no way to climb to it. The wind is still too strong to fly. I will have to jump and pull myself up.

My hands have just about lost all feeling at this point. The cold has numbed most of the pain away, but it has also made my grip unsure. Extending my fingers out sends shooting needlelike pains all along my forearms. I refuse the urge to look down. I already know that it would be a long way to fall.

I have one shot at this. If I had all my strength, this would not be nearly as daunting, but as I am now: exhausted, dehydrated, and starving—my confidence is very slight. I take a deep breath and put every shred of strength that I have left into my shaking legs. I lunge with everything that I can muster and ignite myself forward. Hurling through the air, I feel like I am moving in slow motion, and it is terrifying. One strong gust of wind in the wrong direction could cost me just enough to throw me from the mountainside again. I don't blink. I don't breathe. I don't take my focus away.

After what feels like eternity, my fingers barely grasp the edge. As I am struggling for a better grip with the right hand, the ledge under the left hand betrays me and crumbles away. My eyes go wide, and my body swings out and away. I dig my fingers on the right hand into the ledge as much as I can. I try not to panic, but that seems futile. Wind wraps around me like a funnel and pulls me farther out, so I am almost parallel to the ledge. The howling is worse in the funnel, and grit is hitting me directly in the face. The assault on my eyes makes it impossible to see.

I know it is a risk, but my wings have a longer reach than my arms do. Extending a wing could also catch enough wind to rip me away and send into a tailspin, with no guaranty that I could recover flight, but my grip is down to my first knuckle. The risk must be taken. I extend my left wing a little bit, careful to keep it folded inward, so I don't harness any wind. I have to swing my body slightly to the left to get a good grip. The swing could also dislodge my right hand, my only anchor. Using my legs as a propeller, I throw them over to my left side and shoot my left wing out enough to latch my wing carpal onto the top of the ledge. I quickly grab ahold with my left arm and lift myself up using both arms and my wing, until I get my waist up and am able to get my lower half safely onto the ledge. Relief rushes over me. I roll into the entry of the cave and lie on my back for a moment to rest and catch my breath.

I start to relax enough to notice that the howling wind is much quieter on the inside of the cave, and I feel lighter. The heavy force that has been beating down on me since the forest has finally lifted. It gives me new energy I didn't know I had.

Before going any farther, I take a moment to tend to my injuries. The cut on my leg isn't bad, but if I don't properly attend to it soon it will begin to fester. My hands are in bad shape, but there isn't much else I can do except redo some of the bandaging. My left arm is sore, but healing. I touch the spot on my chest where the pendant burned. It is still tender. I wish I had it with me. I don't know why it is so reactive to the place. It was impossible to bring the rest of the way, but leaving it feels wrong.

Sitting against the cave wall, I go through my pack to see if anything was lost during the climb. I find a couple bites of bread, which I greedily shove in my mouth, and wash down with a small swallow of bitter water that Aryl was kind enough to give me. The Red Book is still securely in place.

"At least I still have you," I say to it, almost hoping for validation.

I check that my kama are still in place and tighten up the strap on my harness. I sling my pack across my body and get up to go deeper into the cave. To the right, the cave seems to dead end rather quickly, making the left side the only passageway. The tunnel is big enough to stand up straight in, but not much bigger than that. There is a damp smell, which I find odd since there is a drought in these lands. It is very dark and the small amount of light from the opening is quickly wasted. I hold my right hand up, so all fingers are pointed toward the ceiling, and ignite a small fire from my fingertips to light the way. The fire doesn't affect me now that I am not wearing the pendant. I pull my dagger from my belt. I may have light to see the way, but I do not know what lies ahead.

The ground declines and I have to turn to the side to keep from sliding. My injured leg slows me down. I can't put my full weight on it. Limping down through the tunnel frustrates me.

I wish I could run or fly! This trip has been one painful step after the next. I finally make it here and I still feel like I'm not making any progress.

I look around and try to absorb my surroundings as a distraction. The rock on the walls is dark with silver flecks that shimmer like the stars. This is the cave from my dreams. I'm certain of it. I follow the tunnel for quite a while, until it begins to open up into a large cavern with three other tunnels on the other side. It is still dark, but bright enough that I can put my fire out. Everything is so quiet. I stop in the middle of the cavern and close my eyes, listening for any sound. There is a low rumble from the wind outside, but just beyond that, I do hear something. A steady drip. There is water somewhere. It is ahead of me through the middle tunnel. My thirst speaks to me. The mere thought of water makes my throat ache for it. I do need water, so this seems like the best place to start.

The new tunnel turns a few times before I see a light coming from the other side. Anticipation swells up in me. I walk at a quicker pace. The dripping sound gets louder, and it doesn't take very long before I reach the end to find an enormous opening. The drip is coming from a slow trickle along the rock wall into a small pool of clear water. Prudently, I look around, and once I assess I truly am alone—I run to it.

Plunging my hands into the water stings at first. The many cuts and scrapes protest. I bring handfuls of water to my lips anyway. It tastes so good. It is almost sweet. I look at my reflection in the water. I am a mess: covered in dirt, my lips are chapped and cracked, windburn has marked my cheeks to a splotchy red, and my hair is a windblown disaster. I lean closer to the water to wash and a flicker of something appears and disappears in the reflection above me. I feel the breeze of something running past me, but as I spin around, nothing is there.

I snatch up my dagger again and stand up cautiously. "Hello?" I say trying to keep my voice level.

There is no answer, but I hear some rocks falling in a tunnel on the other side. The hairs on the back of my neck all stand on end. "Sure, why wouldn't I follow the ghost into the tunnel? Seems like a great idea," I say sarcastically to myself under my breath.

I shake my head. *I didn't come all this way to stop now.*

The tunnel where the sound came from isn't far. It's only a short distance before I see the familiar light dancing on walls and smell the inviting fragrance of the fire. The room is small, but comfortable. The fire burns in the middle and puts off enough heat to make it quite warm. There is a bed made of cotton and straw on the far end and a small writing desk and some books next to it. The really interesting part of this room is the walls. There are symbols and words written on almost every surface, even the ceiling. Nothing seems to be in any particular order, and none of it makes any sense to me. I cannot read most of it, but it's remarkable.

Slowly, discomfort creeps up on me. I feel like I shouldn't be looking at this. I shouldn't be in here. I turn to retreat, but she is standing in the entryway blocking my exit. My dagger slips from my hands hitting the ground with a dull thud.

Her hair is long and dark except for a ribbon of silver in the front. She is about my height, slender, her dress was once white by the looks of it but is old and tattered at the ends just above her feet. Her wings are feathered and white and her eyes are green. This isn't a dream, not this time.

My legs go limp, and I fall to my knees. My head rushes. I feel dizzy. She sees me teeter and puts a hand up to help, but it's too late. Everything goes dark.

Khalon

Chapter 20

The many sleepless hours spent wounded with worry and restless with anticipation have been additionally agitated by the slight snore coming from his travel companion. It isn't so much that he is upset that Jae is sleeping while he is awake trying to ignore the many terrible thoughts about what disastrous situation Sigrun might be in; what he's actually feeling, is closer to jealousy that Jae is able to quiet his mind long enough to fall asleep. Exhaustion has never cloaked him so thoroughly before.

The sky doesn't lighten much, but as soon as he notices a subtle shift toward the dawn that is enough for him to get up and continue on. His body aches with movement. It feels like he has just come from the battlefield, from a fight that he has lost. Aching joints, sore muscles, and a heaviness bear down on him. The cold has only gotten worse in the night hours. His every breath is revealed by a frosty cloud. Vivek wasn't lying—this land is harsh.

He lightly kicks the bottom of Jae's foot interrupting the lazy breath dragging through his throat. Jae snorts a little at the disruption and blinks his eyes awake.

"Sleep well?" Khalon asks.

"Not really." Jae sits up slowly and groans a little. "Ugh, I feel terrible."

"Yeah, this place is awful. I say we get going. The sooner we are out of here, the better."

"Agreed." Jae stands up and moves his body in a way that lets Khalon know he feels just as beaten as he does.

Jae reaches into his pack and splits a piece of bread in two for them to share. He wraps his wings around his shoulders to shield himself from the cold like a soft, warm, feathered blanket. Khalon's wings are thin and don't offer much warmth. His jealousy spreads.

Silently, they march forward, every step labored. Khalon has been marching most of his life with Mantus perpetually moving from place to place;

conquering and inhabiting villages all over the land. That is a soldier's lot in life, but he's never had a march like this before. Mantus never traveled to the mountains. Khalon always assumed it was because he knew there were no resources in the mountains and it's a tough place to live. This trip is certainly proving that point. After so many years of being constantly on the move, he doesn't tire easily. With days upon days of walking, flying, searching, and scouting, his body became immune to the aches, but this time, it's different. Not only is he physically beat down, but the thought of her being out here too, all alone and suffering like this, tortures him. He knows she is strong. He knew that the first moment he met her, but he also knows how strong he is and, if he is struggling, she surely is as well.

Hours later, Jae stops and rubs his right shin. His face winces. He is cramping. Looking at the sky, Khalon tries to gauge the time. It is nearly impossible to get an accurate read on the time of day here. There is no visible sun or moon, and the fog shrouds everything, making every moment of the day another varying shade of gray.

"Here," Khalon tosses a canteen to Jae, "this should help."

Jae takes a drink and hands it back.

"We've been walking most of the day," Khalon assess. He takes a drink. "Let me see the map, we have to be getting close."

Jae digs it out of his pack and spreads it out on the ground. "We have to be past the fog by now. Even going the long way."

"Probably. I don't want to risk flying though just in case we're not."

Jae nods and puts the map back in his pack. He pulls a small bundle out. "We should eat," he says, offering some dried potatoes. Khalon sits on the ground and adds his satchel of nuts to the community dinner. Neither of them likes the idea of stopping, but their energy is low already, and not eating will just make it worse.

Khalon hasn't even finished chewing his last bite and is already standing up. "We should get going. I want to get out of this forest before we lose the daylight."

"Yeah, sounds good." Jae stretches out his wings slowly and painfully. "Why does this place make everything hurt?"

The mere suggestion makes Khalon's joints ache. "I don't know. Why anyone would live out here, I cannot figure."

*****

The day is over by the time Khalon notices the air has gotten lighter. The idea of spending one more night in this place makes him agitated. He hates that they already had to spend one night here, putting them behind schedule, but he sees that the forest is beginning to open up. Jae looks over at him, and he knows that Jae is just as relieved as he is, that the end of this part of the journey is not far away.

Reading each other's thoughts, they both take flight. It isn't long before they come to the edge of the forest and finally see the outline of the mountain range. Even with their accelerated pace, it is well into the night before they come across the outskirts of the village.

Khalon lands and Jae follows his lead.

"Does it seem too quiet?" Khalon asks. He keeps his voice at a whisper, even though there doesn't seem to be anyone around that would hear it.

"Yeah." Jae looks around like he is nervous to be here.

Khalon motions with a small nod for Jae to follow him. He keeps one hand on the hilt of his sword. Silently, they stalk the perimeter of the village. They take care be invisible to anyone or anything that may be here: peering into open windows, listening at closed doors, only seeing shadows in the moonlight, and hearing the emptiness of the wind. It isn't long before Khalon and Jae both realize, there isn't anything around for them to be quiet for.

"It's abandoned," Jae says.

"Long ago," Khalon adds.

Jae walks into one of the homes. He looks around and shakes his head. "It doesn't look like they took anything. All of the cookware is still here, books, clothes. Why would they leave all this behind?"

Khalon squats down to get a better look at some toys left in the middle of the living room. He picks up a small frog figurine carved out of wood. The edges are smooth, and most of the paint wore off a long time ago. His large fingers trace the wide grin of this forgotten thing before he puts it back where he found it.

"They left quickly," he answers Jae's question, "and they were traveling very light, which means they were traveling very far. They weren't chased from here, which is obvious, it's too clean. They left in a hurry, but it wasn't forced."

131

"Then why leave?"

"I don't know," Khalon stands back up and shakes his head, frustrated that he doesn't have the answer. "It doesn't make sense," he rubs his chin as he considers the possibilities. "No tribe ever moved in here after. Nothing has been touched in years. It seems no one even knew this place was here," he turns his head to the side and squints his eyes at something on the floor. "Well, almost no one." The corner of his mouth pulls into a grin. He points to an imprint in the dust. "That is a Sigrun-sized footprint right there."

Jae's shoulders relax a bit for the first time in days. "Can you tell where she went?"

"Well, she would've come here looking for supplies, especially coming from that forest and not knowing ahead of time how bad it was going to be. She'd be in pretty short supply," he walks back outside. "She would be tired, hungry, and looking for water and shelter." He stands in the open looking for a sign of her. It is so dark here that, at first, he thought it was his imagination, but then he looked again and saw the faintest of flickers in the distance. He points to it. "There, she went there."

*****

He would have preferred to approach the cabin in daylight for two reasons: first, because he knows from past experience how locals typically perceive him when he bangs on someone's door in the middle of the night, and second, because he would really like to be better rested, in case it does come to a fight. He hasn't slept in days and isn't as sharp as he would like to be stepping into an unknown situation. There most likely is no threat for him, but he never underestimates the possibility.

They approach the cabin slowly and with their weapons stowed, though, Khalon's hand is not far from his sword. The door opens and a man stands in the doorway. Khalon can tell just by the outline of him that he is old and frail. The old man says nothing he just stands casually, almost as though he was expecting them.

"Good evening," Jae greets with his hand in the air.

The old man still says nothing.

Jae and Khalon both stop and look at each other with mirrored expressions of confusion.

Khalon surely expected some kind of response; more specifically one of fright.

"Do you think he can't hear us?" Jae asks quietly.

"I can hear you fine," the old man answers. He sighs. "I gather you've come looking for the girl."

Khalon straightens up and rushes forward. "She was here," he says, more confirming than questioning.

"Umm-hmm, couple nights ago. What do you want with her?" he asks protectively, but his voice wavers a bit.

Again, Jae meets Khalon's look with the same curious brow.

"We are her friends. We have come to get her home safely," Jae explains.

The old man doesn't seem to except this explanation so easily. He stands silently.

"I swear to you, I am telling you the truth," Jae adds.
The old man tilts his head to the side for a moment weighing Jae's account. "Come on in. I'll get you boys some dinner." Satisfied with Jae's testimony, he waves his hand motioning them to come inside.

Jae is just as eager as Khalon and they both rush to accept the invitation, if for nothing more, than to find out Sigrun's next move. Turning sideways and ducking into the entry way Khalon squeezes into the man's home.

The home is small, but Khalon has seen smaller and far less comfortable. In his past vocation, a dwelling was not always an option for him. When the Skars would be scouting new villages to overturn, they would be traipsing through mud, flying through sandstorms, and worse. There were many days and nights when Khalon's only protection from the world was his own skin. Even after they had conquered and rummaged, he always felt uneasy about sleeping in another man's home; another man he had just taken everything from and left for dead. Sleeping in the trees just became a way to ignore the lives he had just taken. This man's home may be small, but it is more than he has ever had for his own.

The old man looks them both over once they are in the house. He pays Khalon a particular type of attention. He goes over his size, and his eyes take in the many markings on Khalon's body. It makes Khalon edgy the way he is looking at him. He still carries quite a bit of shame and it's all on display all over his body. Khalon can tell he has heard of the Skar tribe by the way the old man is looking at him, but this is most likely the first time he has ever been in the presence of one. If he had been subject to the Skars' 'hospitality,' he would not be nearly this calm.

"You say you are her friends?" the old man's eyes still on Khalon.

"Yes," Jae answers.

The old man shrugs and instructs them to sit at the table. "Is it normal for her to run off into dangerous situations by herself?"

"Yes," Jae and Khalon answer in unison with the same annoyance.

The old man's small mouth twitches with the semblance of a smile.

"I'm Aryl."

"I'm Jae, and this is Khalon."

Aryl nods at them both, "Well, you boys should eat something."

"We're okay. We still have some of our rations left," Jae says digging in his bag for a piece of bread.

"You should keep what you brought for the rest of the trip. You still have a long way to go," he insists.

He busies himself to bring them cups of water and he dishes out two plates of what looks like some kind of boiled root. It is a sickly-green elongated vegetable that smells like dirt and looks like it might not taste much better. Khalon is aching for a piece of tender, greasy meat, or a slab of buttery fish, but this will have to do. Jae seems to share his lack of enthusiasm, but hunger trumps desire and they both gratefully accept their rations.

Khalon takes a bite and the taste, which really does bear a resemblance to dirt, is actually made worse by the texture. It is mushy, stringy, and a little slimy. Khalon is almost certain that he is almost as green as the meal. Jae is going through the same struggle. He has his face pointed down at the table, holding his first bite in his mouth, trying to talk himself into swallowing.

Khalon looks up and meets Aryl's eyes. He is intensely watching them both.

"It's good," Khalon mutters with his mouth full.

"No, it's not," Aryl smirks and waves his hand.

Khalon chuckles at his honesty.

"We're grateful," Jae says with some relief. Presumably, some of that relief was that he was able to keep that bite down.

Aryl nods again accepting his gratitude.

"You said Sigrun was here a couple nights ago?" Khalon redirects to the more pressing matter of finding her.

"Yes," Aryl sits on the foot of his bed. "She left at first light the next morning. Heading toward Dragon Claw Mountain."

"*Dragon* Claw Mountain," Jae repeats, with a certain emphasis on the word dragon. He looks at Khalon with his eyebrows raised.

A new urgency strikes in Khalon, "Did she say anything to you about why she was going?"

Aryl shakes his head, "No. I asked her if she was lost and she showed me the map, but she didn't tell me why she was out here," he pauses and takes a breath, "I didn't need her to tell me why she was here. I already know."

Khalon sits so far on the edge of his chair he almost falls off. He wants to scream, '*Well, what is it?*' Instead, he lets the old man continue at his own pace.

"The mountain is evil. More specifically, it houses evil. I told her as much, but that didn't seem to discourage or frighten her at all. That's when I was certain. She did not come here on her own will."

"What do you mean?" Jae asks. "No one else was with her, right?" His concern growing.

"No. No one was with her. She wasn't dragged here. She was led here." Khalon and Jae are both motionless. Stuck somewhere between fascination and skepticism.

"I've seen her. I know she's different, right?" Aryl waits for a nod of validation. "She isn't evil, of that I am sure, which means she must be powerful, or have some kind of gift." Khalon looks at Jae with his eyebrows raised. This old man knows more than they thought.

"She is very special," Khalon confirms. "She is very strong, and she heals rapidly, and ummm…" he looks to Jae for validation that he should share *all* of her qualities. Jae nods, so he continues, "she emits fire." He tries to mask his voice in a way that the fire-starting bit sounds like it is more ordinary than it seems. Almost like he is saying, 'she's a terrific cardplayer,' or 'she's a great fisherman,' but Aryl's eyes widen anyway.

"Fire? She produces fire?" Aryl's question is more rhetorical than anything. Khalon can see he is figuring out the details in his own mind. Aryl's eyes glaze over and go a little dark.

"The dragon," he says quietly under his breath.

After a moment, Aryl shakes his head and brings his far-off gaze back to them. "There is an evil presence that lives on the mountain, and it is attracted

135

to power. If I had to guess, it will use Sigrun, try to manipulate her, and drain her of her strength to escape. Right now, it is held by a binding spell, and it cannot leave the mountain, but it has grown stronger over the years. Finding holes in the spell."

"Could it have reached out to Sigrun in her dreams?" Khalon asks, starting to put the story together.

"Oh, yes, I'm sure. Alone, it could take another lifetime for the spell to wear out on its own but powered by someone as strong as Sigrun. She would, not only give it what it needs to break the bind, she could feed it enough power to ruin this world.

"This place used to be as lush and green as I expect your homeland is. Slowly, this evil has seeped into the ground and the air, poisoning everything it touches. With enough strength, this evil would transform your home into a wasteland too."

Jae sits back in his chair, looking ill, but this time, it has nothing to do with their tasteless meal. Sigrun is marching into a snake pit, willingly and alone, right at this moment, as they sit talking about it. She is handing herself over to some evil deity to be torn apart and sucked dry. What's worse, it has already infiltrated her mind—Khalon is sure of it. While Jae is sitting like a dumbstruck glob, Khalon is starting make sense of the last few weeks: the rage, the outbursts, the tyrannical orating. He knew it wasn't her, but now he's certain that this thing has been speaking through her. He is, at first, filled with fervor. There is hope to get her back, but quickly, it's stifled by the impossible task in front of him. How can he beat this enemy? He only knows how to defeat an opponent with his hands—with his sword. How do you attack something in *her* mind?

He jumps out of his chair and runs to the window, throwing the shutter open, searching in the dark for something tangible, something he can see and feel. He just needs some sign of her.

"The mountain is this way?" Khalon asks.

"Yes, but as impossible as it may seem, you both need to at least try to get some rest." Aryl closes the window latch, once again putting up the barrier between Khalon and the darkness. "As soon as tomorrow comes, you will not have any rest until this is over."

Aryl points to the floor in front of the fire; their sleeping quarters for the night. Jae and Khalon both quietly obey and lie by the fire.

Khalon's thoughts drift as he listens to the crackle of the fire and Aryl's gargling snore. He left the Skar tribe to find peace. Ironically, his life has become more turbulent than ever. He is sharing a sleeping space with a pretty boy that he generally can't stand. They are chasing after a girl that won't stay put and has a knack for getting into trouble, through a wasteland, up an evil mountain that imprisons a force so sinister that it's striving to destroy the world. He shakes his head a bit, and the corner of his mouth lifts to a half smile. He smiles, because he knows that if he had a chance to do it all over again, if he found himself back at the Deadlands and she was face to face with that Gila again, he would save her every time.

Sigrun

Chapter 21

Something cool and wet touches my face. My head feels thick and slow. *What is going on?* I struggle to open my eyes at first, but eventually the darkness fades out much in the same way that it came in. Once I see the rock ceiling, I remember that I'm in the cave, and then I see her again. This time, she is looking over me. I sit up fast, which I immediately regret, as my vision begins to blur again.

"Careful, not so fast," she puts her hands up, but resists touching me.

My head stops pounding, but my heart does not. Looking at her again, she is indeed the woman from my dream.

She looks at me cautiously with her hands up and palms out, showing me, she means no harm. She squints her eyes and tilts her head to the side. She looks me over, much the same way I am looking at her. She smiles and her eyes begin to well up with tears.

"Sigrun? Is it…is it really you?" She reaches to touch me, yet my reflex is to move away from her completely. "I'm sorry," she apologizes, and her hands go back up submissively. "I'm sorry."

I stand up slowly and she carefully mirrors my movements. My hands are shaking, but my breathing is starting to calm down.

"Do you know who I am?" she asks tentatively.

The answer to that question should be as simple as 'yes' or 'no,' but I cannot seem to find the answer. I want it to be her so badly. I've spent my whole life wishing she were here and feeling the guilt of her death every day. Now that she is in front of me, I cannot force myself to believe it. I cannot find any words, so I stare at her silently.

"I'm. I'm you mother, Sigrun," she says softly, and tears stream down her face.

I can see that it is taking everything she has not to rush to me and hold me.

"I knew you would find me," she wipes her cheeks and nose with the back of her hand. "I knew that if I was patient and strong enough, I would find a way to you."

"What…what happened to you? How did you get here? When? How? I…I don't understand." I'm trying to reconcile this new reality and the questions are rolling in faster than I can verbalize.

She shakes her head and looks over her shoulder nervously. "I know it doesn't make sense and I will explain everything, but we have to get out of here."

"Okay, let's go!" I start to move for the tunnel exit.

"No, I can't."

"What? What do you mean you can't?" Again, I try to move to the door.

"Listen to me!" She sounds frustrated, but then takes a breath and calms down. "I am a prisoner here."

I don't know what she means, there are no bars, and no guards. There isn't even one other person here. I walked right in, so it makes sense that we could just walk right out.

She sees my confusion. "I'm bound here. I have been cursed," she says quietly and looks around again. "You have to help me." Her desperation is growing.

"Okay, what can I do?"

She motions for me to go back into her room with her. "There is a creature here, an evil being that has been keeping me here. I cannot leave, and I cannot harm it. It took everything I had to find my way to you."

"What kind of creature? Why does it keep you here?"

"She's actually a witch, a very powerful witch, and she uses me like an energy source. She will never let me leave. I will tell you everything, but we need to find safety now."

I nod. "How do we break the spell?"

"Since I am bound, I cannot harm her. You will need to find her somewhere in this mountain and kill her."

She explains this plan in such a cavalier way that it takes me a moment to really understand what she is asking me to do.

"Wait, kill her? But you said she is a witch. How can I kill her? Won't she see me coming, or be able to put a spell on me also?"

142

"I know it seems crazy. I will do my best to help you. I know that this is a lot to take in all at once, but I have been preparing for this moment for a long time. I have learned a little magic myself. I'm thinking that I can cloak you enough so you can get close to her."

Crazy doesn't begin to explain it. My head is spinning more now than ever. All I have are questions, but no time for answers. I don't know what I was expecting. I didn't fully understand what my dreams meant, but I never imagined *this* was going to be asked of me.

She looks positively desperate. Her eyes are wild. Her movements are nervous and twitchy. This risky, half-thought-out plan of hers seems to be stemming from sheer panic. Navigating through these mountain caves alone would be a challenging task, but then I'm expected to disarm and murder a witch that is so powerful, she has made a prisoner of my mother, along with destroying the surrounding lands without even stepping foot outside. It's almost laughable.

She continues to ramble her ill-inspired plot. "I think she resides in the center cavern, but I don't know for sure."

"I can't do it!" I cut her off. "I…I don't even know where to start. Don't you see how insane this all sounds?"

She seems angry at first. Her body is shaking and her eyes that were just a few moments ago filled with love and hope are now piercing right through me. Whether it is my tone or outright refusal, she is displeased. After a moment, I see her expression slowly melt from anger into disappointment. I suspect she has been wishing, hoping, and praying for this day for so long that, to her, this all seemed rational. It must be a cold truth when the one fine strand of hope is snipped right before your eyes.

"I'm sorry," I say to her, softening my tone. "It's just that we have one chance at this, right? And I don't want to waste it because we didn't check to make sure there was no other way."

She nods and forces a small smile.

"Okay, let's just slow down and figure this out," I say, trying to keep her encouraged. I kneel down on the ground to think for a moment and collect myself. She sits next to me with her eyes on the ground. She looks defeated and sad. Looking around at this cave, this prison that she has been in for all these years, I think about everything she's missed: celebrations, births, deaths, my entire life. She has lost a husband and a son, and she may not even know it. How much can she see when she comes to me in my dreams? She has not mentioned either of them once. Is that because she already knows, or because her obsession with escaping has left no room in her thoughts for anything else? Either way, I have to tell her.

"M…Mother," I struggle to say the word. It is so foreign to me, so much so the word gets stuck in my throat. Not because I don't want this new truth, but it has been so suddenly thrust on me I can't quite reconcile how it feels. "I need to tell you something," I start as gently as I can. She looks at me with concern, and I swallow back the lump in my throat, "Dadda. Father is dead." I look at her waiting for the explosive grief, the heartbreaking sobs that I'm certain are just under the surface, but they don't come. In fact, the lines of her face flatten out and she takes a breath.

"I know."

I feel my own face crease with confusion. "You do?"

She presses her mouth into a firm line and nods. "I know Baron would never let you out of his sight, let alone, come all the way out here if he were still alive."

Her assessment makes me chuckle a bit because it is completely true.

"I have been without him for so long…" she pauses for a moment and looks out into the distance, "I did my grieving a long time ago." Bitterness clings to her voice.

"There is something else. Merik. Merik is gone too." I wrestle with whether I should tell her everything. Dealing with the death of a child is hard enough but learning the details of his tragic end seems like an act of cruelty.

Her eyes squint and her jaw clenches a little bit. "That makes sense," she says finally.

Her reaction is, again, surprisingly stoic.

"I used to reach out to him. I tried to find him in his dreams, but then, he went dark, and I couldn't find him anymore. I was incredibly lucky that I was able to find you. What happened? What happened to them?"

That is the question: What happened? I don't even know where to begin, because I'm not even sure myself. I don't know why Merik did what he did, not really anyway. The truth is, I may never know, and the torture of not being able to give her any kind of relief is stifling.

"I found Father in his den. He was murdered," I pause for her reaction. There isn't one.

"And Merik was gone."

"He was gone?"

"Yes, he would take off from time to time, leaving for a few days, or a week. He never told us where he went, but he always came back. This time, though, he didn't, and it turned out he found the Skar tribe and made a deal with them to take over the village."

She leans back a little and her eyebrows are raised. "He made a deal with the Skars to take over the village?"

"Yes."

This is just one of the tragic events in this story. I don't want to tell her everything, but she will likely find out once we are back in the village.

"You see," I swallow hard and start again, "it was Merik. He's the one who killed father. And I was the one who killed him."

I look at her. I wait for her to cry, to shame me, hate me, to fall into the deep despair that can only come from knowing that while you've been gone, your entire family has torn itself apart. I study her every move, breath, even her stillness, looking for some clue as to how she is feeling.

Her eyes are wide, searching, taking in everything I have just told her.

"Merik was troubled. He became troubled," I try to explain.

"Troubled?"

"I think the loss, well, losing you was too much for him and he was never happy. I tried to bring him back. I tried reasoning with him. I wanted to help him, but he just…he was already gone. The Skars became the home he really wanted, and in the end, he didn't give me a choice." I lower my eyes to the ground. All I can do is hope that she understands. I've never met her before. I've never known what it is like to have a mother, and yet I desire her approval and forgiveness more than anything. When I look at her again, her eyes are squinting almost analytical. She finally looks at me and gives me a small sideways smile.

"Well, you did what you had to do," she puts her hand on mine in a reassuring way. "We'll talk about it more when we get home."

I nod quickly, a little confused. She is so much calmer about it than I expected. Her mind must be so focused on getting out of here, she cannot fully process anything else. We stare at each other for a moment. Me, still reconciling her existence, and her, still reveling in the fact that I'm actually here. She reaches out with her hand slowly and touches my wing.

"So beautiful. So powerful." Her fingers lightly trace over my scales. She looks almost hypnotized. "They thought you were a curse. They wanted to destroy you," her eyes go a bit dark and there is fury in her voice. "They just didn't understand. They never do. Anything powerful or threatening, they just get rid of it." She waves her hand like she is swatting away a fly. "Well, not this time."

"Wait. What do you mean?" I assume she is comparing me to her own story, but I don't have any idea how they fit together. I was always told that she was adored by everyone. Listening to her now she makes it sound like her life had been one of contempt. "Are you talking about members of our village?" I ask.

She shakes her head and waves her hands. She almost looks embarrassed. "Oh, no, it's nothing. I'm just so glad you are okay. Together, we will find a way out of here."

I don't understand her turbulent mood swings. She appears to be clinging to a narrow margin of sanity. It breaks my heart. I smile at her and reach my hand out for hers. Her hands are similar to mine. She has long slender fingers, though she is much thinner, and her knuckles are a bit knobbier, the shape of them is just about the same. I start to feel relaxed for the first time in a long time. To the point that my stomach decides to speak up and ask for food.

"Oh!" I cover my stomach with my hand, embarrassed.

She laughs a little, "Oh, I'm so sorry. You must be starving."

I haven't eaten much for days. The little bit that I had at Aryl's was barely enough to keep me going. "Is there food here?" I ask.

"Yes, one thing I do have is food."

She stands up and helps me to my feet. I follow her back to the large cavern with the water pool. She leads the way through another tunnel that is on the same wall as the small waterfall. I didn't see it when I was in this room before. The way the wall is shaped around the entrance it almost disappears unless you know where to look. The tunnel twists and turns a couple of times, but then a very bright light greets us at the other side.

"This place is a prison and an oasis at the same time," she says as we walk into the room. It is enormous. This mountain is bigger than I realized. Rows and rows of fruit and nut trees, shrubbery, and crops. Most of these fruits I have never seen before. The ground is no longer hard and rocky, it is soft earth, almost like back home. I walk up to one tree that bears a dark purple fruit. I look to her for permission.

"Go ahead," she encourages.

I pluck one from the branch and bite in. It is sweet, and tart, and delicious. The flesh of it is a dark reddish purple, and it is soft and a little slippery. My eyes feel as though they are rolling to the back of my head as I eat. For a moment, I forget all my worries.

"How is this all possible?" I ask, referring to the flourishing vegetation in the middle of a wasteland.

"Magic," she says with a clever grin.

I laugh a bit and then begin to take an inventory of this place. I look at the entrance and begin to feel exposed. I wonder how long I have before the witch knows I'm here.

"It's okay," she validates, "you are safe in here. She won't find us. Go ahead. Eat."

Greedily, I wander through this paradise plucking various fruits, and nuts, and vegetables.

She stays with me only a few feet behind in a way that is likely wonder and protectiveness. We sit and she lets me eat in silence for a while. Once my belly is full, my eyelids begin to get very heavy. I fight it, trying to stay awake and alert, but exhaustion takes hold.

"You need to rest," she says. She takes the half-eaten fruit out of my hand and motions for me to lie down. "I forgot about what it must have taken for you to get here. I was so frantic when you first arrived. I've been waiting and planning for so long that the urgency to get out of here overwhelmed me and I wasn't thinking about how beaten down you must be. I'm so sorry. You need sleep, you'll be safe here," she gives me an apologetic smile.

I grab my pack and tuck it under my head for a pillow. As soon as I shut my eyes my body gets heavy and feels as though I am sinking into the ground, warm and safe, hibernating until it is time to move again. Just before I slip into unconsciousness, I feel her touch my hand. She traces the scar that was left by Merik when he stabbed me through the hand at the Skar camp. It is almost as if she knows that, out of all my scars, that is the only wound that still brings me pain.

*****

I wake and I feel refreshed, rejuvenated, like these last few days have been wiped clean of all the pain and exhaustion. I take a good look at this paradise that is nestled inside of a rotting wasteland. It is amazing that something so good can grow within something so vile. Then it occurs to me, since I've been here, actually inside the mountain, it's the first time in weeks that I haven't had the other voice in my head. The lust for power has subsided and I feel more like myself than I have for quite some time. Maybe that's how the prison works—you are so immersed in the utopia that you hardly notice your life source is being milked from you slowly. Now that I am rejuvenated, I feel more motivated than ever to find a way to get her out of here.

I sit up and see her not too far off putting together a breakfast for us. I spread my wings out for a long stretch.

"Feeling better?" she asks, keeping her eyes on her task.

"Yes, I am."

She looks up at me and tosses me a piece of fruit. I greedily take it. I stand and look around. There must be a way out, an exit she hasn't found. Maybe she's been here so long that she's blind to it. Maybe she just needs a fresh pair of eyes to look at the problem.

"I don't understand this place, or this spell, but there has to be a way for us to escape without confronting this witch."

"There is no other way," she shuts me down coldly. "If I even go near the exit, I am struck down by lightning. This entire mountain is shrouded by an electrical force."

Now that she says it, that *does* seem possible. I certainly felt the physical effects of this place, and it wasn't even tailored specifically to keep me in or out. This may be even more powerful than I thought.

"How do you live here together?" I ask. "Wouldn't you constantly be fighting each other?"

"With her spell, I can only see her if she wants to be seen and she doesn't want me harmed. That would weaken me, and she needs my life source for her power. She only wants me to be contained and controlled."

"This doesn't make sense," I say to myself more than to her. "If she is so powerful, why doesn't she leave? Why does she only keep just you here? It seems like she must have enough power to make slaves out of entire villages."

She slams her hand down hard against the mountain floor. The piece of fruit it was holding is now a pulpy mess oozing beneath it. "Because!" She shouts in anger, her eyes sharp with anger and frustration.

She doesn't like it when I challenge her.

She is breathing hard. She looks down at her hand. The sweet flesh of the fruit wasted on the ground. Her eyes soften and she takes a breath. "Because," she starts again with a lighter tone, "like I said, I learned a little magic too. I keep her here, so she can't escape. We are bound to each other. That's why we must kill her. We can't let her escape either."

I've never known real magic. My father's healing powers, and foresight were the closest things to magic that I had ever seen, except for my pendant, of course. Out of habit, I touch my chest where it usually hangs. I miss its presence. My heart aches for it. I wish I had something to help her, but I am completely outside my depth. I have no knowledge, no experience, and no tools to help.

"Maybe I could go and get help?" I offer. "Your village, maybe I can find them and…" She shakes her head before I can finish my thought.

"No. They can't help. I don't even know where they are." There is contempt in her voice. "No, we are alone."

She drums her fingers against a stone slab. I feel her frustration pounding through me with every tap. I grab my pack to see what I have that might help our situation. As soon as I open the top flab of my bag the cover of the Red Book shines in the light. I pull it out of the pack first. Her eyes go wide, and she lets out a small gasp.

"You have the book!" She snatches it out of my hands in such a way that I immediately want to grab it back, but I don't. She obviously knows about it, which means she might know how to read it, and I might finally get some answers. Still, I cannot shake this protective feeling over it.

"Yes, I found it in father's den, buried behind the bookshelves."

"It was hidden in the bookshelves?" her tone is almost mocking. "He hid it in plain sight." She shakes her head and chuckles to herself.

"I'm not even sure why he hid it. No one is able to read it. Vivek was only able to translate a small bit. I don't even know what the book is, really."

"No. No one else would be able to read it now that Baron is dead."

Her eyes drink it in seductively. Her hands caress the scaled cover in a coveting way. Something in me feels unsettled. I should be thrilled to make her so happy, but I don't like the book being in her hands, and not in mine.

"This is my book. It belonged to my family and then was mine. I thought it was lost or destroyed." She grabs me suddenly holding my shoulders firmly, and she looks into my eyes with a new sense of urgency. "You were right to bring this to me. This changes everything." She stands up and heads back through the tunnel, "Come with me, quickly."

I follow her through a series of rooms and tunnels. We go uphill, downhill, right then left. I am disoriented and not quite sure where I am anymore. This mountain is a web of tunnels and rooms, a giant maze. Finally, we enter a room, which must be the very top of the mountain. The walls all come up to a central point and there is a small opening at the top. The moment she walks towards the center I see the electrical charge of the lightning sparking at the top. The storm can feel her. It can feel that she is close by.

The rest of the room is fairly open. There is a platform in the center of the room directly under the opening with an altar in the middle. On the floor, there are various types of what I can only imagine are magical relics. There are crystals, and bones, and talismans of varying types, plants that have died and dried up long ago. They all look as though they have been neglected for a very long time. The symbolic writing that I first saw in her room is also etched on the walls in here as well.

She rushes to the platform and places the book on the altar. She quickly flips through the pages reacquainting herself with the book. I wander over to the other side of the room and almost walk off a ledge into a black abyss.

"Careful," she says not taking her eyes from the pages. "That is a nasty drop. You might be able to get your wings open in time, but it would be unlikely."

Looking over the edge, I see that it's a nasty drop indeed. The ledge hangs over a narrow canyon. The rocks on both sides are sharp as blades, so climbing would be impossible, and not much room for a wingspan to move easily. I back up slowly as the rock beneath my toes is already cracking.

I walk back over to the altar where she is busily familiarizing herself with the text.

"Here! This one. I can use this one. It should lead you right to her," she points to a page.

"What it is?"

"It is a spell." She looks up from the book for the first time, no doubt she reads the confusion that is written on my face. "This is a book of spells. and medicine. This is how I help people. This is how I heal them."

A book of spells. We always believed it was a book of prophecy and history. A story that might have explained my existence. Now, hearing that it is book of potions and magical nonsense, I feel cheated. I might never know why I was born different. She doesn't look away from the pages. She continues to search for something. My disappointment breaks way for a small curiosity.

"Can you heal *anything*?" I ask tentatively.

"Yes."

"Even death?"

For the first time since I revealed the book to her, she stops searching its pages and looks at me.

"Could you bring father back?" I ask her directly.

She has a weird grin, and her eyes almost look menacing. "Yes, I could, but you have to help me get out of here first."

The idea that I might be reunited with my father again makes me feel warm and chilled at the same time. I could rebuild my family and finally fill the void. I look at her and nod. "Okay."

She runs down from the platform and searches the room for items. She grabs a few small bones from a rodent of some kind, a gray crystal, and a sprig of one of the dried plants. "This will have to do," she says to herself. She moves frantically. She grabs a bag that was stashed under a stone in the ground and a small stone bowl and runs back up the altar. "Come here," she motions for me. "See, look," she invites me to look on with her. She puts the collected items in the bowl and pulls a white feather from the bag. It looks like one of her own, but I can't be sure. She adds it to the bowl. She runs her fingers along the words on the page. "This will reveal her to us. You will be pulled toward her like a magnet."

I shake my head. This is still the craziest thing I have ever heard. "Even now that you have the book, how does that keep me safe?"

"She won't harm you. She will try to trick you. She could use your power to her benefit, harness it, but you would be worth more to her alive than dead."

"How is that any better?" My eyes are wide.

"I can protect you now," she points to the book again. She walks over to me and puts her hand up to my cheek. She smiles. Then she holds a lock of my hair between her fingers and caresses it gently. Her face contorts into a snarl, and she pulls, hard, ripping my hair from its roots.

"Ow!" I take a step back from her, rubbing the sore spot of my scalp.

She smiles again, "I can protect you," she motions to the lock of hair she stole. Her eyes are wild. She begins to braid the lock. "The book changes everything. Now, we don't have to kill her, unless we have to. If you're able to capture her and bring her to me, I will be able to regain more of my strength. I may be able to reverse her spell, but I will need her alive to do it. Listen to me, if she starts any spells on you just kill her where she stands. It is not worth the risk. Understood?"

I nod. I feel dizzy all over again. This makes no sense to me, but what choice do I have?

"We must hurry. Go now, through that tunnel. You will start to feel it soon."

"Feel what?"

"You'll know. Go!" She turns away from me and begins to chant in a language that I don't understand. It's a language from the book.

I back away from the altar, slowly keeping my eyes on her. Her frail form looks suddenly formidable. She stands firmly with her arms reaching to the skies. Her voice is strong and has real purpose behind it. She isn't what I expected. Every story I ever heard from anyone who ever knew her said she was the kindest, most nurturing person they ever met. The evilness of this place and this creature that I am now hunting must be what nightmares are made of. What else could possibly explain the transformation that has been done to her? I must believe that, once I get her home, she will return to her former self.

I slip into the entryway of the tunnel, and I am, once again, in the darkness.

Chapter 22

She was right. It isn't long before I feel a pull at my chest. The magnetic draw leading me where I need to go. How it works, I have no idea, but whenever I come to a crossroad within the tunnels, the pull leads me in the direction I need to go. Every new turn leads me farther into the maze. Every tunnel looks the same as the last: dark, damp, and narrow. I have a similar feeling as did the first time I was in the underwater tunnel to Jae's cavern, like I can't breathe, even though there is no water here. The farther I get, the more lost I become. I'm completely disoriented. Something about this part of the mountain has me off balance. It's almost difficult to determine left from right, and up from down. A drunkenness has penetrated my senses. Even if I tried to turn back now, I wouldn't be able to find my way. I don't have a choice. I have to let this force continue to lead me.

Nervously, I place my hand on the dagger in my belt and reach behind my head to check that my kama are still in place. I was given no description of the creature that I am looking for. What does a witch look like? I've never seen one. Anything that is strong enough to make a prison without bars and destroy an entire land must be incredibly large, a giant even, or something like one the villainous trolls from our bedtime stories. I imagine it would have to be something truly grotesque; gray, sagging, wart-covered skin, long, boney hands, thin, stringy hair, and saturated by the fowl stench of decay.

It's only a moment later that my thoughts are interrupted by a more aggressive sensation. The slight pull at my chest now feels as though something has reached into my chest and has taken hold of my heart. I must be getting close. The tunnel gets colder, so cold that I can see my breath. The hair on my arms rises, whether it's from the cold, or if I'm feeling heightened by something else, I'm not sure. I pull my dagger out of my belt and slowly move farther into the tunnel. The air smells almost metallic, like a mineral mine. Frost begins to spread across the floor. Icicles form from the ceiling stretching their way down. It's becoming winter right before my eyes. If there was ever a question about this being a work of magic, this is certainly the answer.

My teeth are almost chattering now. I'm breathing heavier and heavier, and with each intake, my lungs freeze a little bit more. My entire body is shivering, and my hands are going numb, making my grip on my dagger unsure. *It can't possibly get any colder.* As soon as I think it, the temperature drops even more, and I fall to my knees. The dagger slips from my hand. I can barely move. The cold has sunk so far into my bones that I feel as frozen and brittle as one of the icicles above me. I try to raise my own body temperature by igniting my fire, but I can't. The cold has penetrated me so deeply that even my internal fire has frozen over.

"Why did you come here?" the voice echoes from every direction.

I look around frantically. I see no one. The voice is gravelly, but definitely female.

I open my mouth to speak, even though I don't know what to say, and she cuts me off.

"I know why *she* sent you, but why did you come here? You're not supposed to be here!" she sounds more panicked than angry.

"I-I s-saw this p-place in my dreams," I stutter out. I clench my jaw shut to keep my teeth from breaking against each other from the chatter. "S-s-she c-came to me, s-she needs m-my help, I w-won't let you hurt her anymore." I grab the dagger again and fight with all my strength to stand up again.

"Are y…you going to f…face me or not!" I challenge. I don't know how much longer I can survive this frigid climate, she is clever, fighting fire with ice.

My eyes search for something in the dark, a flicker of anything. I'm an easy target. She can obviously see me. If she wanted me dead, I would be. So, what does she want from me? Finally, I feel a small lift from deadly cold to somewhat bearable. I breathe easier, but I still cannot feel my hands well enough to be at all competent with a weapon. I'm sure she knows this.

"I always wanted to meet you," she says from the shadows. "I thought I might, but I'd hoped it would never come to this." She sounds sad.

The temperature rises back to normal, and I stumble a bit and almost fall again from the unexpected relief. "Thank you," I say under my breath, not to her, but in general appreciation. My vision begins to clear now that the tears in my eyes are not freezing, and slowly, from a soft glow in front of me, a shape begins to outline. I can feel my hands again and my grip on my dagger is sure once again. Standing firmly, I anticipate the worst. If this comes to a fight, I am ready.

She takes a step forward. I hold my place. The soft light around her dissipates and the darkness in the tunnel lifts enough to see clearly. She is fairly small, not just by stature but also by age. She is very old, like that of a grandmother that has lived a long, hard life. She is frail and her shoulders cave in, rounding her back like a ribbed snail shell. Her hair, at least what is left of it, is a very dull white, stringy, and just past her shoulders. Her ratty clothes hang on her like a little girl trying on her older sister's dress, and where her wings should be, there are only featherless stubs, a heartbreaking reminder of what must be something tragic. She is just that—something tragic—I don't see anything evil in her. Her face is wrinkled and sad, with thin lips and a slender, pointed nose. Her eyes are a dull, mossy green, and there is something familiar about them that I can't quite place, but they are kind and disarming. This 'creature' is nothing I expected. The foul, grotesque image that I was preparing myself for, is the furthest thing from what actually stands before me.

She doesn't move any closer to me. I see her looking me over, much in the same way I am with her. Most people look me over when they first see me, so I am used to it. Strangely, I feel at ease. My shoulders sink closer to the floor. I shake my head and tense up again, re-establish my grip on my dagger. *This is just her witch magic.* I think to myself. *She wants me to be comfortable.*

Her thin, wrinkled lips twitch slightly in one corner. She sighs, "You look like your father."

My mouth goes dry, and I feel faint. My hand holding the dagger involuntarily falls to my side.

"What did you say?" I barely whisper the words.

"Your father, Baron. You have the same cheekbones, same unruly hair as him. The eyes though, those are from your grandmother. She was the only other person I ever knew with violet eyes."

"My Grandmother?" I ask breathlessly.

"On your mother's side. Your wings," she smiles and shakes her head slightly, "those, on the other hand, are entirely yours."

My heart feels like it might burst through my chest. The heat in my body is rising. It isn't long before steam is starting to fill the tunnel where we are standing.

155

Her eyes look around at the effects of the increasing temperature. She remains very calm. She puts her hands up to me. "It's okay. You're okay. I know she told you I'm a monster, that I'm a witch," she pauses and shrugs, "well, I am a witch, but not the kind that you think."

"How do you know my parents?" I can't move past how she knows so much about my family. I can't listen or comprehend anything else.

She takes another deep breath, "That's a long story."

If this is some kind of trickery, I am completely entranced. "Are you, are you reading my mind?"

"No. I could, but no."

I try to make sense of what she is saying, but the truth is, I can't remember the last time anything made sense at all. How could this fragile being keep my mother trapped for all these years? My eyes are wide, my breathing is shallow, and I feel like I might faint. This must be a trick. That is the only explanation. As I stand straighter, remembering why I came here in the first place, she doubles over in pain. She clutches her stomach as though an invisible force has just run her through with a knife.

"*Ah!*" she shouts and falls to one knee.

Instinct makes me reach out to her, to help her, but I pull my hand back instead. The pain seems to pass after a moment. She looks up at me. She looks like an old woman and a child all at the same time. She has an innocence about her that is unmistakable. A thin, red line trickles from her mouth. Blood. She wipes it away.

"We don't have much time," she says as she gets back to her feet. She closes her eyes and seems to regain her strength. She turns her back to me and places her hands behind her back, surrendering to me. Looking over her shoulder she sighs and says, "It's time we end this. I'm tired of fighting her."

I reach out and take hold of her wrists that she has offered to me. The moment I touch her I feel a pain run through me. It hits me hard in the stomach, but then, like lightning, it burns through every part of me. It takes everything not to double over. She also stands a little straighter. She feels something too. She isn't inflicting pain on me, it is not my pain—it's empathy—I can feel her pain. She looks at me again with tears in her eyes. Witch, creature, monster, whatever she is, I am bringing her to her death, and we both know it, but from what I feel from her, it will be a mercy.

Everything is backwards. It's like I slipped through the cracks of reality. Even when I was bound and caged in the Skar camp, I didn't feel as helpless, or as lost, as I do now. Is this a game? Is this a trick? Am I willingly walking into a trap simply because I don't know what else to do? I want to talk to her more. I want to question her. She has said more about my family to me in a shorter period of time, than my own mother has since I have arrived. Instead, we walk in a heavy silence, a death march, there is no conversation that fits here.

The closer we get to the tunnel where my mother is, the more intense the pain becomes. That must be how she has been able tell where my mother is. The sensation is overwhelming. I start breathing heavier through the pain. I'm sure the pain would stop once I release her, but I won't let her go.

"We can hurt each other, but we can't kill each other," she says at last, noticing my reaction to the pain escalation. "It is part of the curse. I hurt her by keeping her here, she hurts me physically. It's almost magnetic. You know how you found me. It was like a magnet was bringing you to me, right?" I nod. "Well, it's like that with her and I as well, but instead of us being drawn together, we repel each other. It intensifies when we get closer to one another. She thought I would eventually give up, that the pain would become too much," she grits her teeth, "but, like always, she underestimated me."

"I don't understand, why hurt each other at all? Why keep her here?"

Her mouth twitches into a half smile. "I know you don't understand, but you will." Her response infuriates me. I have been given that explanation for years. Every time I get close to the truth, it is withheld from me. My father said the same thing to me before he died, and now I get the same hollow promise from her. Heat builds in my chest. My hold tightens on her wrists, so much so, that I feel her bones pop in the joints.

She keeps smiling.

I see the cavern where I left my mother just ahead of me. A bluish light flickers into the tunnel from it. The witch struggles, the closer we get. It's almost like a hurricane wind that only she can feel is pushing against her. I have to push her the rest of the way.

When I left my mother, she had just started a chant; what it was for I have no idea, but I hear faint sounds of it as we approach the entryway. The chanting gets louder and louder. I don't understand the words, but I can tell the witch does. She struggles against my grasp. Her eyes are wide.

"Is that. Oh no, did you give her something personal of yours?" she asks me.

Something personal? I search my memory, I gave her the Red Book, but I wouldn't call that a personal item, since it isn't really mine, and I can't even read it.

We turn the corner and I see her standing on the altar, Red Book open, with blue lightning firing above her. She is harnessed in its platinum light, hair whipping in the wind of the storm, arms reaching to the sky. She sways slightly to the rhythm of the chant. Her eyes are rolled back into her head, leaving only the lifeless whites exposed. She looks unreal. Possessed. Her hands are held above her firmly, and then I see the tiny braid, my hair woven into a harmless little ring, wrapped about her finger. Something personal.

The witch looks at me panicked. "The Red Book!" she exclaims. "Sigrun," she starts, but my mother's eyes roll forward.

"Hello sister," my mother snarls to the witch, her voice echoes throughout the room "you look terrible," she snickers.

Sickness creeps into my belly. This is all wrong. I reach for my dagger with my other hand. My mother turns her face back to the sky, chanting louder than before. She expands her wings fully for the first time since I've been with her. Perfectly white feathers shimmer in the electric light, pristine and glowing, but something isn't right. They are too perfect. The heart-shaped birthmark on her right wing is missing.

The realization hits me hard. I feel sick with heartache. Tears well up in my eyes and anger wells up in my heart. I have been cruelly deceived. Rage funnels through me. I feel the fire coming and I yearn for it. This imposter, whoever she is, has tricked me maliciously and I want to burn her to the ground. I want her to suffer.

I go to lunge for her, but I can't. I stand frozen. The witch beside me falls to her knees.

"NO!" she screams. "Merin, let her go! I'm here. I'll give you what you want. Just let her go!" The witch pleads.

"No, sister. I don't need you anymore. *I'll take it all!*" the imposter shouts back, enraged, and vengeful. The imposter points to the witch and, without even touching her, she sends her to the ground, writhing in pain.

I try to move again and again, slamming against my own mind like fists against a closed door, but I don't budge. Rooted to the ground, trapped in catatonic misery, I can't move even one finger. I try speaking—nothing. Shouting. Screaming. Crying. Nothing. Nothing, but the tears rolling down my face, like raindrops down a stone wall.

The imposter walks down from the altar and stands with her face to mine, inches apart, nose to nose. Her eyes are black, and her mouth is in a twisted smile. Everything that was beautiful about her before has melted into this vile figure before me. I feel her breath on my face. She rubs the braid of my hair between her fingers. Her eyes burn into mine with a look of gratification.

"You're mine now."

Khalon

Chapter 23

The morning comes, or what passes for morning here anyway. Whether it is from sleeping on the hard ground of the shack, or just the effects of this place, he isn't sure, but Khalon's body is stiff and sore. He didn't sleep much, and the little bit he did, wasn't restful. Jae begins to stir as well. From the groaning, it seems he did not sleep well either. Jae turns his head to the right, then left, stretching out his neck and shoulders. The grimace on his face is all too clear. He cannot wait to get back to the comforts of home.

"Morning," Aryl says, walking through the front door with fresh rations in his hands. He notices them rubbing the aches and cramps. "Wish I could say you're sore just from sleeping on the floor, but it's this place doing it to you. It won't stop until you leave either."

"How can you live with it every day?" Jae asks.

"I guess you can get used to anything," he replies. He holds up some more roots and what look like some mushrooms. "Got some breakfast for you. It's not potato cakes and huckleberries, but it will put a little distance between you and your hunger."

"We are more than grateful for anything," Khalon declares. Jae nods in agreement. Khalon stands up and stretches as much as he can in the small room; trying to be mindful not to knock over furniture or break dishes.

"This house wasn't really built to accommodate a fairy of your size," Aryl jokes.

Khalon chuckles, "It's fine, really."

Aryl looks at Khalon and then at Jae, eyes a little squinted. "You boys aren't from the same village, are you? Originally, I mean?"

Jae presses his lips in a line and shakes his head. He seems almost nervous about it, like their secret was just found out, and they are about to be cruelly thrown out into the bitter cold. Khalon is incredibly calm. He knew from the moment the old man looked him over for the first time that he recognized his markings.

"Jae is from the Northwoods, same as Sigrun, and I *was* a General with the Skar tribe until about four seasons ago."

"Was?" Aryl emphasizes on the word, making absolutely sure that Khalon is no longer a murdering, pillaging savage.

"That's right. I left the tribe. That's when I met Sigrun, and I have been in the Northwoods ever since."

"He saved her life," Jae throws in awkwardly, trying to further validate that Khalon is friend, rather than foe. Both Khalon and Aryl look at him with shared confusion. Aryl likely finds the over-explanation strange and unnecessary. Khalon has never heard Jae throw any kind of compliment his way, and he has never acknowledged that Khalon actually saved Sigrun. Jae had sworn and protested that Khalon only saved her from the Gila to gain entry to a new village to plunder. At no point has Jae ever admitted that Khalon's intentions were anything other than menacing. Jae looks over at Khalon, who still has a look of perplexity, and Jae shrugs his shoulders, not knowing what else to say.

Khalon had never been to this village before, or this land in general, so he knows that, in his lifetime, the Skars have not encountered the inhabitants that once lived here, but Aryl seems to have knowledge of the Skar ways.

"You have history with the Skars, don't you?" Khalon asks already knowing the answer.

Aryl presses his lips in a line and nods. "I was a boy," he furrows his brow as he searches his memory. Khalon can tell he has not thought about this for a very long time. "I remember the screaming, but I didn't know what was going on. My mother told me to hide in my room until she came and got me. I hid behind my bed with a blanket on top of me. I stayed there for what felt like a very long time, not moving, barely breathing.

"The screaming outside my window got louder and worse. I could also hear the clang of metal. Now, looking back, I know it was swords clashing, but, at the time, I didn't really understand. I just heard the sick sound of butchery and the gargling of so many last breaths.

"My mother finally came back for me, along with my older brother, and baby sister. We managed to make it to the edge of our village and found my father there." He takes a moment to think about the memory, and then shrugs his shoulders. Coming back to Khalon and Jae, "We were the lucky ones. Many of us were able to escape, but we lost a lot. That's how we ended up here. We found this place because we had nowhere else to go. That is probably the only way we made it through that forest. I remember my parents thought we weren't going to make it out, but the panic of having those beasts on our tails pushed us through. Once we finally made it out, we saw this paradise nestled up against a mountain range, and we knew we would be safe here. We were, starving, homeless, and cold, but we were alive, and it wasn't easy, but we made a home here," he sighs, sadly. "As long as we could anyway."

"I'm sorry," Khalon says apologetically and seriously. He looks Aryl hard in the eyes.

"Oh, that was before your time," Aryl waves his apology away.

Khalon shakes his head, "I have done many terrible things. I have trampled villages like yours, and taken lives, and celebrated over it. I can't take any of it back, I can't make it right, but at least I can swear to you, that I will spend the rest of my life trying to atone for the wrongs I have done." Khalon's voice waivers a bit. He is already feeling raw, the effects of this land are wearing on him, but hearing the story, and seeing a survivor of the Skars' cruelty, cuts him deeply.

Aryl's eyes are glassy and overwhelmed. It is obvious that Khalon's promise is an unexpected gift. It was something he didn't know he needed, but by his expression, he has carried the hurt from it for a long time.

Aryl coughs a little and wipes his nose in an attempt to mask his feelings.

"Also," Jae chimes in, "the Skars have been disbanded. They came for our village as well, but we were able to defeat them." He clears his throat. "If it weren't for Khalon, that probably wouldn't have happened."

Two compliments. Khalon looks at Jae with a dumbstruck expression. It's true, if Khalon had not trained the Northwood fairies, they would have been defenseless against the Skar army, but Khalon always felt his presence was resented by Jae. This glimmer of appreciation makes him highly uncomfortable. Judging by the rigidness of Jae's posture and the pulsing of his temple, that compliment was equally unusual for Jae, but this time, Jae keeps his attention on Aryl.

Aryl coughs again and clears his throat, "Well, I should get breakfast made for you boys. You will need every bit of daylight to get where you are going."

While Aryl turns his attention to the pot over the fire, Jae wanders over to the window.

He opens the latch and swings the door open.

"Is that it?" Jae asks, his stare fixed on the outside.

Aryl looks over his shoulder, "That's it alright. It's a pretty clear day. You're lucky. Usually there's a heavy fog that makes it harder to see."

Khalon gets up urgently to set his eyes on their destination. The entire mountain range looks rough, cold, and treacherous, but that one peak off in the distance trumps them all, looking particularly harsh. *Maybe if we fly hard, we can make it before the end of the day.* Khalon contemplates silently.

"The only entrance into the mountain is at the top, and don't get your hopes up about flying," Aryl says, almost as though he was reading Khalon's mind. "The winds will make that impossible for you. You can actually hear them from here, and they've been getting louder ever since Sigrun arrived here."

All three men stand in silence with their ears toward the window. Khalon hears it first, the whipping and whistling has a threatening tone of a truly ferocious storm.

Aryl nods, "Sounds like she is stirring up some kind of trouble up there. The mountain does not like to be disturbed," Jae and Khalon look at Aryl with furrowed brows. Aryl begins chopping up the vegetables for the soup as he explains, "I've tried before to get to the top, for my wife. She died up there, and I thought that maybe I could bring her body down. Bring her home, to bury her at least." Sadness sweeps over him, "I wasn't strong enough, and the mountain does things to you."

"Does things? What kind of things?" Jae inquires. His body leaning forward.

"It will work against you. Pull you apart from the inside. It's different for everyone, targets your individual weaknesses."

"I don't understand. How do you mean?" Jae asks again. His concern is growing.

Aryl stops his task, thinking back, he rubs his temple. "For me, it was fear and self-doubt. It used my love for my wife against me. I believed that every step closer I took, made her suffer more and, once I turned back, she was given mercy. I know now that it was all a cruel trick, that she suffered regardless, but at the time, it felt so real. I had no choice," he continues chopping. "And there was the physical pain. You think these aches that you are feeling now are bad," he shakes his head, "just wait until you get to the foot of that mountain."

Khalon and Jae look at each other with shared anxiety. The closer they get the more obstacles seem to be stacking against them. The three of them mostly eat their breakfast in silence. Both Jae and Khalon silently scheming, while Aryl battles with his own demons. It's obvious he wants to keep them from going there, but he knows nothing could stop them, so instead, he tries to come up with anything helpful. He mostly comes up short.

Jae and Khalon pack up their few things after they eat. Jae holds the map. He doesn't need it though. They know where they're going, but he rubs the canvas between his fingers anyway. Khalon knows that Jae is worried; perhaps even more worried than he is. Jae had always wanted to keep harm away from Sigrun. He always tried to shield her from it—even when they were children. Whereas Khalon tried to prepare her to face it. Khalon knows that his pushing her, and training her, was ultimately the right thing, but today, he regrets it. He wants more than anything to be home with her, drinking tea and eating cake, safe and protected.

Khalon tucks his knife in his belt and adjusts his sword, yet again. He is nervous.

Aryl looks him over. "That terrain is pretty rough to just be wearing your skin," he says looking at Khalon's chest.

Jae snickers, "Good luck with that argument," he slings his pack across his body. "I've been trying to get him to wear a shirt for a long time."

Khalon chuckles, and gives a grin, "I'll be okay." He grabs his pack and heads out the front door.

"Um, one more thing," Aryl says before Jae and Khalon take flight. "What I said about the mountain working against you, with there being the two of you, it might also work you against each other," his eyes dart between them both. "Just something to consider."

Jae nods, "Thank you, again, for everything."

"We'll see you soon," Khalon reassures.

"I hope so," Aryl replies with promise, but his doubtfulness is palatable.

Chapter 24

Jae and Khalon fly as hard as they can, for as long as they can, but just as Aryl promised, it doesn't take long until the winds force them to the ground. Exhausted and winded, they both try to catch their breath.

"Ah, do you feel that?" Khalon sputters out between gasps. He holds his hand against his chest, hoping to relieve the obstruction of his lungs.

"Yeah," Jae also struggles for breath. "It's like I'm tethered to the ground, and I keep getting pulled down. Just standing upright is hard."

Khalon nods in agreement. He feels like he is being pulled to his knees and, just to remain standing, is a fight. He looks ahead. They still have so far to go. He might be stronger than Jae, but he is also heavier, and his weight is not helping him now.

"Do you think we can get there before dark?" Jae asks.

"I don't know," Khalon answers, as honestly as he can, "but, we have to try." They begin their walk one step at a time.

Their pace is slower than what they would like it to be, but in order to maintain their stamina, they have to go at an easy speed. They only get over the first pass when Khalon notices Jae fidgeting again with the map. He doesn't seem to notice that he is even doing it. Strangely, Khalon feels a small wave of compassion for Jae. Khalon was taken with Sigrun from the first time he met her. He assumes Jae has felt the same way, and he has known her much longer. It would make sense that, for whatever fear Khalon is feeling, for Jae, it must be tenfold. "You know," Khalon breaks the silence. His breathing is a bit labored, but he is able to speak. "I, I should tell you something."

Jae looks at him seriously.

"That day," Khalon continues, "after Malyn's wedding, when we went to the field for our workout, she had one of her 'episodes.' We were just sparring, no big deal, and our swords locked up and my hand slipped, and she got hit in the mouth," his tone is apologetic. Telling this story to Jae is not easy for him.

Jae never approved of Khalon sparring with her. One of their biggest issues came from the first time Khalon and Sigrun matched up. He was preparing her for an enemy that would show her no mercy, but Jae saw it as brutality. Admitting now that harm came to her by his hand is hard to swallow, let alone confess it to his biggest critic. "Anyway, she was fine, but she bled a little. Her lip was cut, and she just saw red. She came after me, seriously came after me, and she came very close to taking my head off."

Khalon looks at Jae expecting a smug look, but instead he sees a face of concern and bewilderment.

"She did some ranting also," Khalon recalls. "She just didn't sound like herself at all," he shakes his head. "She has always rejected the idea of being queen, but when she goes 'dark,' she sounds like a true tyrant."

"I know, I've noticed that too," Jae says.

"And she was so strong." Khalon stops, and takes a drink from his canteen, then hands it to Jae. "I'm pretty strong," he continues, "and I'm pretty big, and she tossed me across that field like a children's toy. I don't know what we are dealing with, what has happened to her, but it's nothing I have ever seen, and I've seen a lot of evil in this world."

Jae presses his lips in a line, and nods slightly. "Thank you for telling me."

Khalon starts to walk forward again, but Jae reaches out and grabs his arm. "Um, she talked to me a little bit too. She didn't give me much, probably because she didn't understand it either, but she did say something that makes me a little nervous. She said, when it does take over, that it feels good, and that, um…she likes it." He struggles to say it out loud. The words almost get stuck in his throat. It seems to hurt him tremendously to realize that his longtime friend might be changing for the worse.

Khalon puts his hand on Jae's shoulder, and looks at him seriously. "We'll get her back."

Jae swallows hard and nods with determination to rescue her, not just from this force on the mountain, but from whatever has taken hold of her as well.

*****

Most of the day has gone by. They are getting closer, but as they do, the forces keeping them away are getting stronger. The wind is whipping so hard that they have to lean into the gusts, so they are not blown over. Sand and grit

169

are blown against them burning and tearing their flesh one tiny cut at a time. Khalon has wrapped his wings around his body as a protective shield, but it does little good, since they are so thin, and he knows the damage to his wings could impede his ability to fly if it gets much worse.

Khalon feels Jae tap on his shoulder. He struggles to look up. Jae motions to a rock ledge over to the side that might offer them a bit of shelter for a moment to rest. Once shielded from the majority of the storm, they both try conserve their strength.

"We have to be getting close," Jae says. He grabs his canteen from his pack.

Khalon holds his hand in front of his face to shield his eyes and peaks around the ledge to determine how much farther they have to go. The mountain is close; dark and cutting, it punctures the sky like a threat to the heavens.

He leans back against the rock, and wipes sand from his eyes. "It's close, just a little farther." He thumps Jae on the chest reassuringly and digs out a piece of bread from his pack. He breaks it in half and gives a piece to Jae. "We should eat now. I'm thinking this will be the last chance we get to eat something before we get inside the mountain, and who knows what's going to happen once we are inside."

Jae nods, and eagerly accepts.

Khalon eats quickly. He wishes that he could slow down to savor this small reward, but his desire to get to Sigrun takes priority. Plus, he is more eager than ever to get home, because he cannot help but think how much better the bread would taste with a little bit of honey.

Chapter 25

They stand at the foot of the wretched peak. Both of them look up searching for an easier way, but there isn't one.

"There doesn't seem to be a path," Jae assesses.

"No. So, I guess we climb."

Khalon reaches up to a protruding rock to begin his ascent. The touch from the rock burns through him like a branding iron. The rock breaks open and a stream of blood pours out from it. It covers his hands and spills out on the ground at his feet. He lets go and sinks back to the ground. He looks up again. There is no blood, not on him, and not on the rock that he touched. It was an image—like a memory. His eyes are wide, and he looks at his hand. It isn't burned and there is no damage, but it felt like he had grabbed an ember straight from a fire.

"Are you okay? What happened?" Jae questions, eyes wide and darting.

Khalon takes a breath, "Oh, this is going to be hard."

Jae reaches up to touch the rock as well, and suddenly releases. He doesn't seem to have the exact same reaction. Instead of nursing his hand he is rubbing his eyes like he has a terrible headache.

"Oh wow," Jae takes a breath. "How does it…? I don't understand."

Khalon shakes his head. "Me either. Just remember why we are here," he encourages. "We have to make it."

"Okay," Jae breathes. "Okay."

Khalon grabs the rock again. The pain is still there, and his body feels heavier, but he can stand it. He finds another rock for his foot, and slowly he pulls himself upward. Every step up requires incredible effort. There is no training that prepares you for this. Determination is the only way to the top. He has only taken a few steps, but he shouts down to Jae, taking care not to actually look down.

"You doing alright?"

"Yeah," Jae replies shakily, "just a little dizzy."

"Yeah, me too."

Khalon reaches up to grab a hold of another rock and a feeling surges through him. It is familiar, and primal, like how he would feel after conquering a village. An odd combination of victory and shame. Then he hears screams. Women and children—shouting for their lives.

"Do you hear that?" he asks Jae.

"What? Do I hear what?" Jae shouts back.

Khalon shakes his head, shaking the sound away. "Nothing, never mind."

He continues on. The storm proceeds to get worse. The sky is getting darker, and the storm clouds are swirling above them. Flashes of lightning are beginning to reach out. Their circumstances are getting more dismal every moment.

Khalon's current footing is very loose, and if it fails, not only will the rock he is standing on fall, but he will also fall with it. Carefully, he looks up and sees a small ledge that he might be able to grab hold of. If he is able to get there, he will have better footing off to the side. The problem is, to get there, he will have to jump a bit to make the distance. The small boulder trembles beneath his foot. He takes a breath and holds it. Building enough strength in his leg, like a coil, he lunges up. The rock that was under his foot is released from its resting place and plummets down to the bottom. He just barely grasps the ledge with his hand, just enough to find new footing and his other hand finds another rock to hold onto as well. He closes his eyes and rests his head against the mountainside. He breathes again and opens his eyes.

Blood. He sees blood. Dripping down the rock again, as though the mountain itself is bleeding. It is on his hand, pouring over his arms, and across his chest. He looks up and around, it is everywhere. Then he sees that the ledge that he is holding is not a ledge at all. It's a bone—a leg bone. The leg bone of a fairy. In a panic, he pulls his hand away, and the bone comes with it. He closes his eyes hard again and opens them. The blood is gone. It was never there. The bone that he was holding is actually a dead tree root. He lets it go. As it falls down to the ground, he watches it, and he is entranced. The ground gets closer. He could make these horrible images and feelings end. All he has to do is let go. It would be a short hop to the bottom.

Let go. A voice whispers on the wind.

"Hey, you okay?" Jae has climbed next to him. He looks worried.

Without reason, anger reaches into Khalon's chest. A vibration rattles from the mountain through his body all the way to the back of his skull. He looks at Jae's face and sees smugness, as though he enjoys Khalon's struggle. This fuels the anger, urging, maybe even demanding, that he reach out and rip out his throat.

Crush him. He doubts you.

He fights the urge and shakes his head attempting to eliminate the thoughts that have recently burrowed their way into his mind. Looking at Jae again, his expression is not smug at all. It is one of true concern. Khalon takes a breath.

"I'm fine," he manages.

"You sure?"

"Yes."

Jae looks him in the eyes. He looks worn down also. The pain is starting to get to him too.

"Go ahead of me," Khalon ushers. "I'm okay."

Jae takes the lead, and Khalon looks down again. The ground that looked so close and easy to get to just a moment ago is very far away and would have been a fatal fall. He gets his bearings. This place is worse than he thought.

*****

Jae is struggling. His wings are thicker, and the feathers catch the wind more, which helps him in flight where he can maneuver easily just by shifting his wings the slightest bit, but here, on the mountain, the wind is working hard against him. The winds are getting worse and, every so often, a gust will catch his wing just enough to pull his grip loose. He's been lucky so far that every slip has been one he could recover from, but Khalon can see that he is wearing down. Jae is laboring to breathe. His hands are shaking. Whether his recent struggle is from sheer exhaustion, or if he is feeling the same radiating pain that comes from the mountain itself, Khalon is unsure.

Khalon looks down again, the ground is a very long way down. He dares to hope that they are close. For the sake of his sanity, he has not looked to the top in quite some time. As hard as this climb has been, it would be incredibly discouraging to be nowhere near the finish. He has been only looking far enough ahead to get his next couple of steps. Taking his chances, he leans back just enough to get a good look. He sighs and hangs his head. They are maybe only halfway there.

Once he has a good footing, he takes a moment to gather his will. Releasing his grip from the mountain feels painful and good at the same time. The muscles in his hand and forearm cry out as he slowly stretches out all fingers. They have been clinched and cramped for so long that merely straightening them feels foreign. Looking at his arm, his gaze fixes on one of his Skar trophy brands. Every mark on his body tells a story about someone else's pain—every village conquered, every battle won, and every King killed is mapped out on his body. They were supposed to be markings of pride, but now, every time he looks at them, shame washes over him. This brand is an outline of a sword that spans from wrist to elbow in the inside of his forearm. It was given after his first victory on the battlefield. He was so young, he had probably only seen 14 winters, but by that spring, he was already bigger than most of the men. Mantus had put a sword in his hand practically from the moment he found him, so he was more than a competent fighter by that point.

The fear and excitement that he felt that day is as clear to him now as it was then. He had worked so hard to make Mantus proud, to earn his place there, and this was his chance to prove himself. And prove himself, he did. His sword claimed the lives of 37 men that day. He'll never forget the first. He was a younger man, probably had a young wife, maybe a child on the way. Khalon remembers that this man did not seem afraid of him. Likely, he saw Khalon and thought of him as only a boy, easily disposed of, and gave it no further thought. The man seemed to regard him with very little care, let alone any degree of fear, and that attitude continued until the moment Khalon's sword swiftly executed a fatal blow. The smugness that was so saturated in this man's eyes poured out of him as quickly as his blood flowed onto the ground. That was the moment that Khalon swore he would never underestimate an opponent the way this man underestimated him.

The battle was quick and bloody. He was tired by the end, but that didn't keep him from joining in on the victory cry with his fellow soldiers. Mantus had noticed him too. As his men celebrated, Mantus stood at the edge of the field with his pinchers casually at his sides, arms crossed in front of his body, standing tall, looking at Khalon with a smirk of satisfaction spreading across his mouth.

It wasn't until later that night Khalon first felt the pang of self-doubt and regret. On the battlefield, he felt justified. The men he killed were warriors just like him. Kill or be killed. They wouldn't hesitate to take his head if given the chance, so why should he? After the battle, they ran to the heart of the village and began pillaging. That was when he saw the true consequences of what he had done. Women crying for their husbands. Children screaming—scared and confused. The elderly mourning the losses of their sons and daughters, and their legacy of what took generations to build dissolving before their eyes in the span of one day.

Khalon also got drunk for the first time that night. He watched as the rest of the tribe celebrated by drinking and taking liberties with some of the local women. He knew then, what they had done was wrong, but it was too late, he was as guilty as the rest of them. So, he knelt in front of Mantus and accepted his reward. This brand, a sword of valor and bravery. The pain was unlike anything he had ever felt before. The iron, red-hot from the fire, scalded his flesh, hissing and smoking. Strangely, it felt cold at first like diving into a frozen river, then searing heat began to pulsate through his entire body. The stench of it burned almost as bad as the iron. Cold sweat trickled down his face and back, nausea rose up in his stomach, but he didn't make a sound, and he didn't move an inch. Later, he went looking for comfort and relief in a wine bottle. He drank to drown out the screams, to wash away the feeling of shame, but he found no reprieve until he passed out.

He looks at this marking now and he can still hear those screams. Especially, here, on this mountain. The pain of the lives he has crushed seem to be written in the wind here, and with every gust, comes the reminder of every horrible deed he has ever done. The wind comes again with a wicked scream and his body trembles. The sounds of pain in the air reach through his body and he feels the despair of his victims. Not only does he hear the sounds of their agony, but he feels their physical pain as well. His flesh burns for every fire set. His insides feel shredded for every stab wound he ever inflicted. His muscles ache for every fight he ever won. It hurts so much. He just wants it to stop. This pain would drop any ordinary fairy to the ground, but Khalon has spent a lifetime tolerating pain, so he is able to withstand it enough to not let go of the rock he is anchored to.

"Hey," Jae shouts from above him, Khalon looks up at him, "don't let it mess with…" Jae doesn't have time to finish his sentence. His footing gives way and his hold crumbles beneath his hand.

Jae shouts out and tries to get his footing back, but it is in vain, he is already sliding downward. He is coming down fast on Khalon's right side. Instinctively, and without hesitation, Khalon releases his right hand from the mountain, swings his arm out, and snatches Jae from the air before he falls into the abyss. At first, he wasn't sure that he actually caught him, but now he sees his hand securely wrapped around Jae's wrist. His left hand has a pretty good grip on the mountain rock, but likely, not for long. Khalon's left hand is now the only anchor supporting the weight of two grown men.

Even though Khalon has him, Jae is dangling freely over the open chasm with only Khalon's hand as his lifeline. The winds aren't settling down either. In fact, they seem to be intensifying. Jae's eyes are wide and panicked. He looks to be in a state of disbelief, almost as though he can't believe he is still alive.

Khalon's chest muscles and shoulder joint cry out with the strain of holding him. Khalon's grip is starting to shake.

Let go. The voice whispers again to Khalon. The first time it urged him to let go so that *he* would fall, but this time it encourages him to let Jae go. *Your pain will go away, all of it. All you have to do is let go.*

The voice is hypnotic, almost seductive, and it promises relief. All he has to do is *let go.*

So simple. So easy. His eyes close and his grip loosens. Jae's wrist slips an inch from his grasp.

"KHALON!" Jae cries out.

Khalon opens his eyes and looks at Jae. Jae's face is riddled with the most heightened fear. He is completely unsure whether Khalon will be able to fight whatever demons are swarming him right now, and Jae's life is completely in Khalon's hands. Jae's look of terror snaps Khalon out of his trance and his grip, which had begun to slip, tightens again and he twists Jae around enough that Jae can grab onto Khalon's wrist for a better hold.

"AH!" Khalon shouts as he uses all his strength to lift Jae up. The muscles in his chest ripple and the veins in his arms pop up under his skin with the effort of lifting Jae with one arm. If his grip on the mountain slips with his other hand, they will both fall down the mountainside. He gets Jae up and over enough so that Jae finally gets his foot on a small ledge and is able to give Khalon some relief.

Once fully back on his own ground, Jae rests his head on the rock wall. Both men gather their breath.

"Thank you," Jae mutters out between breaths. "I thought, I thought you might let go there for a moment," he says with slight suspicion.

Khalon huffs out a small laugh. He's not sure what amuses him more, that Jae actually knew what was going through Khalon's head, or that he called him out on it.

"It was a little shaky there for a moment," he finally admits. He looks up and spots a ledge big enough for them to sit and gather themselves. "Let's rest up there for a bit," he points to the ledge.

Jae nods in agreement, obviously grateful for an opportunity to rest.

*****

The ledge is small, but at least both of them can fit well enough to sit somewhat comfortably. Khalon sits with his back against the mountainside. He rests his head back. Once he catches his breath, he takes a drink from his canteen and goes to hand it over to Jae, but Jae is still on his hands and knees as though his is coming to terms with his own near-death experience. He does take the offering, but does not drink right away, instead he keeps his gaze at the rock under his hand.

Khalon turns and looks out at the landscape. It is as close to a wasteland as it can get. There is nothing green or alive here. There is no color, no richness. Nature provides beauty in all colors, even the somewhat less remarkable ones: black ebony, gray metals, and beautiful stones, and a variety of brown woods from light to dark, from warm to cool. Here, every shade of black, gray, and brown is dusty, dull, and rotten. What trees are left, died long ago, and the barrenness of the country under the mountain's foot is tragic. Against the backdrop of the dreary and lusterless is a glint of something catches the corner of his eye.

Sitting up, he sees something shiny that does not belong to the mountain. He rolls over onto his knees and blows some dust away. He recognizes the small bauble right away. The white rose is closed up tight since it is not connected to Sigrun. The sight of her pendant brings him a feeling of warmth, actual evidence that she was here and that she may be close, but at the same time, the fact that she is not wearing it causes him a greater concern.

"Jae!" he shouts out. Jae looks over at him alarmed. "Come over here. Look at this."

Jae shuffles his way over and kneels beside him.

"What? That's her necklace," Jae exclaims.

Khalon nods, and sighs heavily, getting confirmation that he isn't hallucinating and that the necklace is real, carries the joy that she was here and the worry that something caused her to leave it.

"Why would she leave this? She loves this necklace." Jae's concern is also rising.

"I don't know," Khalon answers, his eyes fixed on the marble. He reaches out for it. Jae grabs his hand quickly.

"Don't touch the actual marble. It might shock you," Jae warns, as he remembers when she first received the necklace. Jae had extended a curious finger to touch it and a small volt reached out to touch him back.

Khalon nods in compliance and instead grabs the ends of the silk cord. As he tries to lift it, he feels the weight and how it feels tied to the mountain surface.

"What the," he tries again, and again. It barely moves. "You have to check this out."

Jae's brow furrows in confusion. He grabs the cord himself and tries to pick it up. The weight is the same for him also.

"Whoa, that's crazy. Why is it so heavy? It can't always be that heavy right?"

Khalon looks around, and shakes his head, "No, it's this place. It forced her to leave it."

"Why?"

"I don't know, but I feel like we have to take it with us."

Khalon takes the cord again and pulls up. It's a struggle but he gets it off the ground and drops it in his pack. Instantly the weight of it pulls him down, but he is strong enough that he can stand. The strap of his pack presses hard into the meat of his neck and shoulder, but it is tolerable.

"You're not going to be able to carry that the whole way," Jae assesses.

"Well, I have to try."

Khalon starts his incline once again. Now, with even more weight on his shoulders.

*****

Every step is harder than the last. Khalon was struggling before he took on the extra burden of the pendant. Now it takes every bit of strength to make the smallest progress. Jae is ahead of him, but not by much, he is wearing down also. When they had stopped on the ledge, Khalon noticed that the color had drained from Jae's face and his eyes are bloodshot. Whatever demons he is battling, they seem to be winning.

The night has come. Every unsteady move they make is even more treacherous in the dark. There is no moon to light the way, only the sporadic threatening flashes of lightning from the storm above.

Khalon looks up, finally the top is within reach. He has never been this tired in his life and everything hurts. His fingers are cut and bleeding from the rough rock edges. The flesh of his body has been slashed and abraded by the whipping wind and the grit that is carried on it. His muscles ache and the strap of his pack, which now houses the additional weight of Sigrun's pendant, has rubbed the skin of his neck and shoulder raw. He can finally see that the end is near, and he gets that final push to keep going. As they have gotten closer to the top, the storm that is erupting around them continues to get more threatening. The lightning strikes are getting closer, dancing around them, and they are becoming increasingly more frequent. With every strike, deafening bursts of thunder roll, vibrating through them. The rain has not come yet, but it feels as though the clouds could open up at any moment and pour over them.

"HAVE YOU EVER SEEN A STORM LIKE THIS?" Jae shouts over the roar of the thunder.

Khalon shakes his head. "NEVER." He looks up, "ALMOST THERE."

Jae is just ahead of him and the encouragement that they will soon have shelter, fuels him to go faster. The thought of getting into the cave and getting that much closer to finding Sigrun brings an eagerness that is barely containable, but a nagging doubt creeps up on him, and an edginess consumes him. Jae is just ahead of him. Sigrun's feelings for Jae have been unpredictable and unclear. Jae, on the other hand, has been very persistent and direct with his intentions.

With him out of the way, she could be all yours.

The voice that was carried on the wind before is now in his head.

It would be easy. Just reach up, grab him, and fling him to the ground.

Khalon shakes his head. The voice confuses him. He is starting to doubt whether these thoughts are a product of this evil place, some nasty side effect from being here too long, or thoughts of his own. He takes a deep breath. "Keep it together, you're almost there," he encourages himself quietly.

Jae makes it to the cave's ledge, turning around to help Khalon. Jae's hand is extended to help him to the top.

Don't take it, the voice warns, *he will betray you.*

Jae's eyes do look devious. He must have voices of his own.

Khalon ignores the warning and accepts Jae's assistance. Out of all the hard steps they've taken, this last one is the hardest. The sensation for Khalon taking this last step feels like he is pulling himself through a pool of liquid rock, sharp and unmoving. When he finally breaks through this invisible barrier, both men lie on their backs at the outer lip of the cave, drinking in this small victory.

Jae starts to move first.

This is your opportunity, before it's too late, just one swing of your sword.

Without even willing himself to do it, Khalon finds his hand on the hilt of his sword.

He will kill you as soon as he gets the chance. You have to strike first. You have to kill him. It's the only way.

Holding the sword feels good, a sensation rushes to his head, and it makes him feel light and euphoric. It's the resisting that hurts. When he tries to lower his sword, shooting pains attack his arms and there is a physical force that pushes against him that is so strong, his body shakes when he moves against it. Jae has his back to him and is oblivious to this struggle.

Not only will he kill you, but he could hurt her too, and you won't be here to save her. Do it. Do it for her. Do it now!

He brings the sword up a little bit and twists his wrists so that the swords edge is lined up beautifully with Jae's neck.

"Jae," Khalon says fairly calmly, despite the seriousness of his thoughts and intentions. Jae turns to face him. As soon as he sees Khalon there with his sword drawn, his brow furrows with confusion and his eyes light up searching for the threat that has caused Khalon to react this way. It doesn't dawn on him that the threat, to Khalon, is him.

"You have to go without me," Khalon manages to say. Just resisting the intention hurts him.

"What?"

"If I go with you, I will hurt you."

"I don't—"

"Jae! I will kill you. You have to go!" his voice trembles. As he struggles to hold the sword steady, the resisting force that desperately wants him to swing the sword fights him so adamantly that his body begins to tremor violently. Lightning fires around him. It strikes the ground and cracks the mountain surface. Rocks break loose and start to roll downward, making the one and only entry point an unsure exit. If they don't move fast, they may be trapped within the mountain forever.

"I can't control it," Khalon tries to explain calmly. "You have to go without me, before it is too late. You have to find her."

Jae finally takes the warning in all its severity, turns, and runs into the mouth of the cave. He slips into darkness and disappears from sight.

"Okay, you bastard," Khalon says to the voice in his head. "Let's deal with you next."

Jae

Chapter 26

As soon as Jae is through the threshold of the cave's entry, he feels lighter, and even though the enervating headache begins to lift, he still feels a heavy uneasiness, especially leaving Khalon that way. He remembered what Aryl said about the mountain working against them; in particular, how it might get them to work against each other. He took the warning seriously but could never have imagined that he would be eye level with the edge of Khalon's sword.

Shaking it off, he runs as fast as he can through the web of tunnels looking for Sigrun. This is not as easy as he had hoped it would be. The darkness makes it nearly impossible to see, and the rocky surface is hard to move quickly on. There is a smell in the air, similar to how it smells before a storm hits, almost acidic and burnt. Several times, he has to turn around after hitting another dead end just to navigate all over again and get no farther.

"*Sig!*" he shouts without care through the tunnels. He knows that there is something evil here, something so powerful, that it has destroyed the very land he is standing on. He knows that stealth would be better than blatant, but the feeling that she is so close overrides his need to be prudent, so he keeps shouting in anticipation that, at any moment, she will shout back. He hears nothing in return and begins to feel a sickness in his stomach. *Am I too late?* Fear seeps into his mind. He doesn't know what he would do if she were gone. She has been in his life for almost as long as he can remember and, to him, a world without her, would be a world without color.

Time seems to pass differently here. He knows that he has only been inside for a very short time, but it feels as though hours have gone by. He stops running for a moment to catch his breath and find new momentum. Once his breathing slows down, the quiet around him begins to envelope him, and it is then, that he finally hears something other than silence. It's subtle at first, but once he really starts to focus on it, he can hear a similar whirring as the wind from outside, and maybe voices.

"Sig," he says quieter this time. With his first real clue to where he is going, he moves fast toward the sound.

Several twists and turns later, the sounds get louder. Cracks of thunder shake the rock beneath his feet, and the voice gets louder. It is definitely a woman's voice, but not Sigrun's. He can't understand what she is saying. It doesn't seem to be a language he knows, and it resembles a chant, more than speech. He slows down. A light flickers ahead of him at the mouth of another opening.

Stopping short of the entryway, he flattens himself against the tunnel wall trying to hear more, hoping to get some clue as to what he is about to barge in on.

"Merrin, stop it. Let her go!" A voice shouts over the chant. It's not Sigrun, that is certain. She sounds old and tired.

"Oh, Mara, you know I can't do that," the other voice taunts. "Now keep quiet or I will do a spell to remove your tongue."

Jae reaches for his sword and steps into the doorway. The blue and white flashes of light coming from the altar are blinding at first. His eyes finally focus to see the woman chanting. She doesn't see him at first. She is too enthralled in her task. Another woman, one who is old and frail looking, is on the ground with her hands and feet bound with what looks like bolts of lightning. Scanning the room wildly looking for Sigrun, his heart pounds violently when he sees her on the other side of the room on the opposite side of the altar. She is on her knees with her hands palm up in a resting position on top of her thighs. Her eyes are closed, and her face is pointing down to the ground. She definitely looks worn. The climate of the mountain seems to have been just as perilous for her. She wears a similar amount of scrapes and cuts all along her visible flesh as he and Khalon. The overwhelming desire to run to her is only held back by the confusing scene laid out in front of him.

"What do we have here?" Merrin coos, breaking her chant to acknowledge Jae's presence. Jae looks at her and back at Sigrun. His confusion is very apparent.

"Sigrun?" he says trying to get her attention. She doesn't budge.

"Oh, I see. A rescuer. How very valiant, and how very foolish," Merrin's voice is threatening. "Kill him," she orders.

Sigrun, who looked as though she had been turned off, suddenly turns on, and she is not the same. Her eyes are black, entirely black, even the whites of

186

her eyes are now filled like a pool of black ink. The blackness is even bleeding through her veins spreading down onto her cheek bones and up to her eyebrows. She looks emotionless and lifeless, and that scares him.

Like a string from the ceiling pulling her upright, she stands and begins walking toward him. She reaches behind her and pulls her kama loose from her harness. Jae has his sword in-hand, but has it lowered. He would never intend to use it on her. It seems she, on the other hand, only has bloodshed in mind. She charges at him with blades drawn.

Sigrun

Chapter 27

Jae! How did you get here? I can't stop! You have to run! I'm screaming a warning at him, but I actually say nothing. I can't speak. I can't control my own body. The feeling is like trying to keep a tree from falling using only a single thread of string. It is an impossible feat. Merrin commands and I have no choice, but to obey. I can feel her in my head. It is the same feeling I had when the anger would overtake me and I would act out in an irrational way, only now, I am fully under her spell, and I can't find my way back.

Everything went dark after she took control of me and I lost consciousness; for how long, I'm not sure, but the first thing I see once that veil is lifted is myself running toward my closest childhood friend with weapons drawn, and murderous intent, and there is nothing I can do to stop myself.

"Sig, it's me. It's Jae!" he shouts, but I am already there. He has no choice, but to raise his sword in defense. My kama clashes with his blade.

"SIG!" he shouts again pushing me away.

I come back and swing my blades again. He deflects both blows and moves to the side, circling around me. Like a deranged brut, I keep coming for him. I feel her arrogance. I feel her anger and determination. She almost feels giddy at the idea of running him through. Mara wriggles madly on the ground, trying desperately to free herself from her electric bonds.

"Merrin, stop this!" Mara screams.

"Quiet! You've had me bound in this place for decades. It's my turn now." Merrin has one hand controlling me and the other hand containing Mara.

She has to refocus her energy on Mara, now that she has control over me too. She seems divided between controlling us both at the same time. When she does this, I feel a slight lifting of her hold, but it is quickly back in place and just as strong.

"Sig, snap out of it," Jae pleads with me.

I'm trying! I slam against myself over and over again, trying to find a way to get control of my body, but my efforts are futile. I am bound and helpless, with an up-close view of myself attempting to tear my best friend apart piece by piece. I wish I could close my eyes and just not look, but that seems to be another one of her cruelties, she wants me to see. She wants to destroy me from the inside out.

"Let her go, witch!" Jae demands.

Merrin laughs, but I can hear the strain in her voice.

"I'll never let her go. She is going to make me stronger and more powerful than you can possibly imagine. It's too bad I have to kill you. You're such a beautiful specimen. You would make such a lovely pet."

I can tell Jae wants to cut her down, but it takes every bit of his focus and strength to deal with me. I am her perfect henchman. I became so much stronger once she took me over. I know that Jae will only be able to defend himself for a short while before he gets too tired to fight back. By the panicked look in his eyes, he is figuring that out as well.

I swing again, he blocks. I keep pushing him back blow after blow. He deflects every swing, but he won't attack. He won't swing back. I want him to hit me. I want him to fight back.

If I can feel her, maybe she can feel me, and if I get hurt, then maybe she gets hurt.

I swing the kama in my right hand down which would potentially sink into his upper chest. He blocks with his sword. With my left arm, I swing my kama sideways to rip out his throat. He ducks out of the way barely in time, and I nick the skin at the top of his shoulder at the base of his neck, just enough to open up and bleed. The blood trickles down his chest and stains his shirt a dark red. The look on his face shifts. He is realizing that she will not stop, and he that he must fight back.

He stands with his sword up and ready. She has me run toward him again. This time, he is ready for it. He swings my blades away and kicks me square in the chest, hard. It knocks me down. It hurts. More importantly, it hurts her. I was right. I can feel her hold weaken, just not enough. She has me back on my feet and charging after him again.

Hit me again, Jae. You must hit me again! I plead to him through this lead veil that has me tied and silenced. I know he cannot hear me, but I plead anyway.

That little setback has amplified her urgency to deal with him. She has me fight him with everything. There is nothing beautiful or fluid about this fight. It is ugly and savage, swinging steel at each other again, and again. Two lifelong friends forced to fight each other, both unwilling, and hoping to find a way out. She has me pushing him toward the cliff's edge at the far side of the room. I know what she is doing, but I can't stop her. I can't warn him.

His heels are to the edge now. The unsteady terrain threatens to crumble beneath him. We stand there, eyes locked on each other. His breathing is labored. He is exhausted and I'm not sure he can even raise his arms anymore. Merrin sees the window and strikes, but not before Jae swings with his left and punches me under my lower jaw, sending my head back. My teeth smack against each other hard and I see stars for a moment. The force of it causes me to drop both kama and stumble backward.

He lowers his sword. I can tell he is wrestling with himself, and what he is supposed to do with this narrow opportunity. Merrin does not waste the chance. She sees his sword lower, and she has me punch him in the chest with so much force that he flies backwards and over the cliff's edge. I see his eyes. They are wide with disbelief. He can't believe this is happening any more than I can. He flies back, almost floats, in a way that looks like all I have to do to snatch him out of the air, is reach out and pull him back in, but I can't.

No! I'm screaming in my head, I'm clawing at my insides, but it makes no difference.

She has won.

She feels satisfied. I can feel her arrogance pulsing through my body, and I feel disgusted and heartbroken. This is so much worse than I could have ever imagined. Devastation doesn't even begin to explain it. I have just flung one of greatest loves of my life to his death. I want to cry. I want to sink into the ground. I would jump over the edge myself if I could, but I am paralyzed. The realization that I am to be her puppet from here on out, has me breaking apart on the inside. She will use me to kill everyone precious to me and I will be powerless by her side as she destroys the world.

She has me turn and head back to my place of submission. I don't make it, but a few steps, when I hear the disturbance of the rock's edge and a grunt.

"You are a stubborn one," Merrin hisses. "Finish it," she orders.

"Merrin, you wretched troll," Mara snarls. "I swear, I will find a way to stop you." This time, Merrin does not waste her time to respond. She merely fires a bolt of electricity through her sister. Mara screams out in pain. The jolt weakens her, but she is still alive. Merrin directs her attention back on me. She has me pick him up by the throat and hold him over the void.

I can feel everything. The hate and sense of justification coming from Merrin, the desperate helplessness that seems to be all that I have been reduced to, and the pulse of Jae's heart that is growing weaker and weaker every moment. She is going to have me hold on to him until he passes out, and he will not be able to save himself again.

Jae, I am so sorry. I wish you had never come here. You may have had a chance to save yourself, to run from her. I will suffer for this moment for the rest of my life. I never deserved you.

My face is emotionless and as still as stone, but I feel tears begin to run down my cheeks.

He sees this and the last expression in his eyes before they roll back and close, is pity, for me.

Just as I start to release my grip, sending him down the cave's edge, something grabs me by the wing and flings me and Jae, backwards so that both of us are on the ground. Jae coughs and starts to get his wits back. I look up to see Khalon standing over us. He has a look on his face that can only be described as lost, and I can't speak to tell him that he is in incredible danger.

I don't have much time to dwell on it. I can feel Merrin's wrath, and she is particularly upset by Khalon's emergence. She has me back on my feet. Khalon backs away from me, slowly positioning himself between me and Jae, his hand is on the hilt of his sword, and he has his eyes on Merrin.

"Sigrun?" he says cautiously. He knows it's not me in control. "Jae, you okay?" he asks, without taking his eyes off me and Merrin.

Jae coughs again and then gets to his feet. "I'm okay."

"What is going on?" Khalon asks.

"I don't really know."

"You two, obviously, are sticking your noses where they don't belong," Merrin growls.

She still has her energy divided between controlling me and keeping Mara bound, so any new complication puts a little more distance between her finishing her spell.

194

"No bother. She's stronger than both of you anyway. Get them," she orders.

She makes me grab the dagger from my belt and start moving toward them both. Khalon still does not draw his sword. Instead, he holds up his hand to me in surrender. Merrin has no intention of taking prisoners. His other hand is down by his side, and I see something dangling from it. My pendant! I'm not sure why but it gives me relief to see it again.

Merrin has me charge them. As Khalon ducks out of the way, he drops the pendant on the ground so he can use both hands. The moment the marble smacks on the floor both Merrin and Mara notice it.

"The pendant," Mara says quietly, with a sense of wonder. She also now has a new resolve. She seems more energized. "The pendant!" she shouts this time to Khalon and Jae. "You have to put it on her body, on her chest, and hold it there until she takes it."

Jae and Khalon look at each other and silently exchange a plan of action. Khalon grabs my arm with the dagger and tries to constrict me while Jae goes for the pendant, but I'm much stronger and I easily overpower Khalon, then kick Jae in the face before he can reach it. Khalon grabs me in a choke hold from behind, trying to make me lose consciousness, but I am able to jump and flip around so that my leg wraps around his neck, and I pull him down, throwing him into Jae, once again keeping them away from the necklace.

Khalon gets up fast and, this time, takes a more aggressive approach. He runs into me and tackles me hard. The dagger is knocked away from me. I kick wildly and punch him in the face.

"I give you credit for trying so hard, but really, your efforts are futile," Merrin boasts, but I can feel the truth. She is getting tired.

"Keep fighting her," Mara coaches. She is wriggling her way up to her knees. "She can't keep this level of energy up forever. She's not strong enough."

"YOU! BE QUIET!" Merrin zaps another ripping bolt through Mara, but this time Mara fights it harder and resists it more. By doing this, she diverts some of her energy away from me. I feel a flash shoot through my body, different than her control. It almost feels electric.

Khalon grabs me again and slams me on the ground. "Jae! Grab it! You have to hurry. She's too strong."

She has me fight Khalon off and scramble towards the dagger. My fingertips just touch the blade when both Jae and Khalon snatch me off the ground and throw me back.

The storm circling above the cave is getting stronger. Lightning is beginning to strike down onto the cave floor surrounding Merrin.

"You have to do it now!" Mara shouts. "We don't have much time!"

"Jae, get the pendant," Khalon instructs.

"No, she's too strong!"

Together, they both pin me to the ground. It is harder to fight them both at the same time, but she doesn't give up, and eventually, I am able to force them back. They are both grunting with exertion trying to keep me contained.

"Jae, you have to get the pendant now."

"You can't hold her alone!"

"It's okay, I have an idea. Go now!"

Jae lets go and runs to where the pendant sits. As soon as he touches the marble, it burns his hand.

"AH!" Jae screams in pain but does not let it go.

Khalon punches me in the gut, trying to knock the wind out of me. I feel it, but it is not enough. She has me fighting him again.

You have to hit me harder. Hurt me!

He slams me to the ground again and looks me in the eyes. Regret washes over him.

"I'm sorry," he says.

I don't understand what he means.

He grabs my wing with both hands, and he looks away with pain painted across his brow. He jerks his hands hard. I hear the snap of my bone breaking first, then a rush of what I can only compare to ice water coursing through my veins, and then finally, the pain takes over.

I'm still not in control, but I do finally break in some way. I scream out a blood-chilling scream and Merrin drops to her knees.

"DO IT NOW!" Mara hollers.

Jae kneels down in front of me and slams the marble onto the center of my chest just below my collar bone. The marble sets on fire as soon as it makes contact with my skin, but this isn't *my* fire. It's burning me. I scream again and louder. Jae panics and starts to lift it off.

"HOLD IT ON HER!" Mara screams.

"IT'S HURTING HER!" Jae screams back.

"TRUST ME! DO IT!"

Jae holds the pendant on my skin. The pain is so intense, I feel sick, I can't breathe. It feels like my heart is roasting inside my own body.

This has Merrin off kilter as well. She has weakened enough that Mara has been able to break her electric ties and she has shifted the storm in her favor.

"KEEP HOLDING! IT'S ALMOST DONE!" Mara is gaining strength.

The crystal continues to blaze, but the rose inside the marble is still perfectly in bloom. The marble starts to liquefy, and just as the form of the marble changes, the rose inside begins to spark as though it is brewing a storm of its own.

The pain never stops. The crystal is melting over my flesh. Khalon and Jae hold me down despite my screaming, and kicking, and writhing. The ball breaks and, like water, the crystal and the rose absorb into my body. All that's left of it is a burn on my skin.

I feel her pulling away from me; her hold slipping away like oil. The feeling is like finally breaking through the water's surface after being under for so long. The relief is immeasurable, but it also hurts, too. The burn of the first free breath. Then, suddenly, the pain just stops. More than stops. I feel energized and refreshed, my skin tingles, and I feel lighter and stronger, at the same time. The darkness that was holding me is gone. I'm back.

"NO!" Merrin cries. She is shaking with rage. Her face morphs into something, almost beastlike, and she growls.

Mara is also fully released and is weaving the tentacles of the storm around her, through her, and into her. She is absorbing the power of the storm. She begins her own chant, a different one from Merrin's.

"You can't do this!" Merrin howls at her, "You weren't strong enough then, and you aren't strong enough now."

"You're right, I wasn't strong enough. I wasn't strong enough to do what I should have done all those years ago. But I am now, because of her," Mara points to me. "Maia's child—you worked so hard to bring her here, because you thought she was going to be as rotten as you, and you thought she would help you bring the world into darkness, but she's not. She is the light."

The winds circle them both. Merrin reaches up to the sky and pulls lightning into her body and fires it at Mara. Mara is pushed back by it, but not pushed over. She's able to hold the beam in her hands and control it enough to throw it back at Merrin. They both stand equally matched, pushing against each other.

I feel a tension in my chest. I'm being drawn to them like a magnet. I don't understand why. I came here to find my mother, to find answers, and, instead, I found more secrets. One thing that is clear to me is that Merrin must be eradicated from this world.

Mara sees me moving toward them and the corner of her mouth pulls into a smile. She controls the beam that Merrin is throwing at her with one hand, and she reaches up to the sky and grabs another with the other hand and sends it to me. It strikes me in the chest where the pendant was absorbed by my body. I brace myself for the volt, but it isn't hurting me. It is fueling me. I feel the same sense of warmth and ease with it, as I do when I ignite my own fire.

I see real fear in Merrin's eyes, but not a shred of remorse. The lightning is pulsing through my blood, merging with my body. Mara and I exchange a glance and we nod to each other. She pushes her beam against Merrin harder. The beam is starting to hurt Merrin. Without having to ask it to, lightning shoots out of my hands and my chest driving three more beams of light into Merrin.

More and more shards of light strike into her from above, and she begins to change. She begins to crystalize. She knows what is happening, but by her face it would appear she does not believe it. At first her movements are slower, stiffer, and then she stops moving completely, until her flesh is fully transformed into a statue of glass.

The storm stops and I finally breathe out. My hands are still up in defense, just in case there is more trickery ahead. I approach the statue cautiously. The glass beings to crack and fall apart. I watch as Merrin dissolves into a pile of fine white sand. A gentle breeze comes through and quietly carries the remains away, making Merrin's mark on this world an invisible one. As the last of the dust is blown away, Mara collapses.

I run to her and prop her up on my lap. Jae and Khalon kneel beside her also. Her breathing is raspy and labored. She coughs and a thin line of blood drips from her mouth. She brushes it away.

"Our fates were t-tied," she struggles to speak. "It was part of the binding spell."

"So, she dies, you die?" I ask.

She nods. A surge of pain ripples through her and she clutches her chest. Then her body begins to glow. Her skin gets smoother, her eyes get brighter, her hair thickens, and her wings, feather-by-feather grow back and fill out. She is still a woman of an older age, but no longer the shriveled old woman that she was. She looks like Merrin. She looks like my mother.

"There, that's better." She chuckles a bit, but another wave of pain hits her. "I…I don't have much time." She spreads out her wings now that they are fully feathered and the perfect white span is only stained by one mark, a small brown sideways heart inside her left wing. I feel dizzy. I hold my breath, and close my eyes remembering my dream. I see her again standing in front of me, but the birthmark from my dream was inside her right wing, not her left.

"Wait, it's on the wrong side." I start to feel sick, like I have been tricked again.

"That's correct, your mother's mark was on her right wing. Your mother, Maia, Merrin, and I, are triplets, but your mother and I are what is called mirror twins; like two halves of a heart. Together, we were very strong, much stronger than Merrin, and she hated us for it, so she began to find ways around it. Dark ways."

The pain comes for her again, and I feel frantic. We are running out of time. I want to ask her so many questions. I want to know everything about her. I want to save her.

"How can I help you? What, what can I do?"

She shakes her head. "You've already done it. You freed me. You ended my suffering. I worked so hard to keep you from this place, to protect you, but I am so glad you are as stubborn as your mother."

I start to cry. I try not to, but emotion and exhaustion have overwhelmed me. Most of all, the strangling feeling of helplessness has me at a complete loss. She reaches up and touches me on my chest where the pendant burned me. Tears run down her face.

"I made that for you," she smiles. "Your parents weren't the only ones who saw you coming. Let me see your fire."

I snap my fingers on my right hand and ignite my blue flames. I make them dance for her, jumping from one fingertip to the next.

"Amazing. So beautiful," she says in awe.

I wipe my face. "If you knew, then why did you try to stop me?"

"Your brother. Merrin had been poisoning him from a young age. I was worried that the same had happened to you."

I shake my head trying to figure it out.

"Merrin had a connection with your brother from the very beginning. The last time we saw your mother, she was already with-child. It was a fight, her leaving, much in the same way that we merged together just now, and in that struggle, part of Merrin's energy infused with the child, linking them together. In a way, he was more Merrin's son, than Maia's."

Hearing her story explains a lot. Closing my eyes, I try to string together everything that I have learned on this journey. It is still a jumbled mess of a web, but I am beginning to feel easier.

"You've been through a lot," she says. I open my eyes. She isn't talking to me, she is addressing Khalon. "This place was very hard on you, wasn't it?"

He nods. His eyes are very sad. I've never seen him this stripped down before.

"Don't let the demons of this place follow you."

He swallows hard, "I'll try."

She doubles over again. Her skin is clammy, and her eyes are getting darker.

"I, I have one more gift for you," she reaches up and touches my face. "My memories. The good ones," she adds.

Her body begins to glow, and the light collects in her hand that is touching my face. I feel a tingling sensation and a warmth. At first, it's only on my face where she's touching me, but before long, my entire body is radiating with her energy.

I feel disconnected from my body and walls of the cave melt away leaving me in a bright white space with no walls and no ceiling, and I'm all alone. Slowly, the colors begin to fill in. Then sound, and smell, and then I feel a breeze on my skin. I see three small fairies, dark hair, green eyes, white wings, all in pretty summer dresses, holding hands and running through a bright grassy meadow. I see them sleeping—two of them facing each other with hands entwined. I see these girls with their parents, my grandparents, loving and protecting.

Time has no boundaries here. I blink and I see my father and my mother, young and in love. My father is a young man in this memory. His hair is still brown, which I had never seen before. This memory must be when they first met. My heart swells. There is no bigger gift than this. She has given me love itself.

When I finally sink back into the real world, my Aunt Mara has already passed away. She looks restful, with a smile on her face. She looks happy.

I cradle her and cry. "Thank you. I'm going to take you home with me," I whisper. "I am going to bring you back to your sister."

Jae puts his hand on my shoulder. I look at him and his eyes are filled with tears. Khalon has his head down. I can feel that his heart is heavy.

The lightning has stopped, but a low rumble ripples through the land and the skies finally open. The cleansing sound of rain surrounds the cave. I find joy in the rains washing the poison away from these lands and hope that all scars will heal here.

Chapter 28

Jae and Khalon help me wrap Mara in cloth, and we fill our bags with fruit from the garden before we depart. As I'm filling my bag, Khalon comes over to me. "We need to reset your bones."

He is talking about my wing that he had to break. I hadn't thought about it much since it happened. Now that everything is settling, it is getting very sore, and my wing hangs limply behind me. He doesn't look me in the eyes. I can tell he feels bad about hurting me, and he will have to hurt me again to fix it.

"Let's do it," I say.

Jae holds my hand while Khalon assesses exactly how to proceed. Once he has a good feel on how the bones are sitting, his grip gets tighter.

"Okay, ready?"

I nod, and I'm already sweating. "Ready."

"One, two, three." On three he pulls hard, and my bones snap back into place.

It hurts just as bad the second time. I'm hit with a wave of nausea. Pain needles all the way to the back of my skull. I groan and sink my face into Jae's chest.

"Alright, hard parts over," Khalon assures. He rubs my back in a soothing way. "Let's get you wrapped up."

He wraps up my injured wing in a sling and ties it to my torso, so I can't move it at all until it has completely healed. Just as he finishes tying the last bandage, he moves the neckline of my shirt and armor to see the burn on my chest.

He winces a little, "Does that hurt?"

"Yeah, but not too bad. It feels like it is already getting better."

"You two ready?" Jae asks throwing his pack across his body.

"Definitely," Khalon answers.

Standing at the mouth of the cave, and looking out, the land already looks different. The rain has washed away the decades of dust and left the ground healthy and rich. The sun is just starting to find its way through the clouds, and I feel confident that new life will spring from the ground soon.

The winds have completely stopped, and the rain has halted enough for us to fly out of here. Khalon carries Aunt Mara and Jae carries me.

Being off the ground in these lands, rather than on it, lends a new perspective as to how majestic these mountains really are. Now that the foreboding presence is gone, this place feels transformed.

Aryl is outside when we arrive. I'm certain that he is relishing in the first real rain fall that these lands have seen in a very long time. Surprise and relief shine on his face when he sees us flying towards him. It takes a moment before he notices that we have brought Mara home as well. He falls to his knees when he sees Khalon holding her and begins to cry. Khalon very carefully lays her in his lap. I kneel beside him.

I choke back tears of my own and put my hand on his shoulder. I had realized on the flight back that Aryl was my uncle and that returning his wife to him was going to be as painful and as necessary, as it was for me to find her in the first place. He holds her close to his chest and rocks her slightly. I choose not to tell him the details. He will ask me if he wants to know, but something makes me think he knows everything anyway.

"I'd like to bring her home, home to my village. To bury her next to her sister."

He nods in agreement.

"I would really love it if you would come live with me." The tears that I had been working so hard to hold back, break free down my cheeks.

He looks around at his dismal shack, and even though it is nothing anyone should live their life in, he has made a home here for many years. This small room holds everything he owns, and everything tied to his old life. He takes a moment to consider the move, and quicker than I had expected, he accepts.

He packs up his books, some clothes, and a few other personal items that he can carry, and closes the door on this life forever. He shakes his wings out a little bit. He, likely, has not flown a long distance in quite some time, and they are not in good shape. He will not have the stamina for the journey.

"Why don't you two go ahead," I say to Jae and Khalon. "You can take Aunt Mara, and since I can't fly right now anyway, Aryl and I can walk together."

Neither Jae nor Khalon like the idea of letting me out of their sight. They look at each other and their bodies stiffen. Jae raises his eyebrows and Khalon clenches his jaw. Before they can protest, Aryl puts up a hand, "I won't let anything happen to her, I promise."

"We'll see you in a couple days, then?" Jae adds uncomfortably.

"See you in a couple of days," Aryl confirms. "You take good care of my beloved."

Khalon smiles, "You have my word."

They hesitantly take flight and Aryl and I begin our long walk together.

*****

"Did you know?" I ask, once we are well on our way. "Did you know who I was?"

He scratches the tip of his nose. "Sigrun, when you showed up on my doorstep, do you remember my surprise when I saw you clearly for the first time? Well, it wasn't your wings, or that you are a dragon, it was because I knew exactly who you were. Mara had a lot of gifts, and she saw you in Maia before Maia even met your father."

"Why didn't you tell me?"

He chuckles. "Which part?"

"Well, all of it, but we're family, why didn't you tell me that?"

He sighs, "Lots of reasons. It was hard for me to even reconcile that you even existed and were there, standing in my home. I knew you were heading into an extremely dangerous situation. I couldn't risk that you might lose your focus. To be honest, I also was worried you wouldn't believe me."

I chuckle, "Good point." He gives a small smile. "Well, I'm glad I met you and that you are coming to our village. It means a lot to me. I went from having a family, to not having one overnight, and it has been very hard."

"Me too. I lost everything much the same way. I've been alone for a long time. I'm glad you found me." He grabs my hand and gives it a squeeze. I see a tear in the corner of his eye, and it warms my heart.

Chapter 29

We arrive home late on the second day. The journey was a slow one, but much easier the way back. I had explained to Aryl the hardships of the journey there, and he believes that Merrin's reach was getting stronger and, once she was gone, the hold over the forest had lifted. I hope he is correct and that the forest will, once again, thrive.

Jae and Khalon are at my house waiting for us when we arrive, which I had anticipated, but what I didn't expect, was Falon to be there as well.

"Hello!" I say surprised. He smiles and looks me over and his eyes wear a look of concern. I know my physical appearance must be alarming, with the cuts, and bruises, and broken wing, and I'm sure he has been given the synopsis by the boys and has been piecing it together, but seeing me in this condition, likely gives the story new depth. I also see him look at Aryl.

"Falon, this is my Uncle Aryl." The two men nod to each other with respect. I'm sure the boys told him about Aryl as well, but I can tell he is still getting a grasp on the situation.

"Baron was one of my closest friends and I knew Maia very well," Falon explains. "My son told me a little bit about your story. I am so sorry for your loss." Aryl fights back his emotion and nods with gratitude. "I hope you find happiness here. We are very grateful that you have come." Falon then looks at me. "I hear you have been through quite a bit," he says, in a blanketing way.

"Yes, we have." I say with a small smile. I'm too exhausted to get into the entire story tonight, so I'm hoping that he'll keep this visit short.

"Well, I won't be staying," he says, almost reading my mind, "but I wanted to stop by and give you this." He extends a small wooden box out to me. I hadn't even noticed that he was carrying anything. I take it from him and start to open it. "One of the Bee Queen's drones brought it for you, but you had already left on your, quest," he pauses, not sure if quest was the right word, "anyway, I told him that I would look after it for you until you returned."

I flip open the lid, and the lining is the same purple silk that had enveloped my crown when that was given to me. It the center is a beautiful wide, gold, cuff-bracelet. It's one of the bracelets the Queen was wearing at the dinner reception she held for us. I gasp at the sight of it. There is a note with it.

My Dearest Sigrun,

I wanted you to have this. For me, the symbol of these bracelets is one of a bonding. A bond between us; two queens, who will always put their people first, but will also always stand with the other through everything to come. I will wear mine to remind myself of our connection and I hope you will wear yours to remind yourself to shine.

Looking forward to a long and prosperous bond.

Your friend,
Asherah

My hand shakes a little when I take it out of the box and put it on. "I will never take this off," I say to myself as I wrap it around my wrist and forearm. I squeeze the gold hard so that it adjusts to my arm and feels secure.

"Bee Queen?" Aryl asks, "You must have some important friends."

"Yes, I do," I say with pride.

"I'm sure you are beyond exhausted, so I will leave you," Falon finds a graceful way to take his leave. "But, come for dinner soon," he looks at us all. "All of you."

I give him a kiss on the cheek, which surprises him, but by his smile, it pleases him as well, and we watch him take flight back to his home.

In preparation of our arrival, Jae and Khalon set out bread, honey, jam, and a warm soup to ease the ache of our weary bodies. The four of us spend the meal mostly giving Aryl a rundown of the last year, and how we disbanded the Skar tribe. In return, he gives us small glimpses of the village he came from, before it turned sour. His village sounds like it was very similar to ours. Small, quiet, mostly farmers and gathers. Good people. Honest people. People harshly forced from their homes. It hadn't occurred to me at the time, but now I wonder if Aryl would rather find his village.

After dinner, Jae flies home and Khalon heads up to his room—I suspect, straight to his branch. Even though they arrived before us, I can tell, neither of them slept while I was away. I walk Aryl up the stairs and give him the layout of the house. I lead him into my father's room. Mordecai was the only other person to stay here, until he made his own nest. The room has been empty ever since.

My father's robes and clothes still hang from hooks in his wardrobe. "You are welcome to these," I hold up one of the robes to him. "Might be a little loose, but I can ask Ainia to take them in for you."

"Are you sure?" He seems nervous to overstep. He fidgets with the tattered edge of his own sleeve.

"Absolutely." I smile, "I will have your clothes properly cleaned and mended as well. I'll bring up some fresh water for you and I'm just down the hall if you need anything. This is your home now, so make yourself comfortable."

He looks emotional and a little overwhelmed.

I stop at the doorway. "This might not be the best time to ask this," I start. "You've been through a lot in the last few days, but I started thinking at dinner when you were talking about your village. Would you like to find them? I mean, I would love for you to stay here, but I don't want to keep you from them, if that's where you really want to be."

I hadn't realized, until I started offering to help him leave, how much I want him to stay.

I'm nervous.

He smiles, "No. I said goodbye to that place a long time ago. They are good people, they will always be my people, but I have nothing there to go back to. You are my family, and as you said, this is my home now."

"Good." I try not to be overly excited, but I can't help but to smile. "Get some rest." I step outside and close his door.

I haven't been gone for more than seven or eight days, but it feels like forever since I've slept in my own bed. I wash up before bed. As the layers of soot start to come off me, I finally start to look and feel like myself again. It has been quite some time since I felt like myself. For weeks, I've barely slept, because it was terrifying. Even my mind wasn't mine alone. I can't wait to sink into my bed and sleep, maybe even for days. I go to my closet for my nightgown, but then think of something. I open one of my drawers and pull out the silk nightgown that was given to me by the bees. "I'm definitely spoiling myself tonight." I say to myself as I put it on. Maneuvering around my broken wing is a little trying. It is really sore, but I'm sure it will be better soon.

I plop down on my bed and open my pack. I look at the Red Book, unsure of what I should do with it. For such a long time, it was a connection to something lost, a mystery that I thought I would never solve, and then, so quickly, it became incredibly dangerous. I can't part with it, but I know it can't fall into the wrong hands again either. I leave it there, in the bag, for now. I tell myself that I will resolve that later, once I am rested and clear headed. Next to it, I see something else. I reach down and feel something soft. When I pull it out, I see that it is the rabbit doll that I came across in the abandoned village. I had forgotten I took it with me. I hold one of the small feet in my hand and hold it to my chest.

Lying down, I hold the old rabbit in one hand to my chest, and with the other hand, I touch the new bracelet given to me by the Queen. They both hold a connection to a part of me. The rabbit is part of my families' past and this gift from the Queen is a symbol of my future. I close my eyes and search my new memories for one of my mother and Mara playing as children. They are sitting in the tall grass of a meadow, and they take turns making daisy chains for each other outside of their parent's home. For the first time in a long time, I fall asleep easily and sleep well through the night.

*****

As soon as he made it home, Khalon had left Aunt Mara with my neighbor, Beda, to be formally prepared for the burial the morning after our return.

This day is very different from the day that I buried my father. On the day I put my father in the ground, the skies were almost black, and it rained so hard, we had to rush the ceremony for everyone's safety. Today, the sun is out, the birds are happy and talkative, and I feel better than I have in quite some time.

I pull out a dark blue dress and lay it out on my bed. I look at myself in the mirror. I look terrible. My skin is scraped, cut, and chapped. My hair is still dirty, and I smell like sweat and blood. I look outside the window and determine that it's still early, so I should have time to run down to the river to wash properly before the ceremony. I grab some soap, a clean rag, fresh clothes, and head down the stairs. Both, Khalon's and Aryl's doors are still closed. I'm glad they are sleeping late.

Jae, as it seems, must have been up with the sun. He is outside my house, sitting on a tree stump, fussing with a small bunch of flowers. He sees me and smiles.

"Oh, I must have lost track, is it your turn to watch me now?" I say jokingly.

"Yes, it is," he says, with a sarcastic smile.

I hold up the soap and rag, "Just running down to the river to wash, I'll be back soon."

"Okay." He gets up and starts walking with me.

"What are you doing?"

"I will escort you there, wait around the corner until you are done, and then I will escort you home."

"Are you serious?"

"Oh, yeah. Very serious."

"Jae-"

"No, no, this is not negotiable. You can't be trusted."

"What?"

"I just got back from a trip where I had to cross through the worst forest in the world, climb the most treacherous mountain imaginable, get into a swordfight with my best friend—who almost killed me by the way—and be a participant in the destruction of a witch, who was so powerful, she was on track to take over the world, all because you had a little fit and decided to take off without telling anyone, and because you thought you didn't need any help."

Even though he is being funny about it, I know he is serious at the same time. I gave him a real scare and I do feel bad about that.

"So," he continues, "until we feel that you have learned from this and are trustworthy once again, you better get really comfortable with a lot of extra attention." He bends down and kisses me on the cheek, "Come on. Let's go."

There's no point in arguing. I have no valid argument anyway. I just shake my head and follow him to the river.

As promised, Jae is waiting to take me home once I'm done. He still has the same little bunch of flowers in his hand. "You look much better," he says.

"Thank you. I feel much better."

"These are for you," he hands me the flowers. "I was helping my mom and Yoana put the flowers together for your aunt's burial and I sorted out a few for you."

"Thank you." I bury my nose in them. Sweet Pea, Lavender, and Moon Flowers, some of my favorites. The smell is sweet and comforting.

"Let's get you home."

*****

No one knew my Aunt Mara, but despite that, nearly everyone in the village came to the burial to pay their respects to her, offer support, and to meet Aryl. He seemed a little uncomfortable at first. He'd been alone for so long and now he is surrounded by so many and receiving so much attention. We did our best to smooth his wispy hair, but it really does whatever it wants. I dressed him in one of my father's nicer robes. It hangs on him quite a bit, since he is so much thinner than my father was, but he looks good.

Watching him say goodbye to her is hard. He loved her his whole life, with his whole heart, so much so, that he refused to leave her. He refused to move on. He kisses her one last time through the silk wrapping and puts a pink rose in her hand before she is lowered down. He and I both toss a handful of earth on top of her and take our leave as the grave is filled.

Afterward, Falon and Yoana host a reception at their home for us. It's nice to be with friends, to assure them that I am better. I know they want to ask more questions. I have no doubt that bits and pieces of the story have been circulating around the village with hurricanelike propensity, but they show restraint today, and I'm grateful for it.

I can tell Aryl is tired. Honestly, so am I, so we say our goodbyes and walk toward home.

"Thanks for getting me out of there," he says to me, once we're out of earshot. "It's not that your friends aren't nice. I really appreciate everything that they've done. It's just a lot for me right now."

"I understand. It's a lot for me too, and I'm used to it, so I can only imagine."

"Listen," he stops and turns to me, "I wanted to wait for the right time, but I don't know if there ever will be a *right* time." I look at him confused. "A very long time ago, long before you were even born, your father came back to see me one last time."

"What?"

He reaches into the pocket of his robe and pulls out a bundle of paper. "I wasn't sure why he came all that way just to give me this. It was for 'safe keeping,' he said, and he gave this to me. He wanted to make sure it was not found until he was ready for it to be found. He trusted me to know when that time came." He hands the pages to me, "These belong to you."

I open them and see my father's handwriting. Immediately, my knees go weak. Aryl grabs my elbow and steadies me. The left edges feel rough like they've been torn and there is a date on the top of the first page. *720.3.78*, these are the missing pages of my father's journal.

"I'll keep those boys away from you until you come home." He pats my hand and leaves me to read these in privacy.

I fall to my knees and start reading.

Chapter 30

720.3.88

I have everything in order here and I leave tomorrow at first light to bring back my love. That is, if the sisters let her go. The one is so close to her, and the other is almost possessive, but the last time I saw Maia, she made it sound important that she come live here with me. I would live with her anywhere. I would stay in her village with her, so she could stay with her family, but she wants to be here, so I will do what I have to, for her.

721.1.64

It has taken almost two full seasons, but we finally made it back. The journey back was arduous. This winter has been the hardest that I have ever seen. The temperature is a brutal cold that chills through your bones and beyond. In our weakened state, we were unable to fly for long, and practically reduced to crawling through the snow to make it back. I am changed, and so is she. The wise thing would be to close this chapter and never look back, but I need to keep an account for the future, and I must write this story now, while the wounds are still fresh.

I had not anticipated being away for so long. Had I, I would have followed her advice and ran away together in the middle of the night. I thought it would be different. I thought it would be love, and praise, and well-wishes. Instead, I was met with panic and concern. Maia's parents had aged years in only months. It was clear that their health was failing. I knew I couldn't take her away, even though she begged. I didn't understand. I didn't realize the strength of the bond between Maia and her sisters. The way they feel each other. They feel each other's pain, their grief, their joy. When Maia and I feel in love, Mara and Merrin felt it. Mara was overjoyed for us.

She, herself, had felt the overwhelming sweeping, of love, and had been married also. Mara's man, Aryl, is a good man who comes from the village.

He is quiet and sensitive, which at first seemed an unusual match for Mara, being that she is the most outspoken and sarcastic of the three girls. Merrin had always been a quiet observer. I mistook her quietness for shyness, when in fact, I know now that she has been plotting all along, and my arrival changed things for her. Maia saw me coming. She told me that she had visions of me since she was a young girl. Merrin did not and that made her angry. She did not like being surprised. When Maia's affections split from her sisters to me, Merrin's quietness changed to cruelty. Their parents' health went from failing to failed, in a matter of days. At first, I thought it was a nasty illness, fatally aggressive and untreatable, but now I see it for what it truly was. Merrin. I knew the sisters had gifts, but I did not realize the full extent until that day. Merrin had found a way to feed off her families' energy. It was something that she could keep a secret. She had been doing it silently for some time, building her power quietly. She started with her parents. After all, they were old, no one would suspect if they became weaker, more tired, so she could drain them without suspicion.

Mara and Maia, though, that would take a fight, and she knew it. The benefits for her outweighed the risk, and so she had been calculating a way to harness enough power so that the two of them could not stop her.

When I came into the village, it threatened her plan. If I took Maia away, then she would not be able to feed on her life source, and she would not have enough power to fulfill her plans; the scope of which I'm still not fully sure. I know that it was bad enough to trap her in that horrid place for the rest of her life.

I had convinced Maia to stay in her village, knowing her parents wouldn't live much longer, and I would never forgive myself if I had robbed her of those last precious days with them. We had our wedding there. It was quiet and simple, but I will never forget how she looked. She wore a simple white dress that once belonged to her mother, her hair, dark brown, her eyes, bright green, and she was adorned in flowers. She is sleeping now in the room next door, and I still cannot believe that she is mine. I almost lost her on that mountain, and I will do whatever it takes to protect her going forward.

It was not long after our wedding that Maia's parents passed, and Mara came to see us. She was in a panic. She urged us to leave and spoke of a book bound in red scales and told us she had to get it back and keep it safe or destroy it. It had fallen into the wrong hands, Merrin's, and she was going to recover it. Maia, who had once begged me to leave, was now hesitant. She looked at her sister, and a wave of calmness washed over her, and she said, "We must finish it for good, and that will take both of us."

Merrin had already left for the mountain. I didn't fully understand what was happening, or what was about to happen, at the time, but Mara knew that she was not going to leave that mountain ever again. That night, she stood in front of us and pulled a small object out of her pocket. It was a marble with a small rose inside of it. She said this was a gift for our daughter. I looked at Maia and her eyes were filled with tears. I didn't know it then, but that was the moment that she realized that her sister was saying goodbye. I was confused about everything, I still am.

Maia and I had only been married for a short time. We hadn't even had a chance to talk about having children, but Mara spoke with such certainty about our future child. She threaded a silk cord through it and held it out to me. When I reached for it, she told me not to touch the actual marble, if I can help it. She had a little sideways smile. It will reject everyone, except who it is meant for. I wrapped it in a cloth and put in my pocket.

Mara and Maia held each other, fortifying their bond, they told me to stay behind, but I could never let my wife face anything like this without me. I asked why this mountain was so dangerous. They weren't really sure either, except that all three sisters had felt something there, like an electrical charge, or a magnetic pull. It was a vortex, a pool of energy, something was drawing them to it. Maia and Mara both felt that it was bad, and they were afraid of it, so if they felt it was evil and they needed to stay away, that meant Merrin ran toward it.

We left before the sun came up the next morning. During that flight, I saw the beginnings of a storm unlike any I had ever seen before. When lightning strikes, it strikes everywhere that the storm reaches. The lightning of this storm only struck the very top of the mountain.

When we found her inside, she was standing at an altar just below an opening. The lightning struck all around her. She was controlling it. Terror doesn't begin to explain how I felt when I saw her wielding one of nature's strongest forces. Her body was ridged, and her eyes were empty. She seemed hollow inside. Filling herself with a force I couldn't see, yet I could feel it. I felt the life in me draining, pulling out of me. Mara and Maia sprang fast. Merrin was already much stronger than she had ever been before. Merrin was

214

pulling me toward her. I was getting weaker and more lifeless. My body was diminishing. The muscles in my body were shriveling. The color of my skin and hair were getting paler with every moment. My breathing was getting more and more shallow. I truly thought I was dying. I started to lose consciousness, but as I was struggling to keep my eyes open, I was bombarded by the brightest light. It saturated the room and just then, I felt the hold that was on me start to let up. Mara was pulling lightning into herself and was using it to control Merrin. Mara shot a bolt to Maia. Maia captured the stream of light and molded it into a ball of fiery light, harnessing its power, until she could shoot her light at Merrin as well. Merrin had grown stronger, but it was certain that she was nothing compared to the force of the mirror twins.

Merrin was forced onto her knees, and it was at that moment that Mara shouted to us to leave. Her fight was near over, but she was very clear on her demand. She wanted us to leave her there and never return. It seemed like madness, but I confess, I wanted nothing more than to flee. I know that it was cowardly. I know I left that beautiful fairy, my new sister, to die, but right then, all I could think of was getting myself and my love to safety. Since the hold had been broken, some of my strength had returned. I was still very weak, but Maia had exhausted herself to the point that I had to carry her out of the cave.

I will never forget the screaming; The angry, defeated, shrillness that resounded from Merrin—it was deafening, but what broke my heart, was the sound of Mara and Maia separating from each other. It wasn't just emotional pain, but they were physically suffering, being torn apart from each other. Though the girls were triplets, Maia and Mara shared a connection that no one can understand, unless they share the same unbreakable bond, so for them, leaving each other was like cutting out part of themselves.

At the time, I didn't understand why. Why did Mara make us leave? As I said, I saw the window to escape, and I took it. It wasn't until I began to think of Aryl, and how I would tell him what we had done, that we had left her. Maia didn't give me a chance. She wrapped her arms around him and said that Mara was gone. She had died to save us.

The moment we were well enough for travel, we packed up to come back to the Northwoods. Aryl refused to come with us. He said he wanted to stay close to her. Sickness and shame are thick within me. When we left the mountain, Mara was still alive, but Maia was very firm that she had passed.

Maybe Maia could feel her presence leave this world. I have a feeling I will never know, and that haunts me.

As awful as the journey was, it is good to be home. Everyone was very surprised to see us, and in such a state. It will take some time for me to fully recover my strength, but I suspect that my hair will stay white forever.

721.2.05

Maia is with child. Knowing that I am going to be a father is a feeling that I will never be able to fully express. The joy and anticipation of the new life that I am responsible for makes it hard for me to focus on much else. I am constantly fussing over her, and I know that she is irritated by it, but I can't help it. I find myself resting my hand on her belly as she sleeps, and I talk to my unborn child. Before we went to the cave, Mara spoke of my daughter. Is this the daughter she spoke of? Maia assures me it is not. She feels certain that she is carrying a boy, but either way, I am desperately waiting to meet my child.

When the midwife told us how far along she was, I couldn't help but to run the numbers through my head. Maia was pregnant during the encounter in the cave. I can't help but worry that some damage was done. I just hope our baby is healthy.

Tears are falling down my face at an unstoppable rate. I'm always softer where my father is concerned, so anytime I learn anything new about him, or I'm given anything from him, it always hits a tender spot, and these entries have a lot of information for me to unpack. I see why he hid these pages with Aryl. If Merik had found them, there is no telling what would've happened. I know now more than ever that he was searching for Merrin his whole life.

I think my father was right to be worried. Damage was done. Feeling the energy shared between Mara, Merrin, and myself in the cave, I know firsthand that they both left pieces of themselves in me. As severe as the encounter was when my mother battled Merrin, I am certain that by the time she was able to peel herself from Merrin's energy, Merik had become more Merrin's child than my mother's. I think Merrin infused herself into Merik, and that's how she found him so easily. She only found me after I had ignited my fire—she must have felt my power like a string pulling all that way.

I feel a wave of relief unlike anything I have felt before. I only had Merrin in my head for a short while and, in that time, I truly thought I was losing my mind. I believe now, that Merrin had shredded Merik's sanity a long time ago, and likely beyond a point of repair. His death, which I always carry a sick feeling of guilt about, finally feels like mercy.

I fold the pages and sit back. I close my eyes and let the sun soak into me. I always knew that my father was the best man, and I had always heard that my mother was truly exceptional, but now I know she was also powerful and surprising. The realization that I have that power in me as well makes me unsteady and uninhibited at the same time. It's intoxicating.

Chapter 31

I stay out the rest of the day. It is dark by the time pull myself away from my retreat. Exhausted and exhilarated, I drag myself home. Dutiful as always, Jae is there waiting for me outside.

"If Aryl hadn't been so adamant that you were okay, and that I should give you some space, you would be in a whole lot of trouble right now," he says with squinty eyes, and he is trying very hard not to smile.

"Well, thank you very much for giving me space."

"Are you okay?"

I take a deep breath, "That is a more difficult question to answer than you might think. I'll be fine, just working through some things."

"I'd offer to help, but I know better."

"That's what I like about you."

His eyes get a little bit more serious, and he leans in a little. "Is that all you like about me?"

He makes me blush. "No, you also have very nice table manners."

He laughs and shakes his head. "That's not exactly what I meant, but you knew that." He touches my cheek softly, "I still mean what I said about waiting. I'll be here." He kisses my cheek just at the corner of my mouth.

My face is on fire. He looks concerned for a moment. He puts his cheek on my forehead.

"You're burning up. Why does that happen every time I kiss you?" his question only makes me blush more.

"Look at you. Even your ears are red." He is grinning ear to ear. He is loving that he has this affect.

"Will you just go home please," I laugh.

"Okay, okay, I'm sorry." After a moment, his smile fades a bit, and he looks more serious. "Listen, I have to ask," he is much more serious, "the reason that you think you might not 'catch up,' is that because of *someone else*?" His eyes are very focused on me.

I feel like I can't breathe, and I really don't know how to answer that, but I'm tired of pushing my feelings around. I have to be honest with him and with myself.

"I don't know." That is the honest, truth. "I love you, Jae. I'm always happy with you. We know everything about each other and, honestly, I have always kept you pushed back because I always thought you were too good for me." He starts to protest, but I cut him off. "But Khalon does bring out something different in me, and I like it. I like being with him too, but I'm not ready to explore any relationship with anyone right now. A lot has happened in the last few days, and I still need to figure out who I am."

He sighs. I'm sure that wasn't what he wanted to hear, but I can tell he appreciated it for what it is. "I understand," he says, and gives me a hug, "and I'm still not going anywhere." We both laugh.

We pull away from each other and we're both smiling. He is looking at me, and like an old habit, he looks down where my pendant used to be, his brow furrows a bit. "What's that?" He points to my chest just below my collar bone. "The burn mark, it's changing."

I run over to a barrel of water in the garden to see my reflection. When the pendant melted it burned me badly but scarred up pretty fast. I've just been waiting for the damaged skin to peel away. There is a faint dark line on the edge. I take a handful of water and start to wipe the dead skin away. It flakes away easily and beneath the dead and damaged skin, my new skin is soft and unscarred, except for an outline. A black outline, as I touch it more, it becomes more and more visible. I gasp.

"Oh wow," Jae says amazed.

My burn where my rose pendant absorbed into my body left a rose branded on my skin.

"Do you see that?" I ask.

"That's incredible." He touches it carefully, "At least this one doesn't burn me."

Khalon

Chapter 32

Sitting and waiting for her to come home is harder than marching onto a battlefield. If he didn't trust Aryl as much as he does, he would be tearing the village apart until she was back with him, until he knew she was safe. His hand is shaking again. It has been flaring up ever since he got back. He had buried his past and locked it away. That witch broke the doors open with a fiery axe and everything flooded back to the forefront of his mind. He is sure that, eventually, he can tuck away every bad memory again, but what he can't let go of, is seeing her that way, and having to do what he did to stop her. He didn't have time to think about it in the moment, he had to break her wing to save her, but now it's all he can think about. Seeing her scream like that. Her body convulsing in pain. The rational part of him knows it was necessary, but it has shaken him in a way that he has never experienced before.

Never before has he felt for anyone, the way he feels about her. It is all new to him, and he doesn't understand it. He never gave much thought to the fairer sex before. In his tribe, the fairer sex always gave him plenty of thought, but to him, it was never real companionship.

Trying to reconcile his own feelings is hard enough but knowing that her moment of suffering came from his hands, is destroying him. He now sees himself unworthy. He looks at his hands again, takes a deep breath, and finally brings his hands to stillness.

Sitting in an empty room waiting for her is not making him feel any better. It may, actually, be making it worse. He gets up abruptly and heads upstairs. Just as he walks past Baron's den, he hears voices coming from outside. He goes in and peers out the window.

She's home! Relief rushes over him and, suddenly, his reservations melt away. All he wants is to pick her up off the ground, and kiss her, and sit with her, and be with her. He is going to tell her everything, all the dark things about his past, how he feels about her, and how she changed him, what he hopes for, and how it is crushing him thinking he hurt her. Just as he is about to run downstairs, he sees Jae with her and something about how they are talking makes him stop.

"That's what I like about you," she says to Jae.

Jae leans into her, "Is that all you like about me?"

Her cheeks flush, but whatever she says back is too quiet for him to hear.

Jae laughs and touches her face. Khalon feels a tightness in his chest. Part of him doesn't want to see this. It hurts to watch this, but he can't pull himself away.

"I still mean what I said about waiting. I'll be here." Jae kisses her.

Khalon turns away from the window and rests against the wall trying to calm himself. He feels woozy, like the room is closing in on him. His heart throbs. He clutches his own chest trying to relieve the ache, but it doesn't work.

The next thing he hears is Jae say to her, "You feel warm. Why does that happen every time I kiss you?"

Something in Khalon breaks just then. He slams his fist against the wall and storms out of the den and into his room. He sits on the foot of his bed with his head in his hands. His whole body is shaking, and his breathing is fast, so fast that he might pass out if he does not get it under control. His vision gets a little blurred. It doesn't occur to him right away that tears are brimming in his eyes. He takes a breath and holds it.

He is the better man for her. He tells himself. His breathing goes back to normal, and his eyes dry up. The ache in his chest is still there, but he can manage it for now. He figures that hurt will go away with time, time and space.

He gets up from the bed and grabs his things, fills his pack and puts his sword in his belt. He opens the latch to the large window and looks around the room one more time.

Aryl is here. He will look after her. She will be safe. After giving himself permission, he jumps out the window and flies into the night.

Sigrun

Chapter 33

I run upstairs eager to show Khalon my marking. Even though his marks are no longer markings of pride for him, he is still the one person I want to show my new rose to. I think he will understand it more than anyone. I want to share this with him. It is something that connects us in a way.

Usually, I knock on his door any time I come into his room, but I am so excited to see him that I fling the door open and run in.

"Hey…" I start talking the moment I walk through the door.

I'm disappointed to see he is not in his room. I see his window is open. *He might be really tired. He's probably sleeping.* I poke my head out the window to see if he is hanging from his branch. He's not there. I sigh. He probably went fishing or something, now that Aryl is here, we will need to bump up our rations, so knowing him, he's probably stocking up. I keep the window open for him and sink back into the room.

"Tomorrow. I'll show him tomorrow," I tell myself and I walk out of his room. As I shut his door, I feel something in my chest. A small flicker of some kind. I put my hand on the tattoo and wait to see if it flares up again. I don't feel anything.

I go into my room and look at it again in better light. The black lines are not on the skin, but are rising up under my skin, and it is getting darker. When I first looked at it outside it was very faint, but just in this short time it has become more defined. It is definitely a rose, but it isn't soft looking, the lines are more angular than curved. The petals are sharper and almost look like they were formed by fire. "That is so strange," I say to myself. I don't understand it, but I love it.

I get changed and lie down on my bed. I close my eyes and let calmness wash over me. Everything is quiet. I sink further into my mattress and feel myself slipping into the welcome embrace of slumber. Then, suddenly, I feel something in my chest, like sparks firing. My eyes fly open and I'm breathing hard.

A storm is coming.

Epilogue

A world away is a land as rotten as its inhabitants. Fires burn across lakes of tar. Day and night blend together through layers of scorched darkness. There are no friends here, only leaders and followers. You eat what you kill, and you make no apologies, for anything.

An enormous bird of prey circles the camp. Grotesque and threatening, it searches for something there. The creatures who live there, dwell in in the caves. Slowly, one by one, they all start creeping out of their personal sanctuaries and all begin pooling together. They are all dangerous, menacing beings, with murder in their minds.

The circling bird, which is bigger than anyone of the creatures below, flies lower and lower until its metal tipped talons puncture the ground upon landing. Its eyes are black and empty, its beak is curved and sharp, and it always has an appetite. The bird stops in front of a figure and bows down. As a reward, the bird is given a chunk of bloody meat. Its master strokes its scaled, featherless, head while it enjoys its reward.

The master's tail curves up and over his shoulder. His stinger was severed the last time he saw the Northwood fairies, so he had a new one made, forged from steel. The stinger is a razor-sharp blade made especially for him.

The bird follows him and protects him dutifully. The master looks over the army of savages he has banded together and fresh excitement pumps through him. The army begins grunting and chanting, quietly at first, but then it gets louder and louder, until it is deafening.

More birds of prey start circling, all of them under his control, beasts of a varying sort emerge from the edges of the camp, all answering a call from the one that leads them. This army is bigger, crueler, and more blood thirsty than any other he has ever seen. It is the perfect tribe of heathens.

"We're ready." A twisted smile spreads across his face. "I'm coming for you, Sigrun," he growls. "I'm coming for you."